All Of My

Heart

The Ladies of London

Meghan Hollie

Book Cover by Coffin Print Designs Ltd (Paperback and eBook only).

Book Cover by Kylah Cover Designs (Hardback only).

Copy and line edit by Sarah Baker @ Word Emporium.

Proofreading by Sophie @ Iris Peony Editing / Lisa Hine.

Formatting by Atticus.

Published through KDP Publishing Amazon.

1st edition 2023.

Foreword

Please be aware there are a few sensitive topics discussed during this book.

Content warnings:

Strained relationship with parents.

Sexual content intended for 18+ audience and explicit language.

Just like *All of My Lasts and All of My Firsts* this book is also written in British English (hopefully not a trigger)

Playlist

Wild Thing – The Troggs

Anti-Hero – Taylor Swift

Late Night Talking – Harry Styles

Slow Hands – Niall Horan

Starving – Hailee Steinfeld, Grey, Zedd

Falling In – Lifehouse

Celestial – Ed Sheeran

Not Like I'm In Love With You – Lauren Weintraub

Little Bit More – Suriel Hess

Meant To Be (Acoustic) – Bebe Rexha

Lover – Taylor Swift

Sparks Fly – Taylor Swift

Chasing Highs – ALMA

No Good – Kaleo

Love U Like That – Lauv

Dedication

In case you need to hear it today. You are enough.

Always.

In fact, you are a thousand times enough.

Chapter 1

Zoey

"You can do this. You can do this," I mutter to myself as I walk up to the giant, obnoxious wooden door that has four, yes, *four-door* knockers. I mean, it's so excessive, but that's my parents for you. They live their lives in excess.

I decide to ignore them all and use my hand to bang on the wood instead because I refuse to conform to what's expected of me. "Do not turn around and walk away, Zoey; you've got this. It's only dinner. You can survive a dinner," I say to myself as the giant front door swings open to reveal one of my brother's smug faces.

"Are you talking to yourself, baby sis?" Max asks, raising an eyebrow at my mental state that's clearly on the fray today.

Heat fills my cheeks. "How much did you hear?" I ask, wincing.

The sides of his mouth tilt upwards mockingly. "Oh, I saw you pull up in your car. I was waiting here for you, and then I heard your little pep talk."

"Well, in that case, I'll be going to jump off a cliff now," I say and try to turn, but two hands twirl me right back around to face the door.

"Woah there. You're not escaping this. It's my birthday, and what I say goes."

"Just like any other day in the Bancroft household, then?" I retort sharply, unable to keep the derision from my voice.

Max puts his arm around my shoulders and pulls me into the house. "Come on, you drama queen, step over the threshold." My reluctant feet stomp as he moves us both towards the open hallway. "You know Mum is gonna hate that outfit," he whispers in my ear.

I smile triumphantly. "I know." I look down at my tattered vintage mom jeans and old band t-shirt with holes. She really is going to hate it. If only she knew this whole outfit cost me less than ten quid.

A huge spiralling staircase flaunts itself before me, as does the over-the-top bouquet of peonies on a pointless table in the middle of the room. "Is everyone here?" I ask him as we walk past the first of three living rooms because what screams rich and pretentious than multiple empty rooms?

Max nods and goes to reply, but just as we round the corner, my mother's sharp voice permeates the air, and I plaster on my fake smile that I've mastered over the years.

"Zoey, darling." She approaches and air kisses me twice. *Air kisses are the fucking worst.* Her perfectly straightened blonde hair skims her shoulders, her bright blue eyes—the same as mine—looking everywhere but at me. We are so similar, yet so opposite. "You're late."

It was intentional.

"Mother, how are you?" I grit my teeth through my fake as fuck sweet smile while inside, I'm grimacing. Her signature Chanel scent chokes me, and I stifle a cough. I swear it gets stronger the older she gets.

She wafts the perfumed air around her as though it's offensive. "Oh, you know, busy as a bee. Max, be a darling and get your mother a drink." He wanders off, mumbling something about it being his birthday, and I wrap my lips around my teeth to stop the laugh erupting from me.

I manage to compose myself and glance over to her. "Glad to hear you're well." When I realise she still isn't looking my way, too busy inspecting her perfectly manicured nails, I decide to give up trying to make eye contact because I know she won't even glance in my direction. I've spent so much of my life being a disappointment to both my parents that their lack of eye contact is easier to deal with than their disapproving stares.

Her smile is as fake as mine as I breeze past her, and I wonder briefly if we were actually honest with each other, what would we say? It certainly wouldn't be all these niceties and meaningless conversations.

When we walk into the kitchen, I'm met with the face of my parents' housekeeper, Seren. "There she is, my Zozo. Come, give me a cwtch then." Her accent brings a smile to my lips.

"You get more Welsh every time I see you," I say as I dive into her soft arms and inhale the warm, comforting smell of washing powder that is Seren.

As she pulls back, she pushes my hair out of my face the way a mother would, and something shudders inside me at the realisation that Seren was always the one to give me hugs growing up. She cleaned my scraped knees while my own mother didn't spare me a glance. And it appears nothing has changed.

Seren's brows furrow as she takes me in. "Now, I'm not being funny, but you're even skinnier than when I saw you last. I'm going to feed you up today. Get some more meat on those tiny bones of yours." Her hands wrap around my biceps, and she squeezes with a laugh.

"Mmkay, Seren. You do you. As long as there is booze in this house, then you can feed me all you want."

Looking beyond the worktops to the table in the kitchen, I spot trays and trays of pretentious catered food. Microscopic entrées, amongst other things that I know my brothers will hate. They both have huge appetites, and nothing I can see here will fill them up. My parents would know this if they knew any of us at all.

"Hi, Tink." I'm hauled upwards from behind and judging by the number of tattoos decorating his arms, I know it's Owen. His huge, inked arms destroy any hope I have of breathing as he squeezes me. As he releases me, he ruffles my hair like I'm fucking five, and my throat lets out a growl before I even realise it.

"Get lost, Owen," I swirl around, slapping his chest because, truthfully, I can't reach any higher.

"I think you're meant to say Happy Birthday, big brother." He pops a tiny appetiser into his mouth, and his face immediately scrunches up as he grabs a napkin and spits it out. "The fuck is that shit?" he grimaces.

I laugh. "You mean you don't like..." I pause and lean over to read the label, "... lobster stuffed vol-au-vents?"

He winces as he shakes his head. "Fuck no. Tell me there's real food somewhere." Owen opens the fridge door and brings out two beers, ignoring the ridiculously giant magnum of champagne chilling in a bucket next to him and passes me a bottle.

I'm about to open it and take a sip when Max steals it from my hand. "Hey!" I shriek.

He sips the drink, shrugging. "It's my birthday."

"Our birthday, dickhead," Owen scolds.

They're technically identical twins, but they have some differences. Max has short, perfectly swooped over dark blonde hair, and his eyes are green. Owen, though, keeps his hair short because it annoys him, and he has blue eyes like me. When I was younger, I followed Max everywhere; I made him play Barbies with me, and he'd do it without complaint, while Owen always had his head in a book. They both play the role of the protective big brother well. God knows I'd never introduce anyone to them now. They'd scare them right off.

"How does it feel to be thirty-five then, boys?" Seren asks, breezing into the kitchen again, my mother on her heels.

"I always found that a weird thing to say to people on their birthday, like I'm going to have some sort of epiphany on the day and feel different. I don't, by the way. Still the same me." Owen has always been black and white and more concerned about how he can try and make everything into a mathematical equation than decipher that awkward human nature, hence why he runs my father's finance department for him.

"Dude, you're so fucking weird," Max scoffs as he downs his–no, *my* beer.

"Language, son." I'd know that booming voice anywhere. It made me angry so many times growing up, and even as an adult, it has the same effect. The hair on the back of my neck stands to attention, waiting for the moment he acknowledges my existence.

"Zoey. You look well." He doesn't attempt eye contact either, just like Mum, who has disappeared, likely to feed that Valium addiction.

I take in his broad shoulders—exactly the same as my brother's—the suit he's wearing, as though he's going to the office and not relaxing at home. His greying hair and the wrinkles that have formed on his face. My dad is incredibly handsome, but beauty doesn't make him a nice person, unfortunately.

"Good to see you, Dad." I'm lying through my teeth, but I promised myself I'd be civil for my brother's sake. I lean in and kiss my father's cheek dutifully. I mean, it's no secret that I'm the black sheep of the family, the surprise baby they never should've had, and over the years that's taken its toll on our relationship. My father and I can barely co-exist because I wouldn't join his prestigious multi-billion-pound insurance company like my brothers did, but tonight is not the time to dwell on that. I won't ruin things for my big brothers.

He turns to smile at them, and his hazel eyes soften as I get a glimpse of the dad who used to push me on our garden swing when I was little. My chest tightens at the memory and the reality clashing so fervently in front of me. My dad openly loves my brothers, while all he shows me is disdain. You'd think I'd be used to it by now, but fuck, I'm not. My eyes sting as I force away the tears trying to spill from them. I know I was a wild child growing up, and when it became obvious that I wasn't going to be the perfect socialite daughter they wanted or the future CEO of Bancroft Insurance, their interest dwindled. They think everything I do is to spite them, like spending the first half of my trust fund on the animal shelter I saved from closing down.

I watch as he embraces both boys and then walks outside through the bi-fold doors to the patio area, laughing and joking with them. My heart sinks a little in my chest before I steel myself again. He doesn't get to make me feel bad anymore. I decided that the day I turned eighteen and moved out of this stupid house.

A small hand wraps around my shoulder, comforting me. Seren has always been the one to pick up my pieces every time my father upset me, but not today. I won't let him win. I tap her hand, silently asking her to stop because if she doesn't, I might burst into tears.

"I'm fine, really S." I look down and scoff, warding off more emotions before they bubble up. "Our boys will not make it through the next hour without more food than this." I gesture to the trays of tiny snacks.

Seren shrugs, not wanting to upset my mother, who has joined us again. I turn around and walk towards her, swallowing down my pride. "Mother, do you think we need more food?"

She doesn't look up from her phone. "More food? Don't be ridiculous."

I think she's the one being ridiculous, only giving those two behemoths that are her sons pigeon food for dinner. But whatever, Mother knows best.

An hour later, we all sit around outside. My mother glares as I strum my fingers on the glass tabletop, filling the silence.

"So, tell me, Zoey, how are things with you?" she asks, making my eyebrows rise. She never asks about me. I hesitate because I half expect her to laugh and take the question back. I sit up taller and refrain from strumming my fingers.

"Things are good, thanks, Mum." I honestly don't know what to say. This is the first time she's asked about me in years, and I'm bewildered.

"And your friends? Jess, is it?" I nod suspiciously, wondering where she's going with this. "She got married, didn't she?" she continues. "To Liam Taylor, yes? Such a nice man, too. From a wealthy family. Good for Jess."

And there it is. Give it a second. I'm sure there's more.

"What about you? Aren't you wanting to find someone like Liam? I'm sure he has friends he could introduce you to. It's best to do it now while you're young, rather than spending all your time with rodents. Besides, you know you won't get the remainder of your trust fund until you're married."

My skin prickles with frustration. "Rodents? Marriage? You know that's unfair," I huff like the petulant child she thinks I am.

My mother turns to my father and blatantly whisper shouts so we can all hear. "Perhaps we should stipulate more terms for her trust fund, like what happens to the money after so many years married. We never know what she—"

"Stop, please." Max's voice booms through the whisper, and everyone swings their heads to look at him. Owen shifts next to me, his face continually stoic, though I think I see his jaw tick. They rarely got involved when we were growing up. I don't hold it against them, though; this isn't their fight. So, I'm surprised he's challenging them now.

Silence falls across the table. It's heavy and suffocating. "There's no need to talk about Zoey like she isn't here. She can hear you. We all can," he adds, his jaw ticking again.

The glare from Max to my mother is... interesting. His eyes are fiery, and the way he's gripping his beer, his knuckles are almost white. But when he turns to face me, his whole face softens to look more like my Max, my big brother and best friend.

"How's work, Zo?" I know he's asking because he's genuinely interested in my life, but answering that question after the snide comments from my mother is going to cause problems.

I flick my focus around the table, ignoring the glares. "It's good. The expansion last year has meant we're able to take on more cats now." Of course, it would be great if I had the rest of my trust fund to invest in the business, but alas, I bite my tongue. I'll never tell them I'm teetering on the edge of desperation with the shelter. Donations are slim, and I'm a breath away from selling my car to help fund it, but I'll do that before I ever ask for anyone's help. "Did you know there are over 16,000 animals dumped in London alone every six months or so? Most of them don't survive, and I hate that. I actually have a meeting with another two London animal shelters next month to discuss how we can help them because they're so overrun."

"I know. I read the article you sent to me," he says with a proud gleam in his eyes that's just for me.

I keep staring at Max, grateful that he cares but also completely aware of the eyes on us as I silently plead with him, hoping he might know how to diffuse the building tension.

"You know, if you teamed up with us, I could triple your customer base and actually get you better revenue. You could become a company instead of a non-profit," Owen pipes up, and my head swings to him, my gaze changing from 'help me' to 'shut up' in an instant.

I know Owen means well, and he's a numbers man at heart—I can practically hear his brain already doing the math—but I want to kill him right now.

I grit my teeth. "That's really ki—"

"Zoey has no interest in the family business. She has made that abundantly clear," my father booms across the table, cutting me off without letting me finish. He's not wrong; I can't associate with his business. Not when he'll either squash mine or take over and make it into something it's not.

I turn my head to find his hazel eyes daring me to bite and fuck, I promised myself I wouldn't, but I can't help it. Rage courses through my body like a wildfire, and my mouth moves before my brain can stop me. "Just because I don't want to work for you doesn't mean I don't take an interest in business. My goals do not revolve around money, they revolve around the animals I help, but if you need me to be the bad guy for following my dreams instead of conforming to your wishes, then fine. I'm the fucking bad guy."

"Zoey," my brother Max pleads, but it's too late—heat spikes into my face with a force that propels my body to stand.

"Don't Zoey me, Max. I'm not a fucking child. Despite what *your* father seems to think, I am a successful business owner who actually *helps* animals. I have a heart, unlike him," I shout, flapping my arms around. It took one stupid remark from my father and I'm diving into the deep end, making myself look like a fucking idiot again. I can't help it. When it comes to him, he's like the red flag to my bull.

I glance over to my father again as he purses his lips in that disapproving way he always does, his silence slices through my chest and I give myself three seconds to let him be mad, shout or even give a shit, but when he doesn't, I internally deflate. I'm done. Over it.

I clench my fists once, twice, and then I can't do it anymore. I don't want to spend one more minute in a room with him. "I'm sorry, boys, I can't stay here any longer." Max protests in my ear, begging me not to go, as I quickly pull him into a hug to say goodbye. I've already said too much, letting my anger bubble over tonight, so it's best I leave before I do anything worse. Like cry.

I rush outside, pushing down the lump that's settled in my throat. One single tear threatens to fall from my eye as I storm towards my car, and I pray that it doesn't fall. *Not yet, not yet. Not before I can get to the safety of my car.*

"Zoey, wait," Max calls after me, and I pause, swiping at my eye to make sure that tear is really gone. He spins me and puts his arms around me, instantly making me emotional again. "I'm sorry about them."

I sniff and bury my face into his t-shirt, gripping onto my brother for dear life. "It's not your fault, Max." I pause, not wanting him to feel the burden of the fractured relationship that me and my parents share. "It's just how it is." I sigh.

He squeezes me tighter, and I have to fight more tears. "I'm still sorry, you're the best baby sister, and I love you. So does Owen."

My brothers have always been there for me, especially when our parents weren't. They love me for me, and I'm always so confused about how two heartless people like my parents have children with such big hearts.

"Come to Vegas with O and me next week," he mumbles into my hair. I pull back to look at him and before I can protest, he continues, obviously on a mission. "I know you said you couldn't, but you need a break. And before you say no again, I already spoke to Sam and Lloyd, who are more than happy to run things over at the shelter for you. I know you hate letting go, but you can work remotely for a few days." When he looks at me with his big green puppy dog eyes, I'm transported back in time to when we were kids, and they'd both use their cuteness against me, making me do stupid shit all the time. Turns out, it's still as effective. I dread to think how their future partners will fare against them. I groan. *Can I leave everything for a trip right now?* "Come onnnnnn, please, Zo? Celebrate your brother's birthdays in Vegas?"

I *could* do with a break. I haven't left London in years. Even Jess and Liam's wedding last year was local. Then, their honeymoon in the Maldives made me green with envy. Things have been busy, and I've spent most of my time working or in clubs, living the single life – because all of my girlfriends have husbands or live-in boyfriends now. He's right, I do need this.

"Fuck it–I'm in."

Chapter 2

Zoey

"You're going on holiday?" Nora shouts down the phone.

"What, I'm not allowed?" I tease, balancing the phone between my ear and shoulder as I open my suitcase on my bed with a flop.

"Of course, you're allowed to go away," she laughs. "I encourage it, even. I meant, who will be at the shelter? Wasn't your excuse from every girl's holiday that you didn't trust anyone to run things while you were gone? What's changed, Miss workaholic?"

"I spoke to Lloyd and Sam last night. They're better off without me breathing down their necks anyway," I say, picking up a bikini that's at least ten years old–but it's my favourite one—before throwing it into the case. "It's about time I let the reins go a little. I wouldn't have made Lloyd manager if he wasn't capable, and Sam is the best vet I've ever met, so I know my animals are in good hands. Plus, my brothers are offering me a free trip to Vegas. Remember, they both get the second part of their trusts now they're 35. Lucky buggers," I mutter under my breath.

"Oh, right, I forgot about that. Well, do you want me to pop in to help? I can volunteer if they need extra hands. Rope Grayson in too."

I smile at her offer. "Thanks, babe, but I think they've got it covered. We went over everything last night once Max persuaded me to go."

"I'm still pissed they didn't invite me and Liam," Grayson shouts in the background.

Nora laughs. "Did you hear him? He's salty he didn't get an invite."

"When it's my birthday, you're both invited, and we'll go somewhere better than Vegas," I promise both of them.

"Nothing is better than Vegas, Zo. Nothing. Tell Owen he owes me one," Grayson replies.

"Baby, go check on dinner, please," Nora mumbles to Grayson. "God, he's driving me mad at the moment. I love him, but we're trying to figure out a moving date, and it's stressing me out because we're both so busy."

"Stop, you don't hate it. You love it." I smile, my heart warming with my friend's happiness.

I hear Nora chuckle. "I do. I'm all gross and in love."

"Gross is right." I let out a small sigh. "Anyway, gotta go, baby girl. I'll text you when we land."

"Enjoy Vegas and remember... Whatever happens in Vegas, stays in Vegas."

I bark a laugh at the cliché I know I'll probably live by whilst I'm in Vegas. Hot American guys and sunshine. What more could a girl ask for? God knows it's not just a holiday I'm in dire need of.

"Sure thing. Tell Grayson I'll send him pictures of what he's missing out on. Love you, bye."

We hang up, and I look at my mostly empty suitcase. I have plenty of clothes, shoes, and accessories, but I don't know how to pack for Vegas. It's all glitz and glamour in the movies, but it also feels like anything goes. I love being eccentric with my outfits, but I also don't want it to look like I got dressed in the dark.'. It's a fine line.

I chew my bottom lip, thinking about outfit options, before walking to my small wardrobe. Something pink and glittery catches my eye, my pink denim jacket with the glittery tassels. "Oh yes, very Vegas."

I embrace the theme and decide to pick out the brightest clothes I own, some skimpy, some not. I toss them haphazardly into the case before forcing the zip shut.

"There," I huff, moving my blonde hair out of my face. My phone goes off just as I'm picking my suitcase up, and Lloyd's number flashes across the screen.

I swipe to answer him. "Lloyd, I've just zipped my case. Please tell me you're calling to wish me a safe flight," I ask, heaving my case to the living area.

"Zoey—"

"Noooooooo. That's the voice you use when you're telling me something's wrong."

"There might be something wrong. I have it under control. I just need you to approve the cost."

My heart leaps into my throat. "Cost? I'm guessing you're not talking about your overtime."

Lloyd grunts. "There's been a leak in the new cat houses. It was like the Titanic. I had to stop myself from playing Rose and shouting 'Come back, Jack' whilst Sam was trying to save all the kittens and I was trying not to get wet a—"

"The cost, Lloyd," I moan, rubbing my temples, praying that I don't have to sell a kidney.

"Right." He lets out a sigh as if he's preparing himself to give me the bad news. "The whole section at the back needs replacing, and the guy said it will cost at least five grand."

"Five... grand... Jesus. Is he also giving our cats gold boxes to shit in?" I huff. Sweat forms at the base of my neck, making my skin itch. It's not that I don't have the money, it's that I need the second part of my trust fund even more now. I suck in a deep breath. Then another. "Okay, it's going to be fine. Charge it to my account. I'll have to win big in Vegas or maybe be a stripper for a night. It is Vegas, after all," I ramble, my pulse still thumping loudly in my ears.

"Hey, if any boss I know could strip, it's you," he mocks, but I ignore him.

"Right. I should cancel the trip," I say, not really listening. My mind whirling with a mountain of thoughts.

"You're not cancelling. I'm only calling to make sure I can charge your account. I was going to do it anyway, but Sam told me that's fraud or whatever." I can practically hear him rolling his eyes.

I smile, even though I feel like I'm hanging on the edge of a cliff.

Brushing my hands through my hair, I let my brain cogs turn for a second. *That section of the building is new. It shouldn't have had issues this soon.*

"Lloyd, book the plumber, email the insurance company. There's no way the pipes in a new building should explode like that and make sure those kittens aren't hurt. Put them in the old room with their crates for now."

"Cats are already safe in the backroom, boss."

"Thanks." I sigh, feeling a little bit relieved. This is going to be okay.

"Oh, and Zoey?"

"Hmm?"

"Sam and I can handle this. Go enjoy your time off."

"I need—"

"Daily updates, I know. Get gone."

"The leather is sticking to the backs of my legs, look... I sound like I'm in a sex show with these noises." I demonstrate my legs making slapping and suction noises against the chair, and Owen just glares at me, unimpressed. Max, however, stifles a laugh.

"I don't know how you're having sex, Zo, but those are not the right noises." Owen huffs then stands to walk towards the front of our family's private jet as we idle on the runway. It's mainly used for business, and I've not been on it since I was sixteen, but I hate it now just as much as I hated it back then.

My leg jitters up and down just as Max passes me something from the minibar opposite him. "Here, down this. You're making me nervous."

I gratefully accept the tequila, unscrewing the cap. "These tiny bottles are funny, aren't they? Look, they're so small and pointless but serve a wonderful purpose," I ramble, knocking back the fiery liquid before studying the now empty bottle. The truth is, after this morning's drama with the shelter, I need a drink. I may have already hassled Lloyd on the drive here, and he's told me he's blocking me if I carry on. So, alcohol seems like a good plan.

"Yeah, like getting you to chill the fuck out," Max laughs.

"Maximillian Laurence Bancroft, you better watch that potty mouth," I gasp dramatically.

"Don't full name me. And I do swear, just not around our parents if I can help it," he says, smoothing down the front of his tie.

I tilt my head to the side, watching him. "Why did you wear a suit on a plane? It must be uncomfortable."

"I've got other clothes to change into in the back. It was more of a formality. Owen and I always travel in suits, then change if it's a long flight. It's a habit now."

Something hits me out of the blue, but it stings my chest. I don't know my brother's that well when it comes to work. I've actively distanced myself from that part of their lives because it's connected to our parents, but in doing so, it feels like I've missed something. It's silly to have a pang of regret over seeing my brothers in suits, but it still reminds me of the choices I've made in my life and how they affect our relationship.

"Heyyooooo!" A male voice gains my attention just as Owen comes back to our seats. I look up to see three guys come on board. Three very good looking guys. Max stands welcoming some of his friends, all bro hugs and laughter.

One of the guys is wearing a grey t-shirt that clings to his broad shoulders and tapers down to his dark jeans. I have to force a swallow because, *damn*. Then, as I look at his unruly beard and big brown eyes, realisation and an unwelcome memory hits me. I flirted with him at Jess and Liam's wedding. I remember because he had a girlfriend at the time, and I still flirted like my life depended on it. *Ohhh crap.*

"Why did you invite him?" I hiss, leaning into Owen, who hasn't got up yet to greet anyone.

He looks up at the group and frowns. "Harrison?" he questions. "Why wouldn't we invite him?" He turns and assesses me for a second, seemingly judging my blank stare. "Are you telling me you don't remember Harrison?"

I look at Harrison again. And my pulse increases as sweat forms at the nape of my neck. I *do* know him, but not from the wedding, from when we were kids. I can't believe I haven't put two and two together until right this second. Actually, I've seen him twice, at the wedding and the stag/hen party, in the last year and a half. Why didn't he say something at the wedding? Preferably before I threw myself at him.

Oh, right, because you were drunker than a pirate, Zoey.

My face burns as I stare at Harrison Clarke. The boy I used to have the biggest crush on when I was a kid. He was nineteen the last time I saw him, and I was only twelve. His dark brown hair is slightly wavy and a little longer than the other guys. The ends have this cute flick to them, and the totally inappropriate thought that I'd like to run my hands through his hair or tug on it whilst it's between my legs makes me feel a little lightheaded. *What the fuck am I doing? I need to stop.* But I'd challenge any other hot-blooded person *not* to react the same. This isn't the Harrison I remember from growing up, not that he wasn't always gorgeous—he was—but he was gangly and geeky. Grown-up Harrison is... beautiful.

"Holy shit, Harrison!" I accidentally blurt, my eyes widening as I realise everyone is staring at me.

Max chuckles. "You remember Zoey, our baby sister?"

God, why did he have to say that? Younger fine, but baby...

Harrison passes Max and stands in front of me. I should stand too, but I'm ninety-nine per cent sure that my legs won't work. "Zoey," The way my name sounds on his lips is like a spell that transports me back to being that twelve-year-old girl with a crush. It's low, gravelly, and far too sinful to be real.

"W-w-what... what are you doing here?" *Good one, Zo. Smooth.*

"We invited him, I told you," Owen says, his brows lifting in confusion from the seat opposite.

"Oh... right... yeah, that's awesome." *Have I ever described anything as awesome in my life before? Nope. Do I hate myself for it? Yep.*

The two other guys who I now recognise from Max's Instagram and a few other events in the past are Aaron and Nate. They step out from behind Harrison, who is practically taking up the entire aisle with his huge self.

Aaron, the blonde-haired, fresh-faced cutie, pushes past Harrison and smiles brightly at me. "Zoey, finally, I get to meet the most gorgeous Bancroft," he winks, charm oozing from him as he takes my hand and kisses it like we're in an episode of Downton Abbey. "Pleasure is all mine." Heat rushes to my cheeks. *God, why do my brothers have so many hot friends? And why are they all in front of me right now, witnessing me blush?*

"Don't kiss my sister, dude. I don't know where your lips have been." Max swats at Aaron as he releases my hand.

"Thinking about my lips, Max? 'Cause you know I'm all about the free love." He says, walking away before he plonks himself into a seat behind me, and I can't help but smile. I like him already. Nate walks past too, with an awkward wave that I return as he scurries to the seats near Aaron and Max.

Harrison turns to Owen, who stands, and they hug and chat. With his back to me, it gives me more opportunity to ogle him. He must be around six-foot-three, measuring him against Owen. He's not dressed like my brothers, his causal jeans and t-shirt leaving little to the imagination. Those broad shoulders, I noticed first, fill the sleeves of his shirt, showing off some seriously sexy forearm porn. Longer hair on guys usually puts me off, but this man owns it, and it's not too long, just enough to make him a little dishevelled. His matching dark beard makes him look like some sort of rugged mountain man who uses an axe to cut wood on the daily... *oof, that image.*

He's fun to look at but he's my brothers' friend, so looking is all I'll be allowed to do. No fun in the mountains with this man. Or the desert, since that's where we're going.

Just as I'm mid-way through my assessment of him, he turns, his eyes landing directly on me. I still can't believe I didn't realise he was Harrison Clarke. I'm such a basket case,

My cheeks burn hot once more as I stand up, extending my hand finally to shake his whilst he removes his sunglasses from the top of his head, and it all happens in slow motion. I don't miss the curve of his lips when he sees me swallow hard.

Lord, save me.

He extends his hand to me, slutty forearms and all. "Look at you," he purrs in this perfectly deep and raspy voice that could easily lull me into an orgasm. "All grown up."

He holds my hand longer than necessary, his thumb ghosting lightly over the back of my knuckles. Images of him griping my throat with that hand invade my brain like a tsunami, and I find myself clearing my incredibly needy oesophagus.

"So have you," I croak.

Max suddenly barrels into the side of Harrison, almost knocking us both over before getting him into a headlock. "Come on, H. Need to get some booze in you." And then Harrison is dragged behind me towards Aaron and Nate, who already have a drink in hand. Which, I decide, is probably for the best.

I sit back in my seat opposite Owen, rubbing my hand that still tingles from his touch and taking a deep breath. Owen taps my foot with his, jolting me back to the real world. "You okay over there with your heart eyes?"

I scoff. "I do not have heart eyes." *I definitely have heart eyes.*

"Huh," he huffs, going back to pretending to read his book. "Could've sworn I read those signals differently. You were practically drooling on the leather."

I laugh a little too unconvincingly, twisting in my seat, feeling uncomfortable with his assessment. Owen or Max thinking I have a crush on their friend would end with someone getting a bloody nose, I'm sure. "And that, big brother, is why you are perpetually single. You'd never know when a girl is hitting on you, unless she asked you out with 'E=mc squared'."

Owen stiffens slightly, something passing over his face, but it's gone just as fast as he tips his head to me and smirks, rubbing his chin. "Like you know what that means, wait... Are you a secret brain, Zo?"

"I'll never tell."

Owen looks over to Harrison and the others. "I'm glad he came, actually. Wasn't sure he would have."

"Why? Worried he finally came to his senses about being friends with you two losers?"

He narrows his eyes mockingly. "No, smartass. His ex has been causing a few problems lately, so we weren't sure he'd want to up and leave while she's up to her shit."

I glance toward the man currently pinning Max to the short alley of the plane as he tries to tap out from under him. Harrison's laugh carries as he shoves Max's shoulder and runs his thick fingers through his hair. But when I really look at him, dark circles line his tired eyes. Maybe I'm not the only one who needed this trip.

"Excusing me, gentlemen, the pilot is ready for take-off."

Chapter 3

Harrison

I finally sit across from Max and place my headphones in to listen to the latest episode of my favourite podcast.

My head falls back onto the soft leather pillow behind me, and I close my eyes. Fuck, I'm tired. I've been working for the last month straight; this new bug in our app system just won't fucking die, and it's kept me awake for days on end. That and the utter shit show that is my private life has made sleep feel impossible. Vanessa, my vindictive ex, calling me at all hours of the day, turning up to my flat, my fucking office, acting all sweet and innocent one minute, then like the spawn of Satan the next. I can't even begin to calculate how much damage she's cost. My poor Aston Martin has had more keys scored across the beautiful black paint than I've had cooked dinners.

But no more. Enough is enough. And that is exactly why I'm here on this trip. No work. No drama. No Vanessa. When Owen called me inviting me to celebrate his and his brother's birthday, I jumped at the chance.

Aaron catches my eye and taps his ears to tell me to take the AirPods out.

"So, what's the latest with she who will not be named?" Aaron asks from the other side of the aisle.

I sigh. "Same shit."

"She still claiming you cheated on her?"

I nod, running my hand over my face. "I found out the guy she cheated on me with works in my company. Or he used to. Apparently, he was a disgruntled employee because he had to work his way up, and I didn't promote him last year."

"You're serious?"

"Deadly."

"Man, that's shit. Good job we're about to spend a good few days getting fucked up in Vegas then," Aaron sing songs.

I laugh along with the others, but in reality, I'm exhausted enough that I'd sit by the pool every day and sleep. My shoulders ache and my brain feels heavy from working so much. Having said that, being around this lot will be good for me. I need to let off some steam, and they're the best kind of fun.

I glance around the plush private plane, and my eyes land on Zoey. When our gazes connect, I catch the faint pink flush creeping up her cheeks as she looks away, and I smile. I didn't expect to see another woman on the trip since I know neither of the guys have partners. But fuck, Zoey... I haven't seen her up close since the night she flirted with me at Liam Taylor's wedding, which she's clearly forgotten about. Plus, she didn't seem to remember me from when we were kids. Yeah, that might've dented my ego a little because I remember a lot about her, like her wild hair she never tamed, her rainbow braces that decorated her teeth for a year and how she was adorably shy about them. Or those bright pink Converse she wore all the time. But now, the reality of an adult Zoey in front of me? She's fucking hot. Tight little body, showcased in a blue bodysuit, a delectable arse cupped in black denim shorts, and those sexy little cowboy boots... Yeah, I'm trying to act as cool as possible, but my insides are heating up. She's any man's wet dream. But she's one hundred per cent off limits, and eye-fucking her is all I'll do this weekend.

I place my AirPods back in, closing my eyes again while I try and get some sleep and push the thoughts of the hot little blonde out of my head.

A loud thud has my eyes springing open, and I look out the window and see... tarmac. That can't be right. Glancing at my watch, it lights up when I tap it, and I notice I've been asleep for ten hours. I've never slept on a flight before, but I've also never slept that long, even in my own bed.

I extend my arms and let my body stretch, relishing the burn.

"There he is, sleeping beauty," Max teases as he unfastens his seat belt and stands.

I stand too, picking up my AirPods that had fallen out and returning them to their case. "Mate, I've never slept that long on a plane."

"You've been working like an animal. I'm not surprised." He slaps my shoulder and smiles.

"Now you've had all your beauty sleep, *princess*, you ready for Vegas?" Aaron asks whilst shouting the last part and whooping and shaking my shoulders. Aaron is a pure party animal; works hard, plays harder kind of guy. If you need a good time, he's the one you call.

"Aaron, I feel like you and I are kindred spirits. We live for the chaos," Zoey declares, standing in the middle of the aisle looking at him incredulously. Those denim shorts are more like scraps of material. I'm sure if she bent over, I'd be able to see the curve of her arse cheeks. When she notices me staring, she tugs at the hem of them, and I avert my gaze, hoping her brothers didn't see me.

"Yeah, we do baby!" Aaron hoots loudly.

"Coming from the queen of chaos. You, my dear sister, know how to have the most fun. I've seen you on a night out. You're wild." Owen says, poking at her shoulder ahead of us.

I hum a laugh, watching Zoey playfully swat her brother. Collecting my carry-on bag, everyone passes in front of me before walking towards the exit at the front of the plane, trailing behind Zoey. My eyes drop far too many times to her toned legs. I'm going to need to find myself a girl, and pronto. I haven't had a lot of sex lately, not since Vanessa and I broke up over eight months ago, and it's showing in my ogling of Max and Owen's sister.

"Oh shit, wait," Zoey exclaims as she spins and collides directly with my chest. I let out an *oof* noise. Even though the impact was tiny, it surprised me more than anything. "Fuck, I'm sorry. I didn't mean to hurt you. Are you okay?"

Her delicate hand rests on my pec, and searing heat pulses through my t-shirt. I look down at where she's touching me, and her eyes widen, but she doesn't remove it. "Sorry about that too, I mean, touching you. Not that I don't want to touch you. I don't think you have diseases or anything. Oh God, I didn't mean that. I'm sure you're as clean as a whistle." Our eyes connect, hers wild and panicked, mine simmering with amusement. "Please stop me."

She tries to pull her hand back, but I place mine on top and squeeze gently. "Why would I do that? You're cute when you ramble."

"Oh…" She blushes again, looking at our connected hands, then back to my eyes. "I'm so nervous when I'm on a plane. I guess it's leftover nerves." She exhales, but it's rough and has an edge of a shudder.

"Zoey, do you need to get something?" I ask in a low voice.

Tugging her hand from under mine, her clear blue eyes widen again as she obviously remembers. "Yes, my headphones. I think I left them in the little seat compartment." She points behind me, and I stand to the side of the aisle as she brushes past me. I watch her as she bends over and gives me a glimpse of that perfectly peachy arse I've been obsessing over since we got on the plane, and fuck, it's better than I thought it could be. I stifle a groan, and Max slaps my chest, gaining my attention.

"Dude, stop ogling my sister," he announces loud enough that I know Zoey heard him.

She snaps up. "Found them," she says, tucking them into her pocket. She walks towards me with a devilish look in her eyes, brushing her body past mine slowly, torturously slowly. Only the lightest of grazes against our clothed bodies when she stops in front of me, and my gaze immediately drops to her lips. My first thought, like it has been the whole plane ride is, *Fuck, she's hot.* My second thought? *Do not get a boner, do not get a boner.*

"Zoey," I say with a little more warning than I'd meant. It's taking every bit of self-control not to grab her hips and push us closer because she's only just touching me, and it's not enough.

She smiles victoriously like she knows exactly what I'm thinking. "Maybe my rambling isn't the only thing you like?"

I scratch at my beard to distract from the groan building. I guess her brother was right; she is a bit wild. And I think I like it.

She pats my chest, laughing carefree. "I'm joking, Harrison, relax."

I'm definitely not seeing the joke. I am crushing on my best friend's little sister, and I shouldn't be.

She walks towards the exit, and I take a deep cleansing breath, looking up at the ceiling of the plane, reminding myself that I'm here to relax and have fun. That doesn't include sex with Zoey.

Stepping off the plane, I'm hit with that stifling Vegas air as I walk down the stairs. "Jesus, I forgot how hot it gets here." I blow out a big breath, trying to acclimatise as quickly as possible.

"Too hot for you, big guy?" Max laughs. "Let's get you by the pool and cool you off."

Zoey is already strutting down towards a waiting car, and the others are already inside another one.

I nod to the driver and crouch to get inside the black saloon. I expect to see Max next to me, but of course, I'm sitting next to the little vixen whose smile is brighter than the 'Welcome to Vegas' sign.

While Zoey applies lip balm and brushes her hair, I try not to stare, taking out my phone and turning off aeroplane mode. There was Wi-Fi on the plane, and I had every intention of answering emails, but that didn't happen, so now several messages and notifications obnoxiously beep in the car.

"Someone's popular," Max chides from the front seat.

"Just work shit," I reply, even though most, if not all, the messages appear to be from Vanessa, ranting in capital letters about fuck knows what.

"Is it Vanessa?" Max asks.

"Nothing I can't handle," I say, squashing the conversation. I don't want to waste energy on her, not when I'm supposed to be relaxing. I feel another set of eyes on me. Zoey's bright blue orbs take me in, filled with curiosity. Before I can speak, she looks away with a frown.

Within forty minutes, we're pulling up outside the Bellagio hotel. The trademark building swoops itself around in a half-moon shape with the famous fountain out front. Zoey stares out the window, watching the fountain go off like it always does in the movies. "This is amazing," she breathes.

"Come on, baby sis, let's go check out how amazing it all is," Max says, exiting the car.

"Stop calling me baby sis," she mutters to herself as she follows him.

All six of us walk into the foyer, greeted by concierges as we approach. When we step inside, the beautiful glass flower ceiling radiates colour into the open space, whilst the botanical conservatory frames the reception desk. "Wow, this place is unreal," Zoey marvels as she spins around.

Walking to the check-in desk, Owen takes charge. "Reservation for Bancroft." The way he says his last name, like he's James Bond, has me chuckling to myself. "There should be four rooms. Two double suites and two single rooms." The receptionist taps on the computer, scowls, taps again, and scowls more, leaving me uneasy.

"I can see we have three of our penthouse rooms reserved. But unfortunately, the suites up there don't split into singles, sir. I can see if we have any singles available on another floor?" She quickly taps her keyboard before looking up and shaking her head. "I'm so sorry, Mr Bancroft, there aren't any suites that would suit your single occupancy."

Max and Owen share a look between them. Zoey, Nate, and Aaron are oblivious to this new revelation. The boys flirting up a storm with my best friend's baby sister. I mean, they're right fucking there, and they aren't being subtle about it either.

Max discusses something with the receptionist, and I'm distracted watching the way Zoey is so at ease with everyone. I don't know if she knew Nate and Aaron before, but if she didn't, she's very comfortable with them already, touching their arms, flicking her hair, and smiling at them. My jaw tightens watching them. She didn't even remember me on the plane, but they're the ones who get her flirty side? Fuck that... and fuck me. I'm not the jealous type. *The fuck am I doing?*

"Guys, come here a sec," Max says, gaining my attention before turning to Owen and sharing another look. Twins are apparently mind readers because one of them nods to the other, and I have no idea what just transpired between them.

"Okay so, we've got three double penthouse suites reserved. We need to buddy up because there's six of us."

Zoey looks nervously between us and then raises an eyebrow at her brothers.

"So I can share with you, Tink," Max says, slinging his arms around his sister's shoulder. Her face contorts into disgust as she shrugs him off.

"And listen to my big brother have sex in the next room–I think the fuck not." She spins to face the woman at the desk. "Are you sure there isn't any other option?" When the woman shakes her head again, Zoey deflates and instantly turns to me, eyes blazing with something I can't quite place... fear, determination? Who knows? Her eyes are so icy blue that I'm lost in a glacier just looking at her. "I'll share with you, but there are ground rules. No loud sex unless we're both having it," she says adamantly, just as Max takes one menacing step towards me, but she raises her hand to his chest placatingly, breaking our gaze. "Separately, I mean, idiot. Not together."

I'm standing completely still, my mind racing, completely unsure what the fuck just happened? Did... did Zoey just claim me as her roommate? Why would she do that?

Aaron comes to Zoey's side, wrapping his hand around her waist, and I frown, watching them. "I'll share with you, baby girl," he says playfully, wiggling his eyebrows.

Zoey swats him away, adjusting the bag on her shoulder. "I'm good with Harrison. At least I kind of know him more than you two goons. Plus, I wouldn't dream of getting in the way of your hook ups."

Aaron pouts. "You could be my hook up."

"In your fucking dreams, dickhead," Max growls, turning to me. "Yours too, H. Hands off."

I practically swallow my tongue at his threat, praying he can't read my mind because my hands? Yeah, I'd like them to be all over his little sister, but I won't. Owen shrugs as he follows Max. "Just don't make her your rebound," he laughs, punching my shoulder lightly.

"I'm here to relax, man." I turn to Zoey, who's assessing me with a curious expression, looking like she has so many questions. Standing in front of her, blocking out the guys behind me so we can privately have this conversation, I lean in. "Contrary to what you think, I'm here for this weekend, it isn't to hook up with a bunch of women. It's to relax. I won't interfere with any reasons you're here either, but I'm happy to room with you," I say, holding her intense stare. Whatever look I give her seems to have her relaxing, her shoulders dropping to a normal height.

"Good. Glad we've cleared that up." She nods, pats my chest and turns toward the lifts. I shake my head, wondering how I'm going to survive the blue balls I'm inevitably going to get by staying in a suite with Zoey Bancroft.

Chapter 4

Zoey

The suite living area, which is as big as my London flat—no, actually, it's bigger—has enormous floor-to-ceiling windows with amazing views of downtown Vegas. I whistle and marvel as I spin around the space, modern décor, gold furnishings, and artwork that probably cost more than my parent's mansion. A bottle of Cristal chills in a bucket on the dining table as I run my fingers over the glass top and spot the complimentary VIP pool cabana reservations. I know I grew up with parents who liked to throw their money around, but I've not realised just how much my brothers like to do it, too.

I look out the windows as daytime Vegas bustles below us when I feel a warmth to my right. For a split second, I forgot I was sharing with Harrison. But how is that possible? The man is right here, taking up all that oxygen I'm trying to hold on to. It doesn't matter that I practically claimed him downstairs. I don't know Nate and Aaron that well, but I can already tell they want to get laid this weekend, and I'm not interested in being around for that. But Harrison seems different.

Yeah, sure, he flusters me a little bit for whatever reason, but he seemed like the best choice. In reality, we shouldn't end up getting under each other's feet too much because of the sheer size of this place.

"Have you been here before?" Harrison asks, awakening me from my gawping state.

"I haven't. Not travelled to the US much. I've only ever been to New York. I'm not my parent's favourite child, remember? They don't like to throw money at me anymore. They still control the boys. I'm a wild card, a free agent, a nightmare in their perfect lives." I internally cringe. *Wow, that took a turn quickly.* I never share that much information with anyone, let alone ex-crushes who I'm now sharing a suite with, but here I go, running my mouth.

Harrison chuckles. It's deep and throaty and completely satisfying to hear. "I know I've known your brothers longer, but I already like you more than those two goons."

I blush uncontrollably hard because did he just compliment my crazy? "Oh, thanks. I've always been this way, so I guess it's good you like me because I don't plan on changing it."

I can't quite figure out the look that crosses over Harrison's handsome features. It seems to be a mixture of happiness and confusion. I think I could spend a long time watching him because he seems like an enigma. He doesn't seem to be a fuckboy, or a party animal from what he said downstairs. He seems kind of serious and quiet, and like I said, has that whole mountain man, axe wielding exterior. I mean, he has done nothing to tell me that he has an axe or has ever held one, but my imagination likes to run wild, so I've pictured him topless, sweaty and throwing an axe down to chop wood almost every hour since he boarded the plane.

"You okay? You zoned out." Harrison shifts on his big feet. *Seriously, now I need to know if the saying is true: big feet...big socks.*

"I'm good." *Just picturing the size of your cock, and what would happen if I ran my fingers through your hair?* "Tired."

"I find it hard to believe you ever get tired. Even as kids, you used to run circles around us."

"I remember..." *I remember you being the cutest boy I'd ever seen in my life*, I think to myself as all these memories come crashing back to me. The way I used to hope I could find a shooting star and make a wish to be older, so he'd finally *see me*. The way he used to help me climb the tree in our garden, or how he'd always bring me a Diet Coke when he knew I wasn't allowed them after dinner. God, I really dropped the ball not recognising my own childhood crush. Especially since now, all I can think of is how good he was to me back then. I flick my eyes across the room, not taking anything in but feeling the need to avoid eye contact with him. "You three always acted like you were too cool to hang around a little girl with wild blonde hair and an attitude problem, I was like the annoying fly buzzing around you all."

He guffaws. "I remember you *were* a little handful. But you were joined at the hip with Max. Even when he brought a girl around, he never ignored you. It was sweet."

It doesn't escape me that *he* never ignored me either, but I smile anyway. "I'm glad I have them," I say a little too sadly than I mean to. He cocks his head at my melancholy, but I continue to smile through it and do what I do best, divert the conversation. "Speaking of women, you gonna tell me about your ex, or do we need more time to get acquainted?"

"I... I don't see the point in wasting more energy on her," he says, his tone full of frustration.

I shrug, acting as though I'm fine with his reply, when really I'm planning ways to get it out of him eventually. "Okay. Message received. Shall we check out the rooms?"

He nods, brushing his hand across his beard-clad chin, and the way his arms flexes with the tiny action sends all the wrong kind of thoughts directly to the apex of my thighs.

Down, kitty.

I walk ahead of him because seeing his perfect arse might just send me tripping over and hoping his dick will catch me, and I'm classier than that. *Ha—yeah, right.* I'm not, but I like to think I can exercise restraint with my new temporary roommate.

We walk around a corner, passing the giant TV opposite the sofa, and find the first bedroom with a king-size bed, yet another giant TV, and a walk-in wardrobe that leads to a, yep, you guessed it, marble bathroom.

"You good with this room?" The low timbre of Harrison's voice vibrates around me.

"I'm good with this room," I repeat, not turning to face him but walking into the bathroom as he lingers in the doorway. "I'm going to take a shower. Get rid of the plane on me. Can you find out what the boys are doing?" I ask, closing the door and standing against the cool wood for a second. My eyes close, and I take a breath. Resisting Harrison is going to be a full-time job.

I wiggle out of my shorts, undressing as I walk towards the bathroom.

The shower cools my over-heated body down, leaving me feeling much more relaxed and in control. When I enter my room, the floor-to-ceiling windows grab my attention, and I walk over to marvel at the Vegas Strip. It's filled with people milling around, and performers everywhere. I smile because in the distance there is nothing but desert, and I find it so strange that such a busy place filled with so much life is just plonked right in the middle of a desert.

A knock on my door breaks my gaze. "Yeah?" I ask.

"Boys and I are heading down to the VIP pool. There's a reserved area, so you just need to tell them you're with the Bancroft party. See you down there?" Harrison says from the other side of the door.

"Sure, be there soon."

Now, what do I wear...

Chapter 5

Harrison

S itting opposite the pool, the sun beams down on us; four guys who are paler than milk bottles compared to most people around us. I'm probably the most tanned, with a slight olive tone to my skin, but compared to all these rich, beautiful people, I may as well be a ghost.

The boys called me after Zoey went for her shower and said they were heading to the pool. It's been about half an hour since we sat down, and she's still not here. I'm wondering if she heard me right. There are several pools here, but I definitely told her the right one because this is the only one that allows reservations on the cabana beds.

Lifting the cool beer to my lips, I take a long drag of the liquid, and instantly I'm on holiday. I close my eyes and enjoy letting go of that feeling of stress that comes from working long hours and dealing with a nightmare ex.

"Holy fucking shit," Aaron mumbles next to me. Following his line of sight, I spot what's got him cursing.

Zoey struts into the pool area, turning heads left and right. Wearing a high-legged bright orange bikini with a matching bikini top that barely covers her breasts. A sheer white kimono drapes over her shoulders—one side hanging low—flowing behind her, making her look ethereal. She moves like she's walking in slow motion, but maybe that's just my brain misfiring. But by Aaron's reaction, I'd say it's not just me.

My eyes snag on the tattoo across her left thigh. It's a sun and moon close together, with what looks like chandelier style flowers falling from the bottom of it. It's gorgeous, and so is she. Only when she stops directly in front of me do I realise that I'm still staring at her tattoo and my mouth is open.

Aaron slaps my shoulder, jolting me forward. "You got a little..." He tries to wipe imaginary drool from my chin, but I slap him away from me and straighten up as I lock eyes with Zoey. A scantily clad and very attractive Zoey. I shouldn't be thinking about her sitting on my lap right now, but if her brothers weren't here, there's no question I'd offer it as the only seating option for her. I want her on me, all over me, and fuck, I should not be thinking about that. I clench my fists to stop myself from doing something really fucking stupid, like trying to touch her at all. But it's useless because she removes her big, dark sunglasses with a knowing smirk. *Are all Bancroft children mind readers? Do they have a sixth sense when my thoughts turn inappropriate?* I am totally screwed.

"Hey, mountain man," she says with her perfect raspy voice. I frown a little at the nickname. I should ask her what she means, but words are barely forming in my head, let alone coming out of my mouth. "Can I sit here?" she gestures to the space beside me on the cabana bed. "We're roommates, after all." The way she says that adds to my many, many impure thoughts of my best friends' sister.

Fuck.

I clear my throat and sit up, hoping that my cock isn't obviously bulging through my swim shorts, but I place my beer there strategically anyway, and Zoey tracks the movement, inhaling slightly when her eyes land on my semi-hard erection. "Sure," I manage to force out, flicking my eyes over to a glaring Max.

Zoey climbs onto the bed and crawls, fucking crawls, to sit next to me. Aaron groans beside me on the other cabana.

"Zoey, baby, you're a fucking snack," he shouts across to her as she settles next to me, her coconut body lotion, or suncream, whatever it is I want to inhale more of it, but I don't. In fact, I might've stopped breathing altogether.

"Thanks, honey." She accepts the compliment with ease and ignores her brother's obvious disapproval.

"Stop trying to fuck her, Aaron." Max barks, frowning at him. Aaron baulks but recovers quickly.

"Like I can't tell her she's gorgeous?" He winks at Zoey, and she obviously warms from his compliments. Unexplained anger surges in my chest, and my fists clench, but when I realise what I'm doing, I release them quickly, trying to hide my weird reaction.

Lifting my beer, I realise it's all gone and reach into the cooler for another. When I sit upright, Zoey is on her knees, undoing her bikini top. "Uhh, what are you doing?" I panic, once again flicking my eyes to her brothers, but they're distracted by something Aaron is saying to them.

"Relax," she laughs. "I'm just going to lay on my front, and I don't want strap marks." She lays flat, pulling out her bikini top and letting it drop to the bed between us. "Could you put suncream on my back? I couldn't reach by myself."

This is a terrible idea. Terrible. *Yeah, sure, tell your cock that.*

She passes me the bottle, and I squirt some onto my hands, rubbing them together. Shuffling closer, I stare down at her pale skin, trying not to focus on the arch of her back or her perfect peachy arse on display in her thong. *Do not think about her naked. Do not think about her naked. Think about I.T systems, coding, and answering client emails. Anything that isn't Zoey Bancroft half-naked.*

Her head turns to check I'm still there. "Caught you checking out my bum, didn't I?" she says, amusement on her face.

I cough, hoping her brothers didn't hear that. "I'm a gentleman. I'd do no such thing." *Except that's exactly what I did.*

She laughs lightly, the sound musical and sweet. "Sure you are."

I press my hands to her shoulders and massage the cream into her skin. Her skin is soft and supple under my slightly calloused hands. That smell of summer and coconut drifts around the cabana as I spread the cream as far as it'll go along the middle of her back until I get to the dip of her lower back. When I remove my hands, she whimpers, and the sound travels directly to my cock. "Ughh, that was too good, your hands..." She trails off with a shiver.

I say nothing because anything I say will be entirely inappropriate. Instead, I keep my eyes trained on the freckles on her back and the way her skin now glistens with the sun cream. Fuck, this is too much. I pause while I pour more suncream and calm the lust surging through my body like wildfire. I watch her breathing change as if she's excited about me touching her again. I rub the cream across her lower back, firmly kneading her hips as I try not to think about pealing her thong off and what she'd looked like naked, laid out in front of me.

"You two enjoying your sex show over there?" Aaron quips, reminding me that we're in public... in front of her brothers. "I'm stiff as a board watching you do that with your big hands, H."

"Fuck you, Aaron," I reply, pointing my middle finger his way.

"Just saying, I'd love to be Zoey right now."

"In your dreams," I volley back.

His eyebrows wiggle. "Absolutely, *big man*," he says suggestively. Aaron is very open with his sexuality, and he's a joker at heart, too, which he uses to his advantage often to make me the brunt of many jokes between the boys. It's usually the runt of the group who gets the beatings, but not this bunch. They pick on the biggest out of all of us. Me. *Cocky bastards.*

Sitting back, I glug my beer again, enjoying how cool it feels against my raging temperature. I will my body to calm the fuck down. I'm not an impulsive guy. I plan and brood and take calculated risks, not make reckless decisions. So, these feelings of desperation that have been biting at my heels for the last ten minutes are unsettling me; I need to chill out.

"Ugh, I'm in heaven. I love the sunshine. Now, if I could just convince you to massage me like that every day, I'd be set for life." Zoey murmurs quietly, as she lets out a contented sigh.

Funny thing is, I'd happily give her massage after massage if it meant I could touch her like that daily. And that is exactly what I shouldn't be admitting to myself.

Chapter 6

Zoey

I f I thought Harrison's touch was torture (of the best kind), it is nothing to watching him getting out of the pool; water running over his sculpted body and his swim shorts clinging to him, outlining his thick thighs and the outline of what looks like his very impressive cock. One I'd very much like to explore. Just the thought makes my mouth water.

Holy mother fucking hell, older men are hot. How am I only just realising this? Older men are it.

Laying on my front, I gawk at him from behind the safety of my sunglasses, drinking in every curve of his stomach that's carved to perfection but not overworked either. He's got a body that screams, 'Zoey, lick me'. Then again, maybe that's just my inner ho trying to fly her freak flag.

His dark hair is long enough to almost tuck it behind his ears and get those fucking cute curls that flick around the base of his neck. Don't even get me started on his beard or the fact that all the hair on his head and face is starting to speckle with grey, which is a huge plus in my books. I watch completely in awe as a droplet of water travels down through the valleys of his pecs and disappears into his abs.

This man—not the boy I crushed on a lifetime ago—is evidently all grown up, and what a fucking grown up he is.

As he moves towards the cabana we've been sharing for the last few hours, I desperately try to tear my attention from him. In my peripheral vision, I see him flick some of the water from his hair, and I have to physically stop myself from opening my mouth to catch the droplets. *No, Zoey, inappropriate.* But when he runs his thick fingers through his strands, pushing it back from his face, I'm done for. I don't even care if I am caught staring because the man is a fucking god among us mortals.

When he sits on the bed next to me, my breathing hitches as heat travels through my body, converging between my thighs. I'm so distracted by his proximity that when his cold hand suddenly lands on my lower calf, I practically leap off the cabana. A zing of pleasure travels upwards and lands directly on my clit with a zap. "Sorry, I didn't mean to make you jump. Drink?" he asks.

My heartbeat thrashes in my ears from his touch. And yet, somehow, I manage to reply. "Please," I say breathlessly, begging my inner ho to calm down and ignore his hand to the best of my ability. When he removes it to grab me a beer, my body whimpers for more of his touch.

God knows how we're supposed to spend a few days together in the same suite and not touch each other. I mean, I do know, and they're called Max and Owen. But aside from them, I'm not totally convinced Harrison wants me. I mean, I thought I saw a flicker of something earlier, like when he watched me walk into the pool area, and they seemed to sparkle with gold flecks against the darkness, and I could've sworn he adjusted in that way that men do when they're rocking a hard-on.

But since the plane, he's been good at being Mr Cool, Mr sombre, and grown up that I'm not actually sure what he's thinking. And since I have the mental age of a teenager, it seems anything between us is likely going to fizzle out faster than I can say, 'What happens in Vegas' because no one ever puts up with my shit. But is that what I'd want? A fling? I mean, it's all I've ever really done, but something about Harrison tells me he is a commitment type. And maybe... But then I realise there's no point in even considering this because it won't happen. Flirting is fine, but that's all I'll allow myself.

I lay flat again to slip my discarded bikini top back on and tie it up, adjusting the material over my chest. Just as I turn slightly to face him, propping my head onto my hand, he passes me a cold beer; a few droplets of condensation drip onto my hip, the cold sizzling from my heated skin, and a gasp escapes my throat with haste. "Jesus, that's cold."

Without hesitation, he leans forward and wipes the cool liquid from my skin, replacing it with a trail of heat where his fingertips have brushed against me. "There," he says casually, as though he hasn't just ignited a fucking raging fire inside me. Honestly, I'm half wishing he'd licked it off me.

"Thanks," I say, tipping my beer towards him and then glugging half of it without a breath.

After a few minutes, he leans forward and lays right next to me. The smell of beer, suncream and something slightly sweet but masculine washes over me as he moves. He turns his head my way, leaving us both staring at each other.

"So, Zoey Bancroft. How has life treated you all these years?"

I narrow my eyes at him. "Piqued your interest, have I?"

He nods. "Very much so." Our eyes stay locked, enough for me to see those golden flecks ignite again like fireworks across a dark sky.

"You're kind of beautiful, you know," I whisper, without really thinking about how he might take my compliment. To my surprise, he blushes. It's hard to see past his beard, but it's definitely there; a cute pink flush colours the tips of his ears and the end of his nose.

"Thank you." He doesn't look away, and now it's my turn to colour. "I don't feel like it'll be genuine if I say it back to you now."

My nose scrunches. "I'm not a words kind of girl. Definitely more into physical touch, so you can call me all the things you like, but as soon as those big, beautiful hands touch me, I'll be a puddle again. So anytime you want to tell me I look good, you can just massage me instead."

"Noted." He smiles genuinely, and the fact I made my ex-crush smile makes my chest swell, and I wonder how much he actually smiles. I stand by my assessment of him, that strong, silent, serious type, and whilst that's insanely hot, that doesn't compare to the effect of this man's perfectly symmetrical smile, which is currently making my tummy flutter.

"So, you want to know what's been going on? I don't know if you realise, but that's sixteen years of catching up."

"You'd best get chatting then."

"Okay, you don't know what you're getting yourself into, mountain man, but you asked..." I sit upright so we're facing each other and take a deep breath because I'm not really sure if he's ready to hear about all the ways my life has changed since I saw him last, but here we go. "I know you said you remember me being a handful.

Well, that never stopped. Once the boys moved out, it was just me in that massive house, and I was bored. I hated being carted around to events with my parents and shown off as some debutant. That wasn't me, and it never has been." I pause, watching his reaction, but when I see he's staring at me intently, it makes me feel more exposed than I've ever been with anyone.

"So, Daddy dearest took to being disappointed in me. My mother was just constantly irritated I wasn't the perfect daughter that she could play dress up on." I laugh to myself, but it's empty. "When I was eight, she dressed me in a white poufy dress, and I hacked it to pieces so the hem was all different lengths. She fainted, like a pure drama queen, but she was so mad at me. In my defence, I'd made the dress better. I looked like a rock chick rather than a debutant. She's never forgiven me for it, I swear."

"I remember that. It's foggy, but I remember Max coming over, being really riled up about it." He stares into the distance, obviously recalling the night.

I play with a thread of cotton from my towel. "Yeah, that doesn't surprise me. It probably upsets Max the most that we don't get on. It used to be a sport, pissing them off, but now it's just..." I pause again, not really willing to admit that it hurts, especially to Harrison Clarke. I shake my head, realising that I'm taking a turn into sad girl vibes. Staring out at the glistening blue pool, a sigh escapes my mouth. "I'm not even sure some of my friends know this much about me. Are you sure you want to learn my innermost secrets?" I say, raising an eyebrow and hoping he doesn't push me for the end of that sentence.

"I'm an excellent secret keeper." He winks, making heat crawl up my spine and settle in my cheeks.

"Okay... So, where was I?"

"The dress when you were eight," he replies.

"Ah yes," I say, finding that piece of string again to keep my hands busy. "So, that was the end of my mother trying to mould me into something I was never going to be. They both put all their effort into my brothers because they were their golden boys; the ones who already worked with Dad on the weekends at the company, the ones who said yes and never no. Once the boys left, everything became a sport to piss my parents off." I scoff at my past self. Thank God I've grown up since then and made a somewhat decent human of myself. "I was the worst kind of teenager, but when I turned seventeen, I realised I wasn't enjoying it anymore. So, I apologised and made a plan to get out of their house. Although my parents still don't approve of what I do. I mean, when I turned eighteen, I used half of my trust fund for a good cause, and that pissed them off even more."

"Are you a do-gooder on the sly, Zoey Bancroft?" he asks, amusement scattered across his face.

I smile widely. "I am, but you can't tell a soul. My reputation as a detached wild child will be ruined." I put my index finger against my lips in a shh motion, and he tracks the movement so intently I want to shiver from his stare. "But seriously, I opened a non-profit animal shelter because if there's one thing I hate, it's the way animals are treated." I feel my blood heat from my passion about this subject. "They're helpless and just want to be loved."

Like me, my subconscious adds—always the voice of reason.

The look on Harrison's face has me feeling raw and vulnerable again, like he's really *seeing* me, and it's unnerving. I don't think anyone has ever seen the real, hidden, scared parts of me. But the look in his eyes—kind, open and calm—has me taking a deep breath that I feel all the way to my toes, and I'm a little more relaxed. Maybe talking to strangers is actually cathartic or whatever.

"I have a confession. I knew you had the shelter. I looked you up after I saw you at the wedding last year."

I squeeze my eyes closed at the hazy memory from that night. "You mean when I shamelessly flirted with you and still had no idea you were *the* Harrison Clarke?"

"I... I thought you didn't remember," he says shyly, running his hand over his beard.

"Pff, you practically were famous to me. Definitely a regular in my dreams growing up, but for whatever reason I never connected the dots until now," I say, and immediately my eyes widen, and I bury my head in my hands, groaning. "Tell me you didn't hear that."

"Oh, I heard it, alright." His voice is low.

When I look up, my face is on fire. Embarrassment curls around me like smoke, but when I look at Harrison, he has a look on his face. It's the same one he wore when I asked him to apply my sun cream. It kind of says, 'I'd fuck you into next Tuesday, but respectfully'. The heat in my cheeks intensifies at the thought.

"Please don't hang that over my head."

He casually sips his beer, and I watch his throat work, swallowing the liquid. "I'd never," he says, smirking.

"Why don't I believe you?" He shrugs, and for a moment, he looks like the boy that I crushed on, full of charm, playfulness, and completely untouchable. "What about you? You obviously haven't managed to shake my brothers?"

He smiles over at them as they continually dunk each other under the water. Honestly, you'd think thirty-five year old men would be more mature in the Bellagio, but no. "Yeah, they're stuck with me just as much though."

"But you work together a lot?" I ask. "I don't have anything to do with the company, so I have no idea. You could be the brains behind it all for all I know."

He chuckles. "I've got my own company. ITC—it's a tech company that develops and implements office software."

"Oooo..."

"You have any idea what that is?"

"No, but it sounds fancy."

He smiles bashfully. "I basically have made different systems, apps and software that companies use across the world to operate their business on. You must have something at work similar?"

I squint to think. "I'm sure Lloyd downloaded something called Officewide, which has a basic system and adoption form we use, but it's not that reliable."

"Hmm, yeah, I've heard of it. I'll hook you up when we get back to London."

Gulping down the casual comment of seeing me in London, I find myself robbed of words, and we manage to fall into a comfortable silence.

Eventually, he speaks again. "Can I ask you something? You can tell me it's none of my business." He pauses.

"It probably is none of your business, but ask anyway."

"You seem passionate about your work. You said only half of your trust fund went to the shelter. What did you do with your other half?" he asks, curiosity marring his face.

"Oh, I don't actually have all of it yet. Don't get me wrong, I need it to invest more into the shelter, but my parents have a clause that

I either need to be married or turn thirty-five." My head thumps at the thought of the shelter issues, reminding me that I need to message them to make sure everything is okay.

"Thirty-five? That means your brothers got theirs this week, which makes sense for this trip." He waves his arms around. "It seems like an outdated notion, though... why bother?"

"Because they live to torture me."

He nods pensively. That strong, silent aura of his emanating so deeply it's intoxicating. "One more question, then I'm done with the Zoey interrogation, I swear."

I laugh, looking at him with a nod. "Go on."

Clearing his throat, he turns his head to look out at the pool. "Why mountain man?" he asks as I tilt my head back to him.

"Because you're built like a sexy mountain man with your ruggedness and... beard and muscles." I gesture wildly at his body as though he won't know what I'm talking about without my flailing.

He smiles that bright smile again and my belly flip flops. "You think I'm sexy?"

"Less so now." I roll my eyes playfully, but when I zone in on him again, his eyes are firmly planted on my mouth, and there's no mistaking what he's thinking when he licks his lower lip and holds it hostage between his teeth.

"You're trouble," he says, growling under his breath. The deep, throaty sound caresses me everywhere, and it's not nearly enough because Harrison Clarke growling? Ten out of ten in the sounds I'd like to remember for the rest of my life.

"With a capital T, baby." I wink and watch him watch me. He's unnerving, and I need to remind myself that sleeping with this beautiful man is a bad idea.

Chapter 7

Harrison

I'm all kinds of exhausted when we get back to the hotel room. It's not that late, but travel, beer, and sunshine have taken it out of me, and I'd love nothing more than a nap.

"Are you as tired as I am, man?" Max huffs, running his hand through his hair as he flops onto the sofa in the living room.

"I am," I say, collapsing right next to him. "Why are you here?"

He shrugs. "Owen took a girl back to the room about an hour ago, and I love my brother, but I don't wanna hear him having an afternoon delight."

"He did? When? How the fuck did I miss that?" I laugh, sinking further into the oversized, soft.

"He's a sneaky fucker. Comes across as the quiet, pensive, innocent one, but it's all a rouse." Max's eyes close, and he stretches his long legs out in front of him. "Goddamn, these sofas are comfy. Gonna nap here if that's cool?"

I nod and go to answer him, but he's already half asleep, his breathing long and slow. I feel it, too; tired in my bones. I stand, throw a blanket over my best friend, and head to my room. When I pass Zoey's room, I hear her laughing. She came upstairs before any of us, and I half expected her to be asleep, but I'm guessing she's on the phone with someone, and I immediately wonder who. I haven't asked if she's seeing anyone but a catch like her. It's highly unlikely she's single.

Thumping my tired feet into my room, my body collapses face first onto my bed, not even bothering to close the door behind me. I hear my phone vibrate on my bedside table, but I don't want to think about anything, especially not Vanessa. She's plagued enough of my time lately and ruined years of my life, and I'm finally in control of the situation, so I'm ignoring thoughts of her indefinitely.

I wake to someone shaking me. "Dude, it's easier to wake the dead than you." Max chuckles next to me, hands still firmly, trying to shake me awake. I roll over onto my back, groaning as I go.

"Fuuuuuuck, dead arms," I grumble, trying to move but failing.

"Cock's not dead though."

My eyes spring open, and I look down to see that I'm hard, and it's very obvious through my swim shorts. "Morning wood, like you've never had it?" I scoff, adjusting myself, ignoring Max's sniggers. *Fucking child.*

"It's like midnight. We all slept so late. We should hit the casinos, or we can order room service together in Owen and my room. His fuckfest is over, and he's hungry," Max says, tapping his phone, acting casual.

"Food. Good," I yawn.

"You neanderthal, food, good." Zoey's mocking, raspy voice comes from the foot of my bed, and I spring upright to lock onto two icy blues and a very amused smirk.

I instantly cover my cock, but it's no use. I spare a look at Max, who laughs. "She's been here the whole time I have."

"Wonderful," I reply, flopping back down onto the bed and covering my eyes with one of my arms, the other over my desperate for attention cock.

"It really was wonderful," Zoey replies with a chuckle in her throat. "I'd say up you get, but clearly that's not the problem here," she lets out that chuckle she held in, and Max barks laughter.

"For the love of—"

"Don't get all bent out of shape. We're all *friends* here. Let's go get food," Max interrupts before leaving me alone with Zoey.

When I remove my arm and see her staring directly at my crotch, which has calmed down, thankfully, she smiles and stands. "I'll leave you to... do whatever you need to." She begins walking backwards.

"I'm going to get dressed," I say, sitting upright and shifting to the edge of my bed. "Sorry about, uh... you know." I can't even say, 'Sorry that you had to get an eyeful of my boner' because I know it'll sound insincere. I'm not even *that* sorry. Horny, yes. Sorry, no.

"All good," she says, closing the door behind her with a swish of her white blonde hair.

I stand and stretch, remembering to head to the gym in the morning because I clearly need to work off some tension.

Once I'm dressed in sweats and a t-shirt, I head across the hall to Max and Owen's room. Knocking on the door, Owen opens it with a shit eating grin. He looks down at my crotch. "How's the third leg? Manage to calm him down?"

I flip him off and push past him. "Not funny. Also, how the fuck have you already had sex? We've been here for..." I check my watch. "Less than fifteen hours."

"He's a manwhore," Nate shouts from the sofa ahead of me, where he's sitting with Zoey, Aaron (who is conveniently sitting right next to her) and Max opposite.

"He's right, he is a manwhore, but mainly it's because women go ga-ga over the fact he can whisper mathematical equations whilst looking like something out of Sons of Anarchy." Max grins widely, and Owen flips him off.

I nod in their direction, head over to the selection of drinks on the small foyer table, and pour myself a whisky.

Zoey throws her head back in laughter at something Aaron says. "Seriously?" he asks, and she shakes her head at him.

What are they talking about? And why do I want her to talk to me, too, not just Aaron?

"Seriously, you gotta stop looking at her like that." A voice startles me. I turn and see Owen.

"Your stealth mode is disturbing."

"How else do you think I sneak out of women's beds so quietly?" He smirks, sipping his whisky. "Seriously, though. She's my sister, and you're eye-fucking her."

I swallow and force myself to stare at the drink in my hand. "I'm not. I wouldn't do that. I just wondered what Aaron said to her."

Or maybe I was, but I didn't mean to be so obvious.

"Listen, I'm not as strict on this as Max, but if you hurt her, then we'll have issues." The serious tone of his voice makes me look back at him.

"What are you saying?" I ask. *Is he saying I'm allowed to hook up with her?*

"Nothing exactly, just that I see the way you're looking at her. If you hurt her, I'll have a whole lot more to say. You're two single people sharing a room…" He huffs a laugh. "I might not be good with people, dude, but it doesn't take a math genius like me to work out that one plus one equals two, if you know what I mean."

I choke on a laugh, and the temperature in the room rises significantly. "I *don't* know what you mean. I'm not going there."

Owen raises an eyebrow as he pins me with a stare. "Okay, well, I guess I read it all wrong then, and we have no issues at all." His hand lands on my shoulder with a slap that feels more menacing than comforting.

"None at all. You might want to have a conversation with Aaron, though. He's not stopped touching her," I say, trying to be casual as I nod towards where he's now got his hand on her leg. I grip my glass tight enough that my fingers ache and definitely don't imagine it's Aaron's neck I'm squeezing. Nope, I would never.

Owen snuffs a noise and walks towards the others on the sofa, purposefully squeezing his huge body between Zoey and Aaron. "Make room."

Zoey grunts as she gets shoved off the sofa, shouting curses at her brother.

"Mate, if you wanted a cuddle, all you had to do was ask." Aaron laughs, wiggling his eyebrows, and they start bickering.

I loosen the grip on my glass. Now that Owen is there, I feel a little less murdery towards Aaron. But I'm still left with burning questions from the conversation with him. I mean, what the fuck just happened? Was that a warning mixed in with permission? I can't even begin to dissect it. I didn't think I'd been as obvious as Aaron when I've been around Zoey today. It's been less than a day, and I'm already failing at hiding the crush I fear is building for her.

A knock at the door has Aaron leaping to his feet, ignoring Owen's glare from their argument. "Food's here."

I walk over to the other sofa where Zoey has been relegated, and she smiles as I sit. Her scent wraps around me, sweet, still coconutty from earlier, and completely mouth-watering.

"Hey, roomie," she coos.

Before I can respond, the food is brought in. We sit and eat like we haven't eaten in years, none of us attempting to make conversation, just enjoying the food taking us to a coma state.

"That was incredible," Zoey sighs, slumping her petite frame into the sofa and patting her cute stomach that she's poking out dramatically.

I'm completely taken off guard though, when she slumps sideways, resting her head on my shoulder, as her blonde hair tickles against my skin. I stiffen, and my eyes scan the room to see if anyone has noticed how we're sitting, but no one is paying us the slightest bit of attention. They're all talking about tomorrow's plans, which I should be listening to, but I can't hear anything except the little puffs of air leaving Zoey's mouth and trailing down my arm.

Dude, you're so crushing on her.

Being this close to a woman feels a little unnatural because, since Vanessa, I've kept things entirely physical and non-committal with women, and even that's been scarce. I felt fragile, hurt, and betrayed by her. And even though I'm over her—I pretty much was from the moment I caught her cheating—it still stung. I think I spent a good amount of time blaming myself and work because Vanessa made me feel like I was the problem in our relationship when it had nothing to do with me, it was her inability to not fuck someone else. Maybe I have been hiding and a little reluctant to put myself out there, but sitting here with Zoey and having her curves against me makes my chest ache in a way I thought I'd never feel again.

"Dude, she's out," someone shouts from across the room, and when I look up, I realise that Owen is shouting at me with a gleam in his eye that I remember well from our earlier conversation. I shift sideways, causing Zoey to startle and groan.

"Nooo, man, warm. Man, cosy," she purrs, nuzzling into me again.

My eyes frantically find her brothers and the other two guys who are staring at me, amused. I put my hands up in surrender, and all it does is cause Zoey to move closer to me. "I didn't do this," I squeal, reaching a pitch completely unnatural given my usual deep voice. All the guys share a look and laugh, throwing their heads back.

"It's cool, man. We know Zoey's a cuddler. She's not picky about who she cuddles. Any warm body will do," Max replies, surprising me, considering how protective he always is. Something in my chest cools. I don't like the idea that she would just search for the nearest warm body. That makes this feel weird. I shake it off though, when Max stands, the chair scraping against the floor as he does, and walks his 6-foot-plus self over to us.

"Tink, it's time for bed," he whispers. She moans, and I decide that it's a sound I definitely want to hear again under different circumstances, as in not in a room with her brothers.

"Don't wanna move," she mumbles sleepily.

"Fine, H will take you back to your bed," Max says calmly, then looks at me. "That cool?" he asks, placing so much trust in me I can't stop the rise in my eyebrows.

"Yeah," I croak, then clear my throat. "Yes, I can take her back."

Shifting us both, I manage to move my arms underneath her and stand with a very full stomach and a very sleepy Zoey, who doesn't protest me carrying her. She just wraps her arm around the back of my neck and nuzzles right there at the base of my collarbone. Goosebumps erupt down my spine and across my arms as she breathes softly against my neck fuuuuuck. I cannot get turned on right now. I give Max one final look of 'I've got her' and carry towards the door.

"Shit, can you reach my keycard and put it in my hand? It's in my back pocket," I say to anyone who will help me. Nate, who has been stoically quiet this whole trip so far, comes to my rescue. I heard from Max that he's dealing with his dad's passing, so I've given him space.

He digs into my back pocket and passes me the key before he moves in front of me and opens the door to the hallway, which makes Zoey shiver and groan in protest. I find myself shushing her, wanting to keep her warm and safe in my arms.

When we get to our room, I awkwardly slide the keycard against the lock and enter our room. I walk Zoey over to her room and place her on the bed, where she grumbles about being cold, so I pull the soft white comforter over her.

I pause in her room for a second, watching her fall back into a slumber deep enough to have her softly snoring. I know I shouldn't make things complicated by crushing on my best friend's sister, but on the one hand, I *think* Owen said it's okay if anything happens between me and Zoey. But on the other, Max's scowl is enough to scare me off completely. *Do I risk my friendship to hook up with their sister?*

Her bright blonde hair is splayed across her pillow like a fan, and her make-up-free face looks beautiful. She's the polar opposite of Vanessa in every way, and even though I've spent most of my life assuming I had a type—brunette and tall—, I'm beginning to wonder if this little platinum bombshell is going to derail me completely.

Chapter 8

Harrison

"Do we have plans today?" Nate asks, looking around at the other tables as the sounds of the distant slot machines echo around us. We've all come to the hotel bar for a quick bite to eat since most of us slept in this morning and missed breakfast and lunch. Well, all of us except Zoey, who went for a swim and woke at some ungodly hour.

"This is the one time I've not planned a single thing for a trip. Business trips keep us both so strict on timings and where to go, so we wanted this to just be chilled and go with the flow," Owen responds. I get that. Both of them work 24/7, like me, and getting downtime is important.

Just as the guys start talking about options, Zoey breezes into the bar, her bright eyes searching for us. She's wearing another pair of barely there black denim shorts that look ripped to shreds and a tucked in sleeveless acid wash grey t-shirt that shows her lace bra when she moves. Her hair is half up, and sunglasses rest on the top of her head.

She looks… really fucking good. Her face lights up when she spots Max and Owen.

"Hey guys," she beams. Her smile makes everyone else smile because she's got this presence about her that is incredibly compelling.

"Hey baby girl," Aaron purrs next to me, and Max shoots him a look of *don't even think about it*, which makes us all laugh. "Nice swim?" he carries on, ignoring Max's glares.

"Lovely, thanks." She glances around the table at our empty plates and glasses. "What are you losers doing? I want to go out and play," she says, excitement lacing her tone.

"Play?" Aaron asks, grinning like a Cheshire cat. The man will never learn.

"Down boy. I want to go out and have fun. Explore. I saw some streetside bars and I'm dying to see Vegas properly. Who's coming with?"

"Did you eat anything yet?" Max asks, his elbows leaning on the table and his fingers steepled together under his chin as he pins Zoey with a look of concern.

She rolls her eyes. "Yes, *Dad*. I had breakfast and lunch from the room service after my swim. Unlike you part timers I had to check in with the shelter too. But I ate, I promise."

Aaron jumps from his seat eagerly, flinging his arm around her shoulders. "I'm in," he purrs into her ear.

She slaps his chest playfully. "Good, the first round of margaritas is on you,"

"I'm in too," I say, standing and earning a bright smile from Zoey. It's not that I don't want to leave her alone with Aaron. It's more that I *really* don't want to leave her alone with him. Which I know is irrational. Aaron is a great guy, but he's a serial flirter. He could have anyone in the room, man or woman, so why is he picking Zoey? I can't tell what his intentions are. Is it to piss the twins off? Or Me? I don't know, but clearly I'm all kinds of green over this whole situation. "I've never had a margarita, but I feel like I need one if Aaron is paying."

"Yes," Zoey shouts and looks down at the others expectantly. They all groan and stand to tag along. We add the bill to our room tab to sort later and head out.

When we step out onto the street, it takes us a minute to join the strip, but when we do, there's no mistaking where we are. Everything is so bright, giant and over the top, but then I guess that's Vegas for you.

In the distance, there's the Eiffel Tower, New York's Statue of Liberty, and a plethora of other knock off sights. The whole place is over the top and kind of hurts my eyes, and it reminds me why, when I've been here with work, I mostly stay in the hotels and casinos. This is a lot.

"Look at all this," Zoey beams. "It's so tacky, I love it!"

"It's even better at night. We should hit the casinos later," Max suggests.

"Great idea, night out. I need to find a willing body, too." Aaron grabs his junk, emphasising his already obvious point.

Zoey chuckles. "You're all going to ditch me for hook ups at some point, aren't you?"

We all answer differently. Owen, Max, and Aaron agree they'll be ditching her, whereas Nate grumbles a nonsense answer. But it's my answer that snags her attention when I reply, "No chance." I'd never leave her alone in Vegas.

She takes three measured steps towards me, glancing at the others as they walk off ahead, tapping her foot to mine and... *is she flirting with me?*

"So, you want to be the one to tuck me in tonight, Harrison?" she says breathlessly.

Yeah, she's flirting.

I swallow hard, watching as she tracks the movement of it. "I want to make sure you're safe and making the right choices." Fuck, could that be more of a dad answer? What the fuck did I say that for?

She chuckles, looking down again. "I can handle myself. I'm a big girl." She pouts, fluttering her lashes at me.

I shuffle slightly closer but have to stop myself from reaching for her. "I know you *can,* but it doesn't mean you *should* all the time. I know you like your independence, but even if for the next few days, I want to make sure you're safe. Okay? Humour me if nothing else."

The way her icy blue eyes spear me and simultaneously soften has me leaning dangerously close. Just when I think I've got her figured out or that she's going to show me more of her vulnerability, she straightens her shoulders and leans to my ear. "You have big *daddy* vibes, you know," she purrs, her voice sounding like sin, then she moves back so I can see her face again.

I tilt my head. "I don't have any children."

She smirks like a little minx. "Oh, honey, that's not what I meant." She licks her lips slowly as her gaze intensifies, burning me from the inside out. "I meant, you look like you could spank me, and I'd thank you for the pleasure... *Daddy.*"

Suddenly, it's difficult to swallow. My tongue is too big for my mouth, and my cock is definitely too big for my boxers. I inwardly groan. I need to actually remember *how* to flirt with a woman. *Right, that's all. Give it back to her.* So I take a breath and let my mouth ghost her ear and whisper, "You have no idea, sweetheart."

The hitch in her breath is everything I wanted from teasing her but the goosebumps trailing over her shoulder, too. That's an added bonus. I like to see her affected by me. Even if this goes nowhere, a guy can live out his fantasies. And the idea of bending her over and spanking that peachy arse is now all I can envision myself doing later.

Zoey

I let everyone go ahead for a second because I need a minute. It's not the Vegas heat that's making me sweat. It's Harrison Clarke and his sex appeal he just flung my way. The man is quickly becoming my newest fantasy, and he doesn't even realise it. Or maybe he does. I know it's probably not a good idea to sleep with him, considering he's connected to my brothers and, by proxy, my father's company. Yeah, best to squash this fantasy and keep it in a box buried deep in my mind.

When I catch up with them, we're on Freemont Street, which has the most amazing light show. Sparks of colour kaleidoscope over our heads, making us crane our necks to watch the explosion.

"This is trippy as fuck," Aaron muses, spinning around, and I join him, loving the way the lights all blur together. It feels freeing and fun, which is exactly what I need. We both dissolve into a burst of shoulder bumps and laughter. When we right ourselves, Max and Owen are busy chatting and watching the show. Nate has moved ahead of us, but Harrison is watching me. Having his attention so intensely gives me goosebumps.

I shake them off though, throwing a wink his way while I try to ignore the effect he has on me.

We walk some more, taking in the giant palm trees, the bright casino lights, and the many street performers dressed up, all whilst the heat stifles us.

"How do people live here?" Aaron asks, moving his t-shirt away from his body.

"You mean the fucking burning ball of hot gas we're currently on? Yeah, I have no idea." Harrison laughs.

"I think I might be boiled alive. This was a terrible idea for location. We're British and have no idea how to act in this hot weather. Look at those two losers buying handheld fans," I say as we all look at my brothers and laugh.

Harrison turns to me. "You want a fan?"

"No," I smirk. "I want two, didn't you hear me? I'm fucking melting out here."

His deep laughter permeates the air around me like a fog, and I'm smiling right back at him like an idiot as he walks towards Max and Owen to get me a fan or two.

There's an easy atmosphere between us all, full of jokes and laughter. I didn't realise how much I needed this, to switch off from daily life for a while and just be.

"Here you go." Harrison appears in front of me again with a handheld fan blowing warm air at me. It's not air conditioning, but it'll have to do. He stands in front of me, blocking my view of my brothers, he presses a button I didn't notice, and a fine mist of cool water blows towards me with the fan.

"Mmfghpifing," I mumble, unable to form actual words from the relief of the heat for a second.

"Are you glitching?"

"I might be. God, that breeze is better than an orgasm," I say, closing my eyes to bask.

"Hmm, seems you've not been getting the right kind of orgasms." His voice is full of sinful promises that I don't think are meant for me, but I want them to be.

"Guess I had better find someone to scratch that itch," I tease, taking the fan and turning to join the others who have walked ahead, letting my hips sway just a little more than usual, hoping his eyes are firmly on my arse.

Chapter 9

Zoey

The boys all begin complaining they need beer to cool off. When we find the margarita truck just around the corner from Freemont Street, surrounded by Stormtroopers, cowboys and Iron Man. I don't even blink at the group together because it's Vegas. "You boys might need beer, but I need tequila and stat."

I approach the colourful truck, complete with red sombreros, paper umbrellas, limes that smell like heaven, and a cheery bartender behind the counter. "Hey there, you want a margarita, sugar?" the lady coos, and I smile at her accent.

"I'll take six please," I say, bouncing up and down on my heels. Harrison appears next to me, his soft masculine scent complimenting the limes.

"This is your favourite drink?" he asks, examining the bottles of tequila behind the bar.

"It is. Tequila in general, but these are the perfect 'hot day' drink."

I watch the women make the drinks in record time. Passing them over to the counter in front of us. "That'll be eighty dollars, sugar."

I turn to find Aaron. "Oh, sugar daddy," I call, and he bounds over to me like an excited puppy. "Such a good boy," I praise jokingly, just as Aaron leans in and pecks my cheek.

"Anything for you, baby," he says, passing the money over and taking a plastic cup. As he leaves, Max taps the side of his head with a light slap. "What was that for? I get it, man, she's off-limits. Fuck, can't a guy have a little fun?"

I hide my smile behind my drink as I watch Harrison for his reaction, but he doesn't give one, he just sips his margarita. "How's the drink?"

"Good. Strong," he answers, staring at Aaron with a scowl. A scowl that's insanely hot on his perfect face.

I put on my best 'Harrison voice' and imitate him. "Man bad, drink good, girls pretty," I mock playfully.

His big brown eyes zone in on me, amused. "Are you taking the piss out of me?"

He steps closer.

"Was I not clear in my impersonation? It might need some work."

I step closer.

"Careful there, Zoey. You don't want to find out what happens to bad girls."

Oh, but I do.

I tilt my head, trying to suppress my smile. "I'm all bad. There really isn't much good in me... bratty to the bone. What you gonna do about it?" I tease.

His eyes ignite with golden flames. I swear I hear a growl build in his chest as his nostrils flare. The way he slowly trails his tongue across his bottom lip has me clenching my thighs together.

"I'm going to—"

"Guys, let's go," Max shouts, interrupting us with a frown, stopping whatever Harrison was going to say. I want to ask him to finish his sentence, but it's probably for the best that I didn't hear whatever he was going to say. I think climbing him like a tree in the middle of downtown Vegas could probably still get me arrested. But would I care? Not really. I'm getting the impression that it'd be worth it.

An hour later, we're buzzed. The heat and the tequila have successfully made everyone happy and loud. My parents used to hate it when we'd all be home for school holidays because I knew how to rile my brothers up the most. We've all got a little chaos inside us, more so Max and I, but even he's subtle with it when he wants to be. Me? Not so much. I thrive off the thrill of doing things I shouldn't. Like right now, I'm only one margarita in and feeling that chaos surging through my veins. Usually, when this happens, I go out dancing and find a random, willing body for the night. However, it's still daytime, and I'm out with my brothers and his friends, so I should probably rein it in.

"Zo, look," Owen shouts, pointing ahead of us at a Ferris wheel in the middle of Vegas because why the fuck not? "Remember when we were kids?"

I look up at the kind of chaos I'm not that interested in.

"Uh, I remember you trying to kill me on one of those things. Both of you fuckers, in fact. Rocking the car so badly, they had to stop the ride and tell you both to pack it in. I also remember Mum blaming me for being a bad influence." I tut at Owen. "You little shits did all that to scare me."

Max chuckles next to me, his green eyes twinkling. "We did."

I cross my arms over my chest. "Which is why I'm not going on there with you again."

"Oh, come on. We're grown ups now," Owen whines.

"Not how I'd describe either of you, actually."

"Rude, sis."

"Guess you're over your fear of them, then?" Max replies, knowing that I hate fairground rides because of them.

But the thing is, I'm stubborn as all hell, and I will not let my brothers back me into a corner. I'll have the last laugh, even if that laugh is hysteria-induced at the top of a Ferris wheel. I bite my bottom lip, ignoring the clawing heat at the base of my throat.

I spin to face the Ferris wheel, determination fuelling my steps as I stomp towards the ticket booth. "Two tickets, please."

When he hands me the two paper stubs, I turn to see the boys all staring at me, so I seek out Harrison and smile.

"Come on roomie, we're going for a ride." I hold my hand out, hoping that he won't mind me using him because, for some strange reason I can't explain, I know he'll calm me down up there.

His brows pinch slightly, and he tilts his head in question but walks towards me anyway. *Thank God for that.* Aaron would have just tried to get in my knickers, and Nate would've probably started crying at the top with me. And I refuse to do it with either of the buggers who gave me this irrational fear to begin with.

"Just so you know," I say, looking at my brothers' amused expressions. "I hate you both for this, but I will not let you win."

With that, I pull Harrison's big frame into the small car, which creaks, and I flinch at the shrill sound. "Jesus," I mutter under my breath but steel my expression, not wanting to give in to my fear.

Harrison remains stoic next to me. His hands rest on his thighs, and he clears his throat as we slowly, painfully slowly, begin to move upwards.

"Sorry," I confess, feeling guilty that I forced him into yet another thing with me. First roommates, now a crux in proving my brothers wrong.

"Why are you sorry?" He turns his head to face me, and suddenly I realise how close we are. It's stiflingly hot, and all I can feel is the furnace of a man sitting next to me with his big brown eyes that engulf me. "Zoey?"

His low voice calms me and simultaneously snaps me from my daydream. "Hmm?" I say, trying not to get lost in the warmth of his gaze.

"Why are you sorry?"

Oh right. "For dragging you into my shit again. I have a tendency to act now and think later. First, I made you be my roommate, now I'm pushing you on a ride."

"If I didn't want to do something, trust me, I wouldn't do it." He sits back, moving his arm around the back of the carriage behind me.

Does that mean he wants to be here right now, with me? I don't linger on that thought because the ride moves suddenly, jerking us forward, and I yelp, practically hauling myself into his lap. I dive into the big, broad muscles of his shoulders as I hear my brothers cackling from below.

"Give it a little shake, big man. Zoey loves it," Owen shouts, and I make a pact to slip something in his drink later as payback.

"Cheeky motherfuckers," I mumble. "I hate having brothers."

Harrison chuckles and I release his torso slightly but can't bring myself to move my hand back to grip the bar over our legs. Not even sure when that was lowered, it's not going to help if this thing makes me fall to my death. I should be strapped in like an astronaut in a rocket, not just free to move around when I'm fifteen million feet in the air. No, I'm much safer gripping onto Harrison's arm.

"I hated having a sister growing up, too."

I glance up at Harrison to find him looking at me and stroking my knuckles that might be death gripping his arm. I loosen them, wincing. "Sorry about that, but I can't let you go because I'll fall to my death." He smiles with a shrug. "Wait, your sister. I remember her. Katie, right?"

He nods, casually wrapping my hand in his and placing it on my thigh. "Yeah, I think she maybe babysat for you once or twice when we were younger." He looks off across the Vegas strip we just walked down, a frown tugging at his lips. "I loved looking after her, but then, as we got older, some of my friends became more interested in her, and I hated the way they all gawked at her. She's beautiful, but she's also my baby sister, so it was a nightmare trying to keep them away."

A light laugh leaves my throat, and I relax a fraction. "I feel her pain." Looking down to my own menace protectors. "Did she hate you for that?"

"Probably. Although it didn't matter, she ended up with one of my mates from school anyway. Happily married with four girls. Turns out I kept the loud ones away, but it's the quiet ones you have to watch out for. Jake just snuck in there and they were inseparable."

I try not to read too much into his protective brother stance. I have two of my own that are currently stopping me from jumping Harrison's bones. And if he's saying nothing can happen with us because of my brothers, then I guess I hear him loud and clear.

"That's really sweet. Tell me about your nieces."

His face lights up and my heart squeezes in my chest. "They're wild. You'd get on well with them. Cassie is the eldest. She's seven. Then Alanna is five, and the twins Ellie and Ophelia are three. They're all so different, but Ophelia slays me. She's this little firecracker, and she gives the best hugs. I love them all equally, but she and I are best mates."

My face softens as I watch him. "I can tell. I bet they love you, too."

"They love the way I spoil them." He laughs.

I look at him, like really look, and I see this man who has kindness radiating from him effortlessly. Yet, he has this bold and powerful exterior, with an underlying intensity that's so alluring, I find myself hanging on his every word. "You're kind of like an onion, Harrison Clarke. You keep surprising me."

"An onion? Isn't that like the ogre from Shrek? Are you telling me I'm an ogre?" His face bunches, but it's not permanent, and when he meets my eyes, he smiles.

I shrug. "If the boot fits," I tease, and he pokes my side, making me yelp and curl back into him, laughing. "I mean, you're deep, but you're also intense. You make me want to peel back more layers to get to know you. You intrigue me."

His brown eyes pierce me with a stare that feels like he's also trying to do the same thing. The issue is my layers are superficial on purpose. I'm flawed, raw and as honest as I am, I don't show everyone everything, so I'm not sure what he thinks he'll find.

"Tell me your biggest fear, besides this ride," he asks quietly.

I run my tongue over my bottom lip, thinking. "That I'll not make enough of a difference with the shelter. Right before I left, we had a leak in the new section of the building and it's not cheap to fix." I remove my hand from his arm and twist my fingers. "You already know I've got years until I can access the remainder of my trust fund unless I miraculously get married before then, and although donations and smart business help, I know it won't be enough."

"Have you talked to your brothers?"

"I haven't," I reply, shaking my head. "It doesn't seem fair for them to receive their money and me to ask for a handout. Besides, my parents wouldn't allow it. They could take it back or worse, shun the boys, and I could never..."

"Maybe I could help?"

I avert my gaze from his. "I can't do that either. I'll be fine, really." I don't know that I will, but I can't accept help from my brothers or their friends. Especially Harrison.

I breathe in a deep breath, letting the view wash over me, and I'm grateful that Harrison doesn't push again. The wheel comes to a stop, and we're right at the highest part, overlooking most of downtown Vegas. The sun is beaming in the sky, and the heat doesn't let up as it beats down on my bare legs.

"What about you? Do you have any fears?" I question, turning to face him.

He contemplates my question for a minute, and I feel his hand flex in mine. "I try not to hold on to fears. They can incapacitate you. But since we're being honest, maybe I'm scared that after my recent relationship, I'm doomed to be a bachelor. Sharing my life and success with someone means something to me, and sometimes I miss that."

"Do you miss your ex?"

"Fuck no," he splutters, shaking his head. "But maybe I miss the idea of what we were supposed to be. She... cheated on me and I realised pretty fast that I never loved her. I need to find a way to get her to leave me alone. My cars get the brunt of her anger, unfortunately, but I've not caught her doing it yet. I mostly get harassing messages from her, usually with empty threats. Lately, I've been ignoring them, not that it's stopped her." He sighs long and deep, and my chest constricts for him. "But that's life, ups and downs. It's how you react in the face of it all. That's what makes you who you are."

I nod and let us both absorb the moment as I look around, not feeling scared of being so high this time, maybe because my brothers aren't here to almost throw me out of the car, but maybe because there's this big strong man next to me, who's presence is like a calming, babbling brook. He releases my hand, moves his warm palm to my knee, and squeezes.

"You doing okay up here?"

My gaze drops to where his hand is, the heat searing me even more than the sun, and yet a violent shiver ripples its way silently through my body.

"Good. I'm good," I force out, clearing my croaky throat. "I used to be so scared because of those two idiots down there, but I forgot that sometimes, at the highest peak, you get the most beautiful views."

I sigh, taking in the beauty in the hum of people below me, relaxing as I bask in the heat from Harrison's hand still on my leg and the miles and miles of desert in front of us.

"Really beautiful views," Harrison echoes next to me. I turn to smile at him, at this shared moment, to find him already looking at me. His stare is molten as it flicks between my lips and my eyes. My breath shallows until I'm almost panting, but for what? *For him to lean in and kiss me?* Wouldn't that be perfect?

Perfect hasn't ever been meant for me, though. I'm used to uninhibited and messy, which is why I look away, returning my gaze to the desert and all the secrets that hide in the sand.

I push away the intense desire to pull his lips to mine and ignore the burning need tearing through my body because this will never happen. I'm pretty sure no one would ever be able to cope with me, so says my history with men and my life. It's best to keep it simple and safe and not pull Harrison into my mess when he's not long out of a messy break up.

Chapter 10

Harrison

I need to get out of my head because I'm having very inappropriate thoughts about Zoey. Things have quickly become familiar and easy between us, but she brings out the side of me I don't often show, and I need to rein it in before I do something stupid, like claim her in front of all these men who think they can have her.

After spending the day sightseeing, we headed back to our rooms to freshen up, and I may have napped for a bit. The day with Zoey spun around my dreams on repeat. I feel drawn to her, and although I know it's a bad idea, I can't help but think we've been pushed together again for a reason.

Like I said, I need to get out of my head and my room, which is why I'm sitting with Owen, Nate and Max at the casino downstairs in the hotel. Aaron and Zoey are still upstairs but will join us soon. Owen is playing roulette next to me and is hitting a winning streak. I'm not a big gambler, but I might see if I can join a poker game later.

A distant ding signifies the lift doors opening from across the casino and that's when I see her—dressed in a pink sequined dress that barely touches any part of her body. It's scraps of material covered in sparkles. Every other hot-blooded human in the room watches her as she struts across the casino. But fucking fuck, does she look sensational.

She shimmers, and it's got nothing to do with the sequins. She's so full of life, the woman is ninety-nine per cent confidence and I like that. My cock thickens at the sight of her. *No, don't go there.*

"Whaddup, motherfuckers," Aaron says, slapping Nate's back as he appears next to us with Zoey—I hadn't even realised he walked in with her. His eyes dance with mischief, and I want to roll my eyes because I can feel it in the air; his aura of crazy biting at our heels and nights when he's like this never end well.

Zoey smiles as she walks past Aaron and stops in front of me. I stand too suddenly feeling very aware of my arms and how badly I'd like to wrap them around Zoey's petite body and haul her to my side away from all the ogling eyes on her, my heart thrashes against my rib cage at the need to touch her.

"Hey mountain man, you're looking very suave tonight," she purrs, brushing her fingers over my dark shirt and chest, looking at me with those bright blue eyes. *God, I want to kiss her.*

Clearing my throat, I tower over her. "You look stunning." I draw my bottom lip between my teeth whilst I let my gaze roam freely over her. That tattoo peeking out from her thigh makes me want to bite her and then spank her for thinking she could ever go out in public wearing such a tiny dress. But I remember that she isn't mine and ain't life a bitch.

"I told you he'd drool," Aaron whisper shouts into Zoey's ear. She whacks his chest, and he rubs the assaulted area. "So violent for such a tiny person."

"*He* is standing right here and can hear you, dickhead," I chastise Aaron, still unable to stop staring at Zoey as he walks away. I lean into her, inhaling against her ear, smelling her sweet but spicy perfume. I watch her suppress a shudder, which makes me gleam with pride. "He's right, though. How can I not drool over you in that dress?"

Her breath stutters as she places a hand on my chest, her eyes flicking over to her brothers. I follow her gaze, watching Max narrow his eyes at our proximity. "Buy me a drink?"

I place my hand on hers and briefly link our fingers together before walking her towards the bar, feeling Max's scrutiny intensify. But right now, I don't think I care. I need to touch her. "Margarita?"

Her lips curl, letting me see that perfect smile of hers. "Of course. What else?"

The bar is brightly lit with blue lights, each shelf laden with an array of alcohol. A waiter approaches us. "What can I get for you, sir?"

"One margarita and a sparkling water."

Zoey turns to face me, a taunting look on her face. "No."

I turn my body to face her. "No, what?"

"You're having a drink. We're in Vegas, Harrison. You aren't allowed to order sparkling water. Let go, have fun. Isn't that why you're here?"

She's right. The pleading and promise in her eyes make me want to give in without hesitation. She has this way of disarming me already, and I'm a little scared. She might be one of the most bossy women I've been around, but she's also got this charm that's linked to her abrasiveness and her stubbornness, and watching her get what she wants is addicting because she lights up when it happens.

"Fine, make that two margaritas," I sigh.

She smiles a big, bright, soul crushing smile at me, and I'm momentarily blinded at seeing her this happy. This right here is why I say yes to her. Even after a couple of days of getting reacquainted, she seems to have invaded my mind and dominated my will.

I pay for our drinks, and we make our way back to the others. Max has a gorgeous leggy brunette on his arm, who is apparently called Cami and is joining us tonight. Dude moves fast.

"Let's go dancing. I have all this pent-up energy that I need to release." Zoey shimmies, holding her drink still, making her dress sparkle as she moves.

She's not the only one with pent-up energy.

"Zoey, baby, you're killing me in that dress. Can I have the first dance?" Aaron slides in beside her, gripping her hip and turning her towards his hungry eyes. She carelessly flings her arms around his neck, still holding her drink in one hand, and kisses his cheek. I feel my teeth almost crack from the pressure of clenching my jaw. *You don't want to kill Aaron; you don't want to kill Aaron.*

When his hands slide down to cup Zoey's arse over her dress, I definitely want to kill Aaron. I act on instinct. "Okay, that's enough of that." I grab her wrist and spin her back towards me. The surprise in her eyes is laced with mischief as I drape my arm over her shoulder.

"Ooo, jealous are we, big man?" Aaron muses, and I want to punch his stupid straight teeth.

"I don't do jealous." *Or I didn't use to.* "I just want to make sure she doesn't catch diseases from you tonight or ever. Isn't that right, Max?"

I nod towards him as I notice his jaw tick and his eyes zone in on my arm around his sister.

Aaron stumbles backwards, his hand dramatically clutching his chest. "Your words hurt, man. I'm clean as a whistle. Don't let him put you off, Zo. My dick is bigger." He winks at her, and she links her fingers with mine as they rest on her shoulder. The simmering fire of need ignites into a raging inferno from her taking my hand.

"Hmm, two men fighting over little old me? That's got me feeling all kinds of reckless, boys, and you'd better be careful, or I'll eat you both for breakfast," she says seductively, ping ponging her gaze between us.

With that, she saunters off with both of our dicks pointing her way.

Chapter 11

Zoey

The heavy bass of the music fills me like no other high. The darkness of the club cloaks my body, strobe lights flickering around me.

This is what I live for. I haven't danced like this in ages.

The boys gambled and drank whilst I watched and bided my time, but now I'm vibrating with energy. I miss dancing; I miss the freeing feeling you get on the dancefloor when everyone around you is caught up in the rhythm, so I told them I was leaving to find a dancefloor. Harrison and Max followed me to the club but left me on the dancefloor ten minutes ago, Max with his pick of the night, who is the least chatty woman I've ever met. The others stayed, too caught up in whatever they were playing in the casino.

"Hey beautiful." A raspy American voice filters in behind me as I feel the brush of connection at my back. I spin to find a tall, typical frat-boy looking male... keyword here being 'boy'. He doesn't look old enough to even be out of high school, and I place my hand on his shoulder to lean in and tell him to find someone his age when I feel another set of hands snake around my hips and hoist me so far backwards, I levitate.

I can't be sure, but I think I yelp.

When I'm hit with the familiar scent that I know because we've been living together the last couple of days, I relax in his hold.

"Move. On." Harrison's deep, growling voice shouldn't make me quiver, but I'd challenge any woman not to tremble when she hears his low timbre. It's a form of unfair foreplay. Well, that and the fact his incredibly hard body is flush with my back, and his big hand is splayed across my stomach, sending heat racing over my skin.

The boy looks between us, hangs his head like he's just been told to go to his room, and vanishes, obviously continuing his search for another willing body.

"Zoey, you're being careless." Heat unfurls in my core from the feeling of his hot breath on my bare skin. Everything feels heightened; the music, his touch, the heat surrounding me. Just everything, and I need air. Stat.

I push away from him, hoping I can find some oxygen in this packed club. "I'm fine. I know how to handle myself," I snap a little too harshly. I don't need a white knight defending me. I definitely don't need one that turns me on, but I can't touch. "Go find the others. I'm good."

Harrison's eyes flicker with something that looks like he wants to argue with me, so I raise my eyebrows at him, daring him to try and push me again. When his nostrils flare, I know he's going to give in. It's one of his tells I've noticed this week. He turns and leaves me and I fill my lungs with a deep breath.

Good, now there's air again.

I dance through several more songs. Alone, vibing with whoever is around me. All the while, though, I know I have eyes on me. I can feel them searing into my body and I can't say I hate it.

When I feel like my legs might drop off, I head towards the bar in search of water. Within seconds, my bodyguard appears next to me. I give him the side eye. "You know, you're borderline stalking me? You should find someone to get rid of all that tension you're radiating. I'm sure someone will drop to their knees for you," I mumble angrily. *Yeah, like me... No. Not me.*

"Are you upset with me?" he asks, his gaze fixed on my face.

"No." *Yes. I don't know.*

"Your face says otherwise. I'll back off. Promise. I just get a bit overprotective of people who are important to me."

And how the fuck do I stay mad at him when he says that? The tightness in my chest loosens as I turn to face him. "Okay, maybe I am a little annoyed. But it's not because of you, it's me."

"Classic line." He smirks, and it's too sexy, enough to break the scowl on my face. I let a small smile sneak free. "Seriously, it's a classic for a reason. I don't need to be protected all the time, but I'm getting in my head."

Harrison stiffens. "About what?"

Shit. I can't exactly say 'because I think I'd like to bang your brains out', can I?

I wave my hand in front of my face. "I'm fine, really. Please, just go have fun. Don't stare at me all night because you're worried about me. I've got skills and pepper spray." I offer a reassuring smile, and he softens slightly.

I think I see a flash of heat in his eyes, but it disappears just as fast. "I happen to like staring at you." He inhales sharply. "But I'll back off."

He takes a step away from me, and my first instinct is to follow him. *God, my brain couldn't sabotage me more if it tried.* I want space, but I also want to be the centre of his attention. Story of my life.

I nod and watch as he continues to retreat, his deep brown eyes never leaving mine. I know it won't take long for a woman to fall into his lap with the way he looks tonight, dressed in a dark charcoal shirt that highlights the grey in his hair that makes him look... well, hot as fuck.

I know I just told him to go find someone, but I would prefer if that someone could be me.

It turns out, I'm stupid. Really stupid.

And an attention whore. Who has issues. I'm enough of a grown-up to admit when I've made a mistake. Most of the time. Like right now, as I sit across from Harrison and a woman. No, a fucking supermodel. I don't actually know if she is, but she looks like she should be. Long slender legs, sculpted body, perfect tits, whiter than white teeth. The perfect shade of blonde hair. Everything screams perfect, and I'm annoyed.

Yes, I told him to find someone to release tension with. I just didn't want to witness it. Yet, here I am. Seething at the situation I put myself in.

The grip around my margarita glass is lethal as she laughs, and as her hand finds his thigh, I almost break a tooth. He's smiling back at her too, but it's not like the smiles I've had from him. They're his practiced smiles. Or at least that's what I'm telling myself.

I need more alcohol. Or a man.

"Zoey, baby!!" Aaron comes barrelling through the crowd to scoop me up and wrap my legs around his waist. "I missed you. Vegas isn't as fun without my chaos buddy."

I laugh, wrapping my arms around his neck. He's weirdly become like another brother to me. Maybe brother isn't quite right, more like a best friend. He's fun, we get on, and I feel comfortable around him.

He lowers me to my feet, spinning us to face everyone, but I keep myself pressed to his side. His gaze darts over to the boys as he nods towards them and the women hanging off them. "H-man, Maxxie boy, how's the selection tonight?"

Max levels him with a glare. "Shut up, man."

Harrison hasn't taken his eyes off where Aaron is holding me to his body or how my arms are still wrapped around his neck. His jaw ticks and I smirk. My mountain man is jealous.

I lean into Aaron, staring straight at Harrison. "Dance with me. Let's make that chaos happen, hm?"

Aaron pulls back, following my gaze as he chuckles. "I'll do anything to get a rise out of our big man. Lead the way, my lady," he whispers, stepping back and extending his hand for me to take.

Chapter 12

Harrison

T he beautiful blonde purrs something in my ear, but I'm finding it difficult to pay attention because Aaron and Zoey have just walked to the dancefloor, looking like they are about to start a mating ritual with how close they are. It's making my skin itch. Even though I have no claim on Zoey, I'm completely unable to ignore the burning sensation in my chest as his hands roam all over her. I flex my fist at my side, feeling every muscle tighten.

"So, what do you think? Wanna get outta here?" The blonde's heavy American accent brings me back to reality.

No, I really don't want to leave with her, my subconscious screams. I didn't come here tonight to get attention, but when I sat down with Max, he was already surrounded by half the female population of Nevada, so it was inevitable that I'd have to talk to someone. I'd rather be talking to Zoey, so it's a shame she asked me to back off earlier. I've done as she asked, but now I'm not sure I can keep that promise. I'll break a tooth with how hard my jaw is clenched watching her grind over Aaron all night.

I tear my gaze from the dancefloor, glancing over to Max, who I silently implore to look at me so I can point out that Aaron is doing all kinds of touching to his baby sister, but he's nuzzled in between two women so there's no chance he'll look up, despite my telepathy skills.

"Listen, I appreciate the offer, but I'm not looking for anything right now." I remove her hand from my chest. "I hope you have a good night. I'm going to get another drink." I stand whilst giving her a polite smile, the kind I've been subtly throwing her way since she sat next to me, but she chose to ignore. Her face reddens as she huffs a response I can't hear because I'm striding away to refill my already full tumbler of whiskey.

I'm about to reach the bar when I lock eyes with Zoey, who still has her hands around Aaron's neck. She's flush to his front and his head is buried in her neck, hands on her hips as they move in sync. Her barely there sequin dress sparkles around her like a disco ball. She moves her hips like a snake against Aaron's front, and my blood spikes to dangerous temperatures. He needs to move his hands; she needs to step away.

Before I know it, I've eaten up the space between us in three long strides. With the music blaring around us, Aaron hasn't noticed me yet, but Zoey has. Her wide eyes flare with mischief as her tongue darts out to wet her bottom lip. "Hey mountain man," she shouts over the rhythmic beat that seems to mirror the thumping happening in my chest right now.

"Aaron," I boom and when he looks up, he's got the exact same look of mischief on his face. "Fuck off," I say through gritted teeth.

He laughs, throwing his head back. "Why would I do that? I'm dancing with *my girl*." He grips her hips tighter, spiking my pulse from thumping to raging.

Releasing a slow breath through my nose, I look up to the ceiling, willing my anger to settle before I forcefully remove him from Zoey's body. I know he's goading me; he does it all the time—but I'm hanging by a thread of control right now. I don't want his hands all over her, and I'm not okay with him calling her his either.

I level my head to look at them again. Zoey's expression has changed from mischievous to devious. She turns to face Aaron, whispering something in his ear. When he looks back at her, he tilts his head, questioning whatever she just whispered to him, but relents when her stare hardens.

He bends and kisses her cheek and my fists clench. Aaron moves, but I don't look at him as he leaves. My focus is still on Zoey. She moves effortlessly to the music and leans in towards me, smelling like tequila and trouble. "Dance with me. I know you want to."

I want to. God, do I want to.

Forcing myself to swallow the lump that's left over from the fury I just felt, I take a deep breath. Zoey strokes her hand down my arm, her eyes following the movement, erasing the remaining stress from my body in an instant. Her warm, delicate hands move to smooth over my chest and snake around the back of my neck, where she links them and pulls me to her with a grin that should be illegal.

Zoey Bancroft is going to be the death of me.

"Don't make me beg, Harrison. I just want one little dance." She pouts those perfect, pink lips and flutters her mesmerising eyelashes and I surrender. I wrap an arm around her waist and pull our bodies flush together, relishing the gasp that leaves her mouth and brushes against the skin on my neck.

Her body relaxes against mine immediately as she moves her hips to the music again. Her softness caresses every part of me as we move, but I want more. I want to explore every inch of her, to feel her yield to my touch. There's a control switch in my head that I'm usually pretty good at keeping in check, but tonight, with Zoey in my arms, my blood hums with the need to be reckless. Maybe it's her, maybe it's the past year I've had, but all I know is that I want more with her, consequences be damned. I'd take all the punches from her big brothers if it meant getting all of her.

"You're tense," Zoey says, lifting up to talk into my ear.

I reply with a simple nod whilst gritting my teeth. My control is fraying, and I'm trying to stay in the realm of sanity as she grinds against me. But all I want to do is drag her to the nearest dark corner and edge the living shit out of her for being such a brat. The thought of my lips on her skin and my fingers being buried inside her has my cock begging for release, white hot need spears down my spine at an alarming rate as I swallow a groan.

"Worried we'll be caught by my brothers?"

I nod again, and Zoey sighs hard enough that I feel the exhale of air against my throat.

"Okay, mountain man, we need to loosen you up. Come." She takes my hand and drags me towards where we sat before with the others. Aaron looks up immediately and beams at Zoey—the bastard. I squeeze Zoey's hand tighter, and she returns the squeeze, relaxing me slightly.

"Hey, baby girl, miss me already?"

"You wish, pretty boy. We want to do shots. Owen, can you get two rounds of tequila delivered to the table? I've got a game to play."

She turns to me without waiting to see her brother roll his eyes. She lets my hand go but places both her palms on my chest, pushing me backwards. The heat from her hands sears through me, making me feel weak, so I move without resistance until my arse hits the leather sofa, and she smirks like a little devil.

Zoey turns around to the group.

"Drinks will be here in a minute," Owen says over the music, staring at the app on his phone where he ordered the drinks.

"Amazing. So, we are going to play truth or dare."

"Zoey, we aren't kids," Owen protests with a groan. Most of the others react in the same way except Aaron, who looks like an excited puppy, but then he's always like that.

"I'm aware, but I don't care. It'll be fun, and we're in Vegas, so don't be whingey bitches. We're doing this," she says, taking the space next to me.

Our tray of shots arrives, and they smell like bad decisions.

"Rules: every time you forfeit, you take a shot. Once we've gone around once, you have to do a shot anyway. Shots are mandatory. I'm just easing you all in for now. I'll go first." She taps her chin and surveys her brothers, Nate, Aaron, and the girls sitting on their respective laps. "Truth or dare... Nate."

My eyes widen. I didn't expect her to pick him, since he's been mostly quiet this trip.

Nate cocks an eyebrow at her. "Dare."

The collective "oooo" vibrates through the group, and Aaron slaps his friend's shoulder, wiggling him in his seat.

"I dare you to give Aaron a one-minute lap dance."

Nate's gaze flies over to his friend, and for a second, I think I see him considering it. Aaron smiles widely, licking his lips as he taps his lap. "Come on man, you know I love it when I get to turn a straight one."

Heat floods Nate's cheeks, but he shakes his head. "Not happening. I respect you too much to grind on your lap. Besides, I can't have you pining for me after I'm done," he jokes as he reaches for a shot and downs it in one. Aaron slumps in his chair, leaning into the girl sitting next to him and whispering something that makes her blush fiercely. *I'm surrounded by a bunch of horny teenagers, I swear.*

Nate continues the game, daring Max to make out with the girl on his lap. Of course, Zoey covers her eyes and Owen makes a gagging sound when he does. *Like I said, teenagers.*

The others take their turns and when it's Aaron's turn, he locks eyes with me and winks. My whole body stiffens, wondering what he's going to do.

"Truth or dare... Zoey?" he says, while I'm sure I hear Max mutter, "Fuck's sake." My pulse spikes to a marching band because I know whatever Aaron is about to do, he's going to do it to get a rise out of me. I can feel it.

Zoey shifts slightly to the edge of the sofa, pauses for a second, then smiles. "Dare, baby."

Aaron's already rubbing his hands together and looking at Zoey like she's a piece of meat and my body bristles from his heated stare. "I think I'm owed a lap dance, and since I don't have Nate to do that because he's a pussy, I pick you. Bring that pretty body over her and gimme a little something to think about later, hm?"

Max stares at his sister with bulging eyes. The air is thicker than it was a minute ago because everyone is wondering if Zoey will take the bait or be a good girl and keep everyone here friends after this is over.

"You got a death wish, honey?" Zoey laughs but it's filled with nerves, a higher pitch than her usual laugh. She glances to Max and then Aaron. "I'm saving your life by saying no. Trust me," she says, picking up a shot and knocking it back.

My shoulders deflate as a wave of relief floods over me.

"Fuck, what do I have to do to get a lap dance?" Aaron whines, his arms flying into the air. Suddenly, the girl next to him leans in and whispers something that turns his expression from downtrodden to excited. He stands, taking the girl's hand and tugging her to stand. He waves. "I'm out. See you fuckers later."

Zoey chuckles next to me. Max turns his attention to the woman next to him again. Owen and Nate have even gotten lucky too. Suddenly, Zoey and I are the only single ones, sitting with a bunch of people mauling each other's faces.

"Fuck's sake..." she mutters, then turns to me. "So, truth or dare, mountain man?"

"I pick truth," I say, moving closer to her as those big baby blue eyes pin me in place. Sure, they're a little glazed from all the alcohol, but the way she's staring at me with such intrigue stalls my breath for a second. Then a smile erupts on her face, making her the most beautiful woman in the entire room.

"What's the stupidest thing you've ever done?"

Chapter 13

Zoey

There's only one thing that can make my brain have a pulse this vicious, and that's tequila. The pounding intensifies tenfold, like a herd of cute little baby elephants that are not cute and not little, and in fact, are making me feel like my ears are bleeding. *Why do I do this to myself?* Assume that tequila and I are best friends when we most definitely are not. She's my hype girl, sure, but she always leaves me feeling like shit.

Tequila and I are on a break, for real.

What the ever-loving fuck is the other taste in my mouth? Champagne? Yes, that explains the cotton tongue. I remember being at the club with everyone. Drinking, evidently. Dancing, playing truth or dare... but my memory is hazy after that.

Wait. Why am I so hot? I slowly open one eye, which feels like I'm pouring acid directly into my retina, to find Harrison in his boxers, draped comfortably across my stomach. I look down at what I'm wearing; strapless bra and thong, which is something I guess. But this man has a body temperature of a million degrees, and I feel like I'm in full thermal wear with him on me.

Fuck, did we... no, no, no. We couldn't have. But is that why he's here? Think, Zoey, think. What happened when you got home? Nothing. My memory is blank.

I run my hands through my hair, which is so knotted it hurts, but my left hand gets stuck in something in my hair. Owwww, I mouth as I try to tug it free. I wiggle it some more, hoping it'll loosen, but it doesn't. It's useless. I need to see what I'm working with. Shifting my body slowly, which is now slick underneath Harrison.

Before I can get free, his eyes spring open. His usual warm brown irises are hazy as he blinks at me like an owl. His brows furrow as confusion mars his face. "Zoey?" he rasps, sleep and last night's alcohol lacing his voice. "Why are you in my bed?" he asks, lifting his head slightly, allowing me to breathe much better.

"Uhhh, technically, you're in my bed, big guy." I quirk the side of my mouth, realising that we are in fact in my room.

He pounces upwards immediately. Looking around, he swallows and then winces. Yeah, I've been there already. "The fuck am I doing in here?" he muses, sounding adorable and then something obviously crosses his mind as his eyes open wider than saucers, and he looks at the bed and to me and the bed again in horror. "Did we? Oh fuck." He collapses backwards onto the bed with a thud.

"I don't think anything happened. Hang on," I say, sitting upright and scanning the room for any signs of sex. Condoms, lube, ripped clothing, but there's nothing except our discarded clothes at the foot of the bed as though we took them off and collapsed in here—sans sex. "I think we're good. No sex was had."

"Do you... feel like we had sex?" he questions, pushing his hair back, but it's sticking up all over the place and I can't help but smile. His eyes flit to my thong that's doing a poor job of covering me. I glance down too and think about what he means.

"No, I feel normal."

"You'd know if we had sex," he says, scratching the scruff on his face. He says it so casually, like he hasn't just piqued my interest to find out what's under my sheets. My gaze drops to where he's rocking something I want to see. Just as I'm about to question it he cocks his head, staring at my hand. "Why are you holding your head? Did you hurt yourself?"

Oh, yeah. "My hand is stuck. Help me."

He leans in, smelling like tequila and smoke and a little sweat, inspecting the mess on my head and then begins pulling apart the knot in my hair. I feel it the moment my hand is free, all the blood rushes to my finger, making it tingle. I pull my hand out and wiggle my fingers.

Harrison's face whitens to match my sheets and I realise it's probably because my hair is sticking up in every direction, and I'm nowhere near as cute as he is to pull it off. I daren't run my hand through it again in case it gets stuck.

"I guess I should probably brush this nest on my head today," I say. When I glance at him as I slowly move to the edge of the bed, he looks paler. Oh God, I really hope he isn't about to throw up. "Uh, you okay?" I ask warily.

He clears his throat, but his face remains as pale as a ghost. He points to my hand. "Zoey, where did you get that?"

I follow to where he's pointing. My left ring finger which is sporting a very large round diamond. It glistens in the sliver of sunshine that's peeking in around the edge of the blackout blinds. "Huh, I have no idea," I reply, examining it with a shrug. "Maybe I got it from one of those gumball machines. Do you think it's real?"

"Zoey, did we... did we get married last night?" he whispers, bringing his hand to my face, showing me a silver band adorning his left ring finger.

I laugh incredulously. I would never. More laughter rises in my throat, except this time tears begin to form in my eyes from the hilarity of the situation. There's no way... but Harrison isn't laughing at all. We didn't get married. We absolutely did not.

I stare at him, willing my memory to return, but when it does, I lose the ability to breathe. Instead, my wedding ring wearing hand flies up to cover my open mouth.

A chapel. A white chapel.

Oh. My. Fucking. God.

"Oh, no, no, no." I spiral at the reality of my memories, hitting me square in the face with a slap.

"We're married," Harrison says as though he can't compute the information, his brows so close together they look joined.

I might throw up. "We can't be married!" I shriek and leap out of the bed, my feet hitting the floor, making my bum jiggle. "I'm... and you... and we... my brothers..." I gesture wildly between us, not making any sense and unable to complete a sentence. It doesn't feel like my limbs are attached to my body. I'm having some sort of stroke, I swear. "I have to..." I speed out of the bedroom, grabbing a white hotel robe on my way to my bathroom slamming the door.

My eyes fill with tears at the thought that I did something so fucking stupid last night, and I didn't even have any clue I did it. "Fuck, fuck, fuck," I whisper under my breath.

Harrison knocks on my door. "Zoey, please let me in."

"I-I'm just going to shower. Give me a minute, okay?" I stand there on wobbly feet, swiping the tears from my wet cheeks.

He doesn't push, and I let out a sigh of relief as I hear his footsteps retreat from the door.

Once I'm inside the shower, I slump against the back tiled wall, letting the hot water rain down over me as I sink to the ground and cry.

Chapter 14

Harrison

I pause outside her door, trying to figure out how I went from making smart decisions like taking care of Zoey to marrying the woman. Pulling on my hair, I try to recall more of the night. She and I left the club, walked—or stumbled, more likely—down the Vegas strip, where she flirted with some actor. Then we walked some more when we went past a couple posing for wedding pictures in front of the fountain. I swallow, remembering the feeling I had when she looked at me. She said, 'I want to get married one day', but I don't remember much after that.

I twirl my ring on my left hand, noticing that it doesn't feel as foreign as I thought it would. I'm guessing at some point we talked about it and went to buy jewellery at some ungodly hour of the night, and went to the chapel because, of course, this is Vegas, where it's apparently never too late to make life changing decisions.

Walking into my room, I open my banking app to see if we used my card to buy the rings. "Oh fucking hell," I mutter to myself. There's a transaction for a hefty few hundred grand spent at Tiffany's last night. But the money doesn't actually bother me. I know I'd want to spoil Zoey if she were mine... which I guess she is now. I huff a laugh at the whole situation.

I decide to shower and take a minute because this is a lot. As I stand in the open wet room and let the hot water beat down on my back, I try to let my body relax and think about last night. It wasn't just us being drunk; I remember talking about Vanessa, and I wish I hadn't. I can't remember exactly what I said, but I remember Zoey saying she would kill her for me. Stress begins to crawl up my spine and into my shoulders, knotting like it always does when I think about my ex. And then, like a puzzle piece finding its place, it all slots together, and I remember everything. I see her. Outside the chapel, Elvis shouts about being pretend married. I'm almost convinced from that memory that we just bought rings and didn't go into a chapel.

Fuck, I need to talk to her.

I grab a towel and dry off, wrapping it around my waist and heading out into my room. I stop immediately when I see Zoey sitting on the edge of my bed, with wet hair and her white robe again. Her eyes are red, and her cheeks are flushed as she stares at a spot on the wooden floor.

"Zo, are you okay?" I ask, my feet carrying me to her before I can deny myself.

When her head lifts, she looks so broken, so sad and disappointed; the complete opposite of how she's been for the last few days. She's so full of wild, untameable energy that seeing her like this has my chest cracking wide open. I suddenly have the urge to scoop her up and go full alpha male on her, protecting her from whatever has her feeling like this. Then it hits me. She looks like this because of me and what we did last night. My chest inflates and deflates with a sigh as I sit next to her. "Please look at me," I beg.

When she does, I take in the solemn expression painted on her beautiful face as she starts speaking. "I'm so sorry I dragged you into this. I-I don't exactly remember what happened, but I'm almost certain it would've been my idea. My whole life I've been the black sheep of my family and they're constantly waiting for me to fuck up. This though..." Her icy blue eyes lock onto mine, the redness around them making them appear even more blue than normal. "I'm so fucking sorry, Harrison."

She falls into my shoulder sobbing, and that possessive need to protect her roars in my chest again. "Listen, Zo. I'm a grown up, I own everything I do. This is not your fault," I say firmly, but her sobs don't let up. Before I know what I'm doing, my hands are hauling her onto my lap so I can cradle her against my chest properly. I run my hands through her wet platinum hair, making shushing noises until she finally calms down. "It's okay, sweetheart. I've got you," I whisper, as I press my lips to her forehead.

Minutes feel like an hour as we sit, Zoey pressed against my chest. I feel her breathing settle and her heart stop thrashing, and in this moment, I know if she asked me to stay here with her all day, I would do it without question. When she eventually lifts her head, her eyes look tired and missing the brightness she possesses. "Thank you for being here. Most men would've run straight to the courthouse to get this shit annulled."

I take a breath, ready to tell her what I remembered in the shower. "I don't think we actually got married."

Her eyes widen. "You what?" She shifts off my lap to stand in front of me, the white robe swamping her tiny frame. "Do you remember everything?"

I run my fingers through my damp hair. "Not everything. But I remember being outside the chapel with Elvis taking pictures. Go get your phone."

Zoey high tails it to her room and is back in a millisecond. Opening her phone, she throws her hand over her mouth and watches the video of us pretending to get married with fake Elvis on the street, complete with Elvis yelling, 'You may now kiss your fake bride' and us yelling, 'Happy fake wedding day'.

"We didn't get married." The deflation in her shoulders tells me she might cry again, so I grab her hands and pull her into my chest.

"Hey, that's a good thing. You're not stuck with an old mountain man for a husband," I laugh lightly.

"And you're not stuck with all my chaos."

"I don't know. I like the chaos," I admit, softly running my hands up and down her back.

"Honey, you haven't seen the half of it yet." She lifts her head and smiles at me. It's sad and happy and everything in between. "Thank you."

"For what?"

"Not being an arsehole about all this."

Instinctively, I move my lips to the top of her head and kiss lightly. "We're good. I mean, I have a dent in my bank account from the rings, so at some point we were stupid enough to do that part, but we're still very much single," I say before pulling back.

She sniffs, wiping her eyes again, and takes a deep breath. "Thank God we didn't become one of those cliché couples that get drunk married in Vegas."

Right.

Right?

Chapter 15

Harrison

As the day went on yesterday, more and more of the evening came back to both of us. We would have done the real thing had we not been so blind drunk. The others apparently found us laughing and joking with Elvis at some point and so far, no one has commented on the fact we were wearing rings. It feels like the twilight zone, but what I can't work out is how I feel about all this. My brain is soup.

"Morning." Her soft, raspy voice filters into my room as she stands, leaning against the open doorway.

"Morning. Did you sleep well?"

"I did." There's a pause in her voice, trepidation that isn't usually there.

"Zoey—"

"I wanted to give you this back. I know it cost the same amount as a small country, so..."

I snap my full attention to her as soon as the words leave her mouth and register in my brain. She holds the ring out for me to take from her as I stand from my bed and stride over to her, I feel a pang of something in my chest. "You don't have to."

"I do. I can't just keep a Tiffany ring, Harrison. That's insane."

I understand her reason, but it feels weird taking it back even though it shouldn't.

"Keeping it would feel wrong," she continues. "Plus, I don't want to make any more of an idiot of myself." She huffs an empty laugh.

"You never made an idiot of yourself." Talking the ring from her hand.

The side of her mouth quirks upwards as she looks at me. "Debatable. I don't usually try to marry my brothers' best friend."

"In your defence, you had a very good reason to want to marry me."

"Your muscles?" she teases.

I laugh. "To get your trust fund *and* have unlimited access to my muscles. We could've had it all, baby." I flex my arm just to see if I can make her smile, and lucky for me, she does. A real Zoey smile. Pride warms my chest as I return her smile.

"Hmm. Remind me why I didn't marry you for real." She fans herself.

"Beats me." I shrug.

"I'm going to take a bath and then pack for the flight later."

She turns to leave, and my first instinct is to ask if I can see her when we're back in London. It's probably not a good idea, considering the last twenty-four hours, but there's something between us, but is it a friendship? Is it just how Zoey is with everyone? I've seen her with Aaron this week. She's so comfortable and approachable. Maybe this is just part of her charm, part of who she is. Maybe I'm reading into something.

I let her go without calling her back, ignoring the voice in my head demanding that I tell her to turn around and come back here. I haven't been possessive over a woman for a long time and it's not a good idea to start now. Not with a psycho ex stalking me and a business that's busier than ever. I shake my head and turn, going into the living area and flicking on the coffee machine.

As the smoky aroma fills the room, I suck in a deep inhale and remember that I haven't done any yoga since being here. Hell, maybe that's why I've been so on edge around Zoey. I drink my coffee, put on my sweats, and head to my room to do a short session to relieve some tension.

I put on my meditation playlist that plays sounds from being outdoors, making me miss the hikes I usually do on weekends outside of London to clear my head. There isn't anything better than being outside of the city and taking that first deep breath of fresh air.

I move slowly through my positions, stretching out any muscles that need it and lingering in poses that make me feel good. Before I know it, I'm sweating and feeling much calmer. Pushing up from Child's Pose, I kneel with my eyes closed, drawing in some deep breaths, as I let my body come down from the session while I reflect on this trip so far.

My mind replays so many moments we've had on this trip, but the one that gets stuck in my head the most is why we almost got married. We both needed to feel in control again, her with her trust fund and me with my ex. It's not the most romantic reason to get married, but it would be a business transaction, a means to an end.

We're just two people who have been dealt a difficult hand right now and found something in one another for a moment. And I can't ignore that something about Zoey feels unfinished, and now that my head is clearer, I've got an idea that could benefit us both. I need to talk to her today, and I won't take no for an answer.

Moving to the bathroom door, I shower quickly, dress, and start throwing my things into my case. I zip my case, check I have everything, and walk into the living area of the suite.

"There he is, my almost husband." She beams, that playfulness I love seeing on her glimmering all over her face.

"We ready to go?" I ask.

My leg is nervously bouncing up and down as I wait for the others to fall asleep. I'm three down, but Owen is being stubborn and refusing to sleep. I might just need to pray he doesn't care if I go and sit next to his sister.

Fuck it, I'm doing it.

Hauling my body from the seat, I immediately gain Owen's attention, his blue eyes—almost the exact shade of his sister's—narrow, but I ignore him as best I can. "Just going to chat to Zoey, seeing as though you're ignoring me," I mumble as I move.

He huffs but doesn't say anything, concentrating on his phone. *Good, ignore me, please.*

I squeeze down the aisle to the seat next to Zoey. She's awake, thankfully, and has her headphones in. As if sensing my presence, she looks up at me, removing one of them with a smile. "Hey, mountain man. Miss me already?"

"Of course I miss my roomie," I say, hoping I don't sound as desperate as I feel. My body hums with nerves because I've had an idea that is either really smart or really stupid.

"Oh, you flatter me." She waves me off, then looks me up and down when she realises I'm hovering. "You gonna stand there all day or?" she says, moving her legs from the seat across from her so I can sit.

I take the seat across from her and stare at her petite frame in the huge leather seats. Her blonde hair that's scrapped up in a bun on top of her head, her freckles are on show, dusting across her nose, and her sunglasses are wedged somewhere in her hair. "So, what's up? You look like you have something to say."

I rub the skin on the back of my neck to relieve pressure, to no avail. "I do... I was thinking about what happened." I look around to check we don't have an audience and lower my voice. "Or what nearly happened."

She leans forward, showing me a glimpse of her lace bralette she's wearing underneath the vest top. "Don't tell me. You're in love with me already and want to marry me for real."

I laugh, but it's a little too loud because Max grunts from the rows ahead of us but snuggles back into his hoodie—no suits on this flight. "Hear me out,"

"Oh God," she gasps.

"No, I'm not in love with you. But I think we can help each other."

Chapter 16

Harrison

Zoey's eyes widen and she flicks her frantic stare around the plane, as though me asking to marry her will somehow summon her protective brothers. "Sorry?" she whisper shouts. "Say that again."

"Marry me for real this time."

She groans, frustrated or confused, I can't tell. "Harrison, you don't mean that."

I run my damp hands through my hair, so I don't have the urge to pull her onto my lap and whisper this conversation into her ear.

"I do. We can help each other. You need access to the rest of your trust fund, and I want my ex to get the message that I've moved on. It's a win for us both. Plus, you don't know this, but I'm a pretty good boyfriend, so I'll make a great husband."

She raises an eyebrow. "Oh, with all that modesty, I don't doubt you." Zoey looks at me with curiosity but also something else. "I don't want you to do this just because you think you can help me."

"I'm not. This will help me too. Think about it, we both win from doing this."

The way she assesses me has me shifting in my seat, sweat forming at the base of my neck. She's trying to get a read on me. I hope I'm not showing her how nervous I am. It feels like I might be signing a death certificate with her brothers, but I push that to the back of my mind for now because I want to help her, and I need help too.

She picks up her water bottle, takes a sip, then places it back on the seat next to her before she speaks again. "Why do I want to say yes?"

I lean forward, finally taking her hand in mine. "Because I'm making an offer you can't refuse. Plus, you can have your own mountain man at your beck and call, for a while, at least."

Her gaze continues to linger on my face. I don't know what she's searching for, but I know that I can reassure her. "Look, you don't have to say yes. I'll carry my broken heart back to London, but I think one year is doable. It'll give us enough time to make sure your parents buy that we're married for real, and it isn't a rouse. We can sort out specifics later, but I think you know this is the best way to get what you need."

"What about what you need? It feels one sided. I don't think you know what you're getting yourself into." Shadows of doubt play across her face, and I suddenly have the urge to comfort her, to touch her and smooth the lines on her forehead.

"If my ex sees that I'm serious with someone else, she'll leave me alone. She'll have to and Zoey," I sigh, looking at our connected hands. "I need peace. It's been over a year since shit went down and I'm fucking tired." I remove my hand from hers and drag it down my face, feeling that heavy weight again. I just want to feel like I'm not constantly looking over my shoulder, and Zoey can help me. "Plus, you'll get your money for the shelter."

She sighs, her bottom lip whitens from her teeth digging into it. "We don't know each other that well," she finally says weakly.

"I know enough to know that I like you. Living with you for a year? Piece of cake. Pretending to be your husband? Easy as pie," I whisper conspiratorially.

"If I say yes, will you stop with the old man food metaphors?"

"If you say yes..."

She narrows her eyes at me, but a smile plays on her lips. "Can I think about it?"

I smile, hoping that this is what we need to solve both our problems. "Absolutely. I'll do whatever you need me to do. Like I said, this is for both of us and if at any point, even before the marriage, you don't want to do it, we don't."

She nods once and smiles at me. "Okay."

And I let out the world's longest sigh at the idea that Zoey might, very soon, be my wife.

Back home, everything is the same, but it feels different, which is probably because I'm more... relaxed than I was before I left.

I drag my case into my bedroom and begin unpacking, throwing things into the wash basket and tucking shoes away. When I turn into my walk-in wardrobe, my mind wanders to what would happen if Zoey said yes. Would she want to live here? Would she take the spare room? It's probably for the best, considering this is all a rouse, but maybe her clothes should be in here in case anyone visits. If they see our things are not together, they might suspect us.

So, feeling hopeful that she will agree to my proposal, I remove some of my clothes and make space for Zoey in my wardrobe. Is it presumptuous of me to make room even though she hasn't said yes yet? Probably, but I like to plan and stay ahead of things.

As I move some shirts to another section, I realise I never did this for Vanessa. We were together for two years, but we were only together when it suited her and, now that I think about it, none of that relationship was on my terms. It should make me feel like I was used, but I feel nothing but relief. I escaped a future with her. Yet, somehow the thought of a future with Zoey, however temporary, feels easier and more natural than it ever did with Vanessa.

My phone pings from where it's sitting on my chest of drawers and I pick it up.

> **Zoey**: Why does this feel like the craziest thing ever?
> **Me**: It's a little crazy, but I'm hoping you'll see the rational side of things.

Rational being that we both get something out of this that benefits us... that's not physical. Despite how tempting she proved she is in Vegas.

> **Zoey**: We need a plan, and it has to be foolproof enough that my brothers believe it's real

She's considering it. A buzz of adrenaline surges through me as I type my response.

> **Me**: Is this you saying yes?
> **Zoey**: I'm definitely in the vicinity of saying yes.

I beam, typing furiously.

> **Me**: I think we need accomplices, and we need people to vouch for us that we were secretly seeing each other before the surprise wedding.

I think for another minute before adding more.

> **Me**: Aaron is out, he's a blabber mouth. Nate probably wouldn't want to keep the secret. Do you have close friends you trust enough with this?

Her reply is almost immediate.

> **Zoey**: I do. I'd trust both of my girlfriends with this.
> **Me**: What if you had to pick one?
> **Zoey**: Probably Nora.

I don't remember much about Nora, but I think she was a bridesmaid at Liam's wedding last year.

>**Me**: If you trust her, then I say let's meet with her
>as soon as possible to figure all this out.
>**Zoey**: Okay, I'll message her.
>**Me**: So, how do you feel about moving in with
>me tomorrow?

My pulse spikes at the thought of this coming together, and I realise Zoey will be the only woman I've lived with.

>**Zoey**: We're really doing this, aren't we?
>**Me**: Fuck yeah, we are.

Chapter 17

Zoey

After texting Harrison last night, I passed out and now I'm rushing before he picks me up. To move. Into his house.

I think I left my sanity in Vegas because this feels crazy. I glance at my watch, that tells me I'm going to be late and I'm not nearly packed properly.

"Shit," I haphazardly throw a bunch of my clothes in a bigger case than I took to Vegas, say RIP to my house plant that I've never been able to keep alive anyway and rush down to wait for him outside. I'm not ashamed of my little flat, but it is just that; small and crowded with my mess and until I can beg Seren to come over and help me clean and tidy, he cannot see it.

A sleek black DBX V8 comes curbside, the door swings open and Harrison exits the vehicle with such swagger that it makes my inner ho do a little twerk in my head. I let out a wolf whistle, and he smirks. "That is one sexy car, mountain man. How can I live out all the axe wielding, flannel wearing, truck driving fantasies of you if you drive a car that says boss man instead of mountain man?"

He steps towards me, eyes dancing with amusement. "I guess you'll have to accept that your husband is a little bit of everything."

My mouth drops open, and I'm not sure if it's because of him calling himself my husband or because he might actually be a real life fantasy come true. "Are you telling me you can actually chop wood?"

He shrugs. "I guess we'll have to take a camping trip for you to find out. I'll even wear my flannel shirt for you."

"Camping?" I ask, scrunching my nose.

"Not a fan?"

"No, I love sleeping on the freezing cold floor, peeing in bushes, and brushing my teeth with a bottle of water. What's not to love?" I raise a sarcastic eyebrow.

"I'm changing your mind about camping. We'll go soon." He leans in to press a kiss to my forehead, and my heart swoops to my feet. Before I can react, he takes the case out of my hand, casually places his palm in the small of my back and ushers me to his car, and I finally register what he said. I stop myself from moving. "Oh, will we now?" His hand slips from my lower back to the top of my arse. A sharp inhale leaves me without my permission.

"Yes, *we* will," he says again. I angle myself towards him slightly, squint my eyes and cross my arms over my chest in defiance, giving him a chance to stop bossing me around. "I forget how stubborn you Bancroft's are." He laughs but doesn't remove his hand that's currently causing a wildfire to spread all over me.

"The *most* stubborn. Also, we're city folk. I have no desire to camp. Even with my future fake husband." I flick my hair over my shoulder.

His eyes briefly flash with molten heat, but he blinks quickly, releasing his hold on me and rubbing his jaw in that insanely sexy way men do. "Now that you'll be my wife, *Zoey Clarke*, you should know I like to spend time outside of the city limits, and you'll have to come with me."

Zoey Clarke. My stomach flip flops at him saying that out loud and with such... heat.

I'm far too turned on by the muscular man in front of me, but my brat side wants to play with him. I jut my chin towards him, trailing my index finger up his pec and along his collarbone, smiling when I swear I feel him tremble beneath me. "And if I don't? What you gonna do about it?"

His finger hooks under my chin, forcing me to look into his deep brown eyes that threaten to swallow me whole. "Turns out, I happen to like tiny blonde bratty women who think they can get their own way. So go ahead, sweetheart, push me and see what happens."

I practically swallow my tongue, unable to stop the amount of flush rushing to my cheeks. An instant wetness pools in my underwear because, right now, I'd love nothing more than to admit that my husband-to-be—the strong silent, protective man—is also a fucking dirty talker who would respectfully disrespect me in the bedroom.

Then I internally deflate, remembering that this is a fake arrangement.

But there's sure as hell nothing fake about my reaction to him.

I clear my throat, stepping back towards his car, taking a full non-Harrison scented inhale. He watches me go with rapt attention, his eyes burning with fire again. His stare is too much and not enough all at once. Sending misfiring signals to my already confused and turned on brain *and* body.

It's fake, this is fake, I remind myself.

"Okay, you can take me camping," I say, trying to diffuse the overwhelming feeling rushing around inside me.

Harrison steps forwards. Once, twice. Until he raises his arms, caging me against his car. He smells like fresh air and soft bedding, and something so inherently masculine I can't seem to get enough when he's this close to me.

"Mmm," he hums, the vibration from his deep voice sparking something in my core. His eyes search my face slowly, his attention lethal and thrilling, making me want to drop to my knees for him. The intensity of his stare feels like a lover's caress, and I feel drunk on it. "I love it when you surrender to me."

I'm fucked. So fucking fucked.

Chapter 18

Harrison

"We are going to have to face your parents at some point, Zoey," I say, watching her sip her fizzy drink through the straw. She picked the place for dinner, a cosy little burger place tucked away in Greenwich. We're meeting Nora afterwards at a bar across the street.

She groans. "You're wrong. I like living in a world where they don't know something about me. Gives me a thrill."

I laugh, taking a sip of my fizzy lemonade. "Let's get it over with and tell them on the weekend."

She side eyes me. "Are you always this sensible?"

"Sensible to a fault." Except when it comes to you. I can't always control where my thoughts go around her and that disarms me and brings out the side that not many have seen.

She relents, playfully rolling her blue eyes. "Fine, ruin my fun."

"I'm definitely more scared about telling your brothers," I admit, staring into my drink.

"You should be."

I swallow the fear lodged in my throat, praying it'll be fine. "Anyway…"

"Anyway…" she repeats, smiling. "I guess I should know more about my secret boyfriend slash husband," she says, tapping her finger on her glass. "Although…" She points a finger at my face. "If I find out that you're a sociopath who folds his socks, then we absolutely can't get married."

"You *don't* fold your socks? You're the sociopath, sweetheart," I tease. *I definitely do not fold my socks.* "You can check yourself later when you come home." She pauses, staring at me like I've just told her something profound. I wait for her to say something, but she doesn't. "What did I say?"

Shaking her head, she blinks. "Nothing. So, your inner most secrets…"

"Right. I guess, thinking about things you should know…" I hesitate, and my chest fills with that same feeling I get when I think about her. "My mum passed away when I was twenty-five. Cancer. Her name was Evelyn, and she made the best banana bread ever. My dad tries to make it every year on her birthday, and he does a pretty good job, but Mum just had the magic touch."

"Damn, here I was thinking you were about to tell me your favourite sex positions." She swallows loudly and winces, piercing me with her honesty shining in her blue eyes. "I'm sorry about your mum. I think I may have met her once when I was younger." She takes my hand and squeezes it, and I'm grateful for her doing that. "I wish I could've known her."

"Me too. You would probably be in cahoots all the time." My chest constricts, but it swells at the same time at the thought of the two of them together. Mum really would've liked Zoey.

"She sounds like my kind of woman." Zoey smiles. It's soft and warm, and I take comfort from it. "I can't believe you're my brother's best friend and I don't know your family. It feels weird."

"Don't forget, there's seven years between us. We weren't friends officially; it would be weird. I only ever saw you at your house when I visited your brothers."

"I had the biggest crush on you," she blurts, then slaps her hand over her mouth. "Oh shit, please forget I said that out loud."

My grin is so wide I'm sure she can see my molars. "You had a crush on me?"

"I'd like to erase the last minute of this conversation, please. I'm ignoring you until you agree to these terms."

I'm still smiling, loving the flush she's sporting. "Your cheeks are very pink."

"I put blusher on this morning. Too much, evidently."

"It's creeping up your neck."

"It is not. It's the light in here." She refuses to meet my eyes, even though I'm silently pleading with her to do so. I want to bask in her adorableness.

"I think I like blushing Zoey."

Her blue eyes flick to mine, and I wilt under the sheer depth of the ocean, staring back at me. "I. Am. Not. Blushing."

Hiding my smile in a sip of my drink, I decide that defiant Zoey might be my favourite. "Okay. Whatever you say."

"I never would've agreed to marry you if I'd known you were this intolerable."

"That'll teach you to make uninformed decisions."

A beat passes. It's not awkward, it's comfortable. Zoey softens the longer I look at her, the frustration from blurting out her inner thoughts dissipates, her shoulders come down from her ears, her mouth parts on each soft exhale and she mindlessly traces the outline of her top lip as she stares at me too. Cataloguing.

"I'm going to pretend that whole conversation didn't happen. So, you were saying..."

"That you're beautiful when you're shy?"

"Flattery will get you nowhere with me. I told you in Vegas, I'm a physical touch girl. Besides, we're getting off track here."

I do remember her telling me that. How could I forget after rubbing suncream torturously over her perfect skin? *Fuck no, don't think about that.* I cough awkwardly, begging all the blood to remain in the upper half of my body and not travel south.

"Right. When my mum passed, he wasn't in a good place for a long time, but he got help, and he's doing good now."

"What's his name?"

"Ralph."

"Evelyn and Ralph. Even their names are perfect together. I feel sad that your dad lost his person."

I nod, lowering my gaze to the wooden table. A waiter appears with our burgers and chips in those American diner style baskets. Zoey doesn't hesitate to dive straight in, and I watch in fascination. Vanessa would only ever eat salads and even then, she'd pick at her food like it was offensive. Watching Zoey eat is so refreshing.

She swipes the blob of barbeque sauce from the side of her mouth. "I know I eat like a pig. My mother likes to remind me whenever I see her. Carry on telling me about your family. Although, I may need a family tree of your sisters' kids. You said she has four?"

I pop a chip in my mouth and chew. "You don't eat like a pig, for the record." I swallow and watch Zoey smile again. "My sister, Katie. You remember her? Her husband, Jake, is an environmental scientist. We went to school together. He was the quiet type and ridiculously smart. Katie teaches primary school. She went back to work part time recently, and my dad helps with the girls when she's working."

Zoey swallows a mouthful. "Right, so let me try and remember their names from when you told me." She licks her full lips as she aimlessly looks around, as if she's searching for the names in her head. "Cassie, Alana, Ellie and... Amelia?"

"Close. Amelia is actually Ophelia."

She smacks the table. "Damn, so close. Remind me of their ages again," she mumbles, popping a chip into her mouth.

"Cassie is seven, Alana is five, and Ellie and Ophelia are three."

"Okay, I've got a handle on your family tree. Hey, it's like we've been dating secretly before we got married."

"Imagine that," I reply with a laugh. "So, tell me more about you. Your love life, what your favourite things are. I need to know more about the real Zoey."

She finishes her mouthful. "I don't know that my life is that interesting in all honesty. I'm a party girl at heart. I spend most weekends out, or I'm at the shelter."

"Well, now I feel bad that I'm actively destroying your sex life." *Or do I?* At least I won't be crazy jealous seeing her with other men.

"Oh, don't worry." She waves me off. "My plan is to seduce you until you crack anyway. It'll keep me busy." She quietens for a moment, staring into the distance. "Hook ups were always... empty."

She refocuses her attention on me and shakes her head. "Sorry, anyway, back on topic. My favourite colour is a toss up between mint green and pink. I love all food, I obviously love animals, I hate feeling cold, I am messy to a fault, so sorry about the mess I'm going to make in your house... I'm a mediocre cook, but I do a mean paella. I'm sure there's more, but I can't think."

"I like learning about you. You're an enigma because, although you're fierce and strong willed, I also think that you can be shy and sweet. I like seeing both sides." I have no idea how she'll take my confession of seeing her vulnerable side. The truth is, there is so much more to her than the party girl image she pushes into the world. I can already see that from the limited time we've spent together.

"Thank you, I think." Her blush spread across her cheeks like the sweetest shade of pink in springtime. I can't help but smile.

"You're welcome."

Chapter 19

Zoey

"It's just over there." I point towards the bar that Jess, Nora and I go to sometimes after work. I haven't been there in what feels like forever, though.

When we enter through the double doors, I immediately spot Nora and Grayson in the corner booth.

Harrison places his giant hand on my lower back and leans in closer. "Grayson is here?"

I turn slightly to see his face marred with confusion. "Yeah, he and Nora are together."

He nods. "I forgot, is all. Grayson got me a big contract last year with Liam's company. We've known each other a while, but I'm about to straight up ask him to lie for me. It feels... odd."

I glance back at my friends, then turn to stand in front of Harrison, resting my palms on his hard chest. His heart is beating a mile a minute as I look up at this big man in front of me. "Remember when you said I can back out at any point? Same goes for you. Do you need a minute?" I take in his dark eyes with even darker eyelashes framing them perfectly. *Seriously, why do men get good eyelashes? It's wholly unfair.*

Harrison breathes deeply, and the rise and fall of his chest under my palms warm my gut as I feel his heart rate even out. Our eyes lock in a moment of weakness. All I want to do is press my lips to his to reassure him. But that won't make him feel better. That'll confuse things, so I pull away and he nods to me. "I'm good."

I take his hand and walk over to my friends. Nora's eyes dart between my face and where I'm holding Harrison's hand. "Hey lovers, how the hell are you both?"

Nora wakes from her stupor of seeing me with Harrison and stands to hug me. "What the hell is going on right now?" she whispers into my ear as the boys greet each other next to us. I pull back to look at my friend, worry flashes in her eyes and I smile my best 'please don't worry' smile.

"Let's sit," I say just as I'm engulfed in a hug from Grayson too. "Oh hey, pretty boy. Hope you're taking care of my girl."

He releases me and smiles at Nora. "Doing the best I can." He winks at her and she rolls her eyes playfully.

We all sit, and Harrison takes the space next to me. I watch him scan the QR code and order me a margarita without even asking. When he looks up, he winks and I melt. Damn it, he's perfect.

"So..." Nora begins, the awkward silence eating me alive. "Are you two together?"

"Oh, we're going straight into that? No warm up. No hey, I missed you. How was Vegas? Vegas was great, the shelter is finally fixed, thanks for asking..." I rush.

Nora winces. "I'm sorry, you're right. How was Vegas? I already know the shelter is fine. I was there on Saturday, the day after you left for Vegas."

"You were? The guys didn't tell me."

"I told them not to. I just wanted to see if they needed any help. I got to cuddle the cutest little ginger kitten."

"Oh, that litter are adorable. I swear I'd take one home if I could."

"Anyway, Vegas... Go."

I look at Harrison, silently apologising for the pitch that Nora is about to shriek at because I need her to know everything. "We almost got drunk married."

She slams her drink down with a thud on the table. "You did what?!" There's that high pitch that makes everyone stare at us.

"I wouldn't normally tell you to be quiet, but people are staring, shorty," Grayson says, loud enough for us all to hear.

Nora glares at him and I chuckle, which only gets me my own Nora Scott glare.

"Explain. Now."

"I said we *almost* did. You should have more of your drink though, because that's not the part that's surprising." She doesn't let up her stare, so I give in. "Fine, we *are* getting married."

"You are?" she yelps again. I glance at Harrison, pleading with him to help me here because I can't seem to stop my friend from yelping.

He clears his throat. "We're getting married, but we need you to know the reasons why. But to be clear, we need your help."

"What do you need?" Grayson asks, his brows drawing together.

Harrison gives me one final look to check we're really doing this. "This is somewhat of a business arrangement. Zoey needs the remainder of her trust fund, and her parent's clause is that she's married or turning thirty-five, but the shelter needs help now—"

"We can help you, Zoey," Nora interrupts.

"Thank you, but I absolutely am not asking friends for handouts. This is why Harrison is helping me because I'll also be helping him."

"How?" Nora tilts her head.

"I have an ex-girlfriend who won't take the hint, and I'm a step away from filing a restraining order. If she sees I've moved on, that will make my life a lot easier."

"Is she dangerous?" Nora asks, eyeing him sceptically.

Harrison shakes his head. "Just vindictive but persistent."

"This is Vanessa, right?" Grayson asks. "Piece of work. I remember her."

Nora pauses, then shakes her head. "Backtrack, I need specifics. Why do you need us?"

"Because we need to convince my brothers that we've been seeing each other in secret. That this marriage isn't a business deal. Plus, we need witnesses for the actual wedding," I tell her honestly.

"This feels weird," Nora replies. "Are you sure there's no other way? Talk to your parents about the issues at the shelter?"

I pin her with a look. "I forget you have parents who love you and would do anything for you."

"Sorry." She looks at Grayson and sighs. "If you need us, we're there for you, of course, but Zo…" Her eyes flick between me and Harrison, then she gives me a look that only a best friend could give. "I don't want you to get hurt."

I grab her hand and squeeze. "Babe, I promise, Harrison is a good man. He's even moved me in and everything. We're working everything out, but I need you in this with me. If it's too much, then maybe I can ask Jess."

"No, I mean, my sister probably will kill me from keeping another secret from her, but I'm in. You know I'd do anything for you."

"Even be my witness to my fake wedding next weekend?"

Nora rolls her eyes. "I don't know how you get yourself into these situations, but this is possibly worse than the time you had that orgy last year and got stuck—"

I throw my hand over her mouth, embarrassment choking me. I glance sheepishly over at the men with us. "She doesn't know what she's talking about."

Grayson's eyes shimmer with amusement. "It's fine. She'll tell me later."

I release my hand from Nora's mouth.

"Why don't we share with the group? Since we're all here?" Harrison muses.

"Kill me now," I declare, throwing my face into my hands.

"So, next weekend?" Nora asks, waving off the conversation.

I nod. "Next weekend, we're getting married."

Chapter 20

Harrison

Sitting on my sofa after drinks and dinner, Zoey is tapping away on her iPad, and every now and then, she scribbles on some post it notes next to her. I'm glancing over emails, readying myself for tomorrow morning. The silence between us isn't awkward or strained; it's comforting. And I realise that this is just another thing I never had with Vanessa.

Speaking of, I had several messages from her waiting for me by the time we got home. She's heard through the grapevine that I'm seeing someone, though she didn't name Zoey, her messages were not kind. But that's the point of this. I need her to take the fucking hint and move on.

"You know," Zoey says, gaining my attention. "It's weirdly exactly how I imagined it would be." She spins to face me, her blonde locks flowing over the tips of her shoulders.

"What is?"

"This. Your place. Dark, sexy, edgy. Just like you."

I lean towards her, something inside me pulling me to her. "Careful there, Mrs Clarke. You keep complimenting me like that and you'll steal my heart. You never asked, but I'm a words of affirmation and quality time kind of guy."

Zoey assesses me with eyes that sparkle something fierce. "You know, I would've guessed that you were about quality time, but words of affirmation surprises me,"

"How so?" I watch as she swings those short, toned legs my way and straight onto my lap. Then I remember she's a physical touch lover, so I rest my hand over her knee and draw little circles with the tips of my fingers, like touching her is the most natural thing in the world.

"You're so secure in who you are. I never thought you'd need more security in that from others."

I tear my attention from her legs to her face, which is wearing an amused expression. "I don't *need* it. But I like it."

She sucks her bottom lip into her mouth and digs her teeth into the flesh there, taunting me without even trying to be sexy. "Hmm, okay. Good to know." She releases her lip and I realise I'm still touching her. "You're too good at that."

I look down at my hand and then back to her face, which is full of heat and unspoken words that we haven't covered yet in our little agreement, mainly sex.

"Touching me, that is."

I know what she meant, but hearing her say that spikes the heat between us. "You're going to be the death of me, aren't you?"

"I might be a handful, but you knew that already going into this, so don't pretend to be surprised," she says before swiftly moving to stand in front of me, her delicate hand outstretched for me to take. "Come on, it's late and we have work tomorrow."

I take her hand, liking how mine swallows hers. "You know, I was under the impression my future wife was a wild child, but you're being incredibly sensible right now."

She smiles and drags me towards the bedrooms. "It won't last, trust me." Looking over her shoulder at me, her blonde hair framing her face so perfectly, she winks, and my dick takes that as an invitation just for him.

Pausing in front of my—our—bedroom door, I turn to face her. "We haven't actually discussed where we'll be sleeping."

Her lips tilt up at the sides. "Worried you can't resist me in your bed?"

Exactly that. "Uhh, I—"

"Relax, I'll take the spare room. Problem solved." She shrugs as she walks towards the closed door next to my room.

Except, problem not solved because why do I want to pull her into my room and make her share with me?

I follow her into the room and take a seat next to her on the bed. We're almost touching, but I don't trust myself to get any closer. "Zoey," I say hesitating, wondering if I should admit this. "I'm really fucking attracted to you. As much as I want you in my bed, I'm pretty sure I'd never let you leave, and that's complicating our arrangement." My skin feels too tight, too hot, too...much from my admission.

Zoey inhales sharply and chews on her bottom lip, her blue eyes not meeting mine.

Longing pangs in my gut. I want her, but I know it's not a good idea. We're already straddling the line between lies and truth. Adding sex to that will complicate things more. And if we both want to walk away from this unscathed, it's best if we abstain. It's a good argument in my head, now I need to convince my body of the same thing.

Zoey stands, taking a step away from me, an expression crossing her face I seldom see as she nods and pouts her lips. "I think it's best I sleep here for now. That way, we're removing temptation."

I inhale and let a long, defeated sigh leave my chest. She's right, and I hate that I was sensible about this. "Okay, if you think that's best."

She nods. "If it keeps those big, thick, rough hands..." She pauses, looking down at my hands, but shakes her head and when her ocean eyes refocus on me, they're full of heat—something I'm sure she sees in mine too. A heartbeat passes between us. "Yeah, we should definitely *not* sleep in the same bed."

"Should we make that a deal that we don't, you know..."

"Have sex?"

I nod. "With anyone." *Why did we agree to do this again?*

"Probably a good idea, although you'll have to put up with my no-sex grumpiness," she says.

"We'll be grumpy together then."

Before my mind can play catch up to the agreement we just made, I step towards her and kiss her forehead. Pulling back, she looks like a deer in headlights, but the pink colouring her cheeks tells me she didn't hate it. It's going to be really hard not to touch her.

"Goodnight, Zoey," I say, clearing my throat.

She steps to the side. "Night Harrison."

Chapter 21

Harrison

As I make my way around the apartment, I see the door to her bedroom open and her bed empty. I didn't hear her leave early, but I guess she went to the shelter.

My phone buzzing from my pocket distracts me and when I pull it out, I see my sister's name. "Hey Katie."

"Hey, big brother. How was Vegas?"

Oh man, I do not want to do this over the phone. "Vegas was good."

I hear Ophelia shouting in the background about her school shoes being too small, and I stifle a laugh. "Just good? Do you have any good stories for me? Anyone do anything so disgustingly cliché like that movie?"

"Uhh, no. We all had a great time." Not my most convincing performance granted, but it'll have to do.

"You're not telling me something."

I sigh internally. Keeping something from her is futile, but I can't do this right now. "Listen, I'd love to stay and chat, but how about we make plans for dinner soon instead? You can rinse me for more details then." *And you can meet my wife.*

"Fine—Ophelia, do not hit your sister with the hairbrush—sorry H, I better go before someone gets a black eye. Sunday is good, though. Maybe you can give Ophelia a talk about being kind to her sisters," she says pointedly, talking to both me and Ophelia. I can just imagine her with her wild brown hair and cute button nose, staring at my sister with attitude in the way she always does.

"Sounds good." I smile. "See you Sunday."

We hang up and I go about my usual morning routine. Coffee, emails, stretching, shower and dressed.

When I'm on my way out the door, I bring up my texts to send a message to Zoey at the exact moment as my phone rings and it's her.

"Zoey, I was just thinking about you."

"Oh, you were? Good things, I hope."

"Always. What's up?" I ask as I get into my car and turn the engine on, waiting for the Bluetooth to pick up the call.

"So, the marriage thing. Lloyd and Sam tell me we need to give notice for twenty-eight days before we get married."

"Shit, we do?"

"Apparently, we need to give people the opportunity to contest it. I don't think it'll be an issue, but it does mean we won't be getting married this weekend."

"How are we so bad at this?" I ask, turning a corner.

"You don't think... this isn't..."

I tighten my grip on the wheel, anticipation thrumming at my skin. "No, this isn't a bad omen. It's happening, Zoey, we're getting married. We're doing this for us."

I hear her breath catch on an inhale, and then she exhales slowly. "You're right," she says. "We're doing this."

"I'll get us sorted for everything. In the meantime, I just need you to focus on work for today. I'll call you later, okay?"

"Okay." I hear someone call her from a distance through the phone. "Harrison, I have to go—"

"Don't worry about this. I've got it sorted."

"Thank you. I'll talk to you later."

And then she hangs up. And I realise I have a lot to do today.

When I arrive at the office, it's busy as usual. We recently moved into a new bigger shared corporate building that's owned by Liam Taylor's company and it's been the best decision. Not only are we closer to the Wharf, but we're also not struggling for space now. I offer my employees a 70-30 balance of working from home and office too. How they split that is up to them, but a lot of them like this new space.

The building is naturally airy and spacious, with plenty of open workspace and then quieter areas. Everyone has their own space but also the opportunity to be in the bustle or not. I have an office and conference rooms for client meetings, but I spend just as much time out here on the floor with the team.

"Good morning, sir." My assistant, Wesley, pops out of his favourite spot on the floor just before I reach my corner office.

"What have I told you about the sir, Wes?" I arch a brow at him, and he smiles, offering me a to-go cup of coffee.

"Sorry, Harrison," he says pointedly. "I got you a welcome back coffee."

I take the coffee, smiling gratefully. "You didn't have to, but I definitely need it."

"Vegas was good?" he asks innocently.

"Vegas was great."

Then it occurs to me that he might be able to help me with my workload today. "Hey, Wes?"

He looks back up at me. "Yeah?"

"Could I get you to run the meeting with the other interns today? You know the ropes, you know the agenda. I can give you all my notes and put Mary with you if that'll make you more comfortable, but I could do with the assist."

He pales slightly but nods his head. "You think I'm ready for that?"

"Frankly, I'm surprised you're questioning yourself. You have as much to do with this group of interns as I do. You know their programme. I trust you."

Wes loses all the nervousness and smiles widely. "Thank you, sir—uh, Harrison—that means a lot to me."

I push the door to my office. "You deserve it, Wes."

When I settle at my desk, I'm immediately flooded with fifty new emails from when I checked an hour ago. Some are HR related, so I forward them to Mary. Some are bugs that are being worked and most of them I'm only copied into, so I open another browser and Google 'how to get married in the UK'.

It turns out that we do need to register. Maybe we should've just done it in Vegas. Damn.

I forward Zoey the page I'm reading and tell her I've made us an appointment for tomorrow so we can officially give notice for our wedding day.

Zoey

"So, you're telling me that the work done by the contractors was faulty?" I say, propping my iPad under my arm.

The guy, who has been fixing the mistake of the previous plumber nods, pushing back his floppy brown hair that has fallen into his eyes.

"Okay, so I'm not going to have this problem again, am I?"

"Not with my guys on the job."

I nod and hope to hell I don't have another issue in six months. Trying to figure out this with the insurance company has been testing. Well, for Sam and Lloyd, since they have been here dealing with it. The irony is the insurance is with Bancroft insurance. Yep, Max made me do it when I took this place over. And now, I hate him for it because not only is the insurance refusing to help with the situation, due to it being the contractor's fault. But I also can't help but wonder why I'm paying for insurance when they don't step in when I need help.

I refuse to ask my brothers or anyone else for help because that means conceding something to my parents somehow.

I take a deep breath and focus on the empty hallway in front of me. "This is fine. Everything will be sorted as soon as you can get your trust fund. It'll even out," I tell myself.

Sam's head pops out into the hallway, making me jump. "Talking to yourself again? That's the first sign of insanity, honey."

"Jesus, Sam. Make more noise next time." I place my hand over my racing heart and exhale. "Let's be honest, I didn't have much sanity to begin with. I mean, I hired you, after all."

"Ouch. Someone didn't take their sugar pills this morning. Seems you chose salty ones."

"Sorry, I'm incredibly grateful for you two. You know that."

"Yeah," he laughs. "You're also paying for our trip to America next year with all this overtime we're doing. So, we love you too, boss."

I don't even want to think about the cost right now. My head is pounding. Moving towards his office door, we both head inside, where Lloyd is waiting with my favourite litter of kittens in his lap. My heart immediately leaps at the sight of these tiny four week old babies who were abandoned.

"There you are. Come here little one," I say, holding out my hands to take the white kitten.

"She's just had some milk, so don't go throwing her around," Lloyd warns, but I'm not listening. I take the beautiful white fluffball and cradle her into my neck, where she nuzzles into me like it's her job. We've had to feed them by hand since they were abandoned at what we think was a few hours old, and this little runt has stolen my heart.

"She missed me," I say, looking between Sam and Lloyd.

They both roll their eyes, but I don't care. I've got my personal serotonin fix from this little fluffball on my shoulder. Everything is right with the world again.

My phone chimes with an email notification and when I pull it out, I see it's from Harrison. There's a link and a message telling me he's booked an appointment at the Chelsea Old Town Hall for eleven tomorrow.

"Excuse me, missy. Why are you smiling at your phone like that?" Lloyd asks, whilst he feeds another.

I'm smiling? Huh. "I have somewhere I need to be tomorrow at eleven, that's all."

"Is that code for 'I'm definitely going to bang my future fake husband and I won't be in work'?" Lloyd asks, amusement lacing his voice.

"I wish I hadn't told you... either of you," I fire back before replying to Harrison and pocketing my phone. I'm not sure why I told them. They caught me in a moment of weakness, I think.

"So, you are going to bang him?" Sam asks, his eyebrow raising.

"I am not. If you must know, he looked into the whole 28-day thing you told me about, so we're going to book our wedding tomorrow," I reply, stroking the little white kitten on my lap, who's finished her milk and is blinking at me sleepily.

"Hmm,"

"Oh, no, no, no. Don't give me that judgemental hum, Sam." He sits across from me with his arms over his broad chest and those dark eyes challenging me.

"I give you two weeks before you end up in his bed," he says matter of fact, like he's just read the weather.

"Two weeks? No chance, I reckon ten days max," Lloyd chimes in.

I place the kitten down gently, watching her fall back to sleep in the blanket filled box. "You're both fired."

Lloyd laughs, but Sam just stares at me with indifference and damn, that annoys me more.

"You can't fire us," Lloyd argues, then flits his eyes to his husband, who's still glaring at me. "Can she?" he whispers.

Sam shakes his head. "Zoey needs us. She's just being defensive. Maybe because she thinks we're both being generous with our time frame for the bet and she thinks she won't even last the night."

"Seriously, get out. Both of you. You're awful humans who have no faith in me at all. I will not sleep with my fake future husband."

A chorus of sarcastic agreement makes my irritation soar. My skin itches with the desire to be right and for both of these dickheads to be wrong.

Except, they really might not be wrong because Harrison Clarke is all kinds of irresistible.

Chapter 22

Zoey - Three weeks later

S o, it turns out, when you're trying to abstain from sex, you notice it everywhere. Several of our male dogs have been nonstop humping the females this week. Luckily, they're all neutered. I see happy couples eating each other's faces on the tube. It's annoying and frustrating. As though a siren has gone off to tell the world, 'Hello, Zoey isn't having sex of any kind at the moment, so please remind her of that every minute of every day'.

If I wasn't so hellbent on keeping this quiet until we're married, I'd insist my brothers had set all this up to torture me, but alas, they're none the wiser. For the last three weeks, we've managed to keep everything secret from both our families whilst still living together, and that suits us until we're ready to tell them we're married and there isn't anything they can do about it.

I worry if my brothers found out earlier, they'd want to kill Harrison. At least, this way, if he's my husband, their anger is easier to dismiss. Well, it isn't, but it'll be impossible for them to stop it at that point.

Harrison has successfully set my body on fire with every little touch, graze, or heated stare we've shared. Last night, he passed me the saltshaker. Our fingers brushed against one another, and I swear, I had to clamp my mouth closed so fast to stop a moan from escaping. He's so big and imposing, I'm hyper aware of him and if I don't get some kind of release soon, my will to stay in my own bed will dissolve pretty fast.

And it's not just his physical effect on me; he makes me coffee every morning, he texts me about dinner, he asks about my day without fail, he's attentive and sweet and... completely off bounds. And I'm incredibly frustrated.

"Zoey?" Nora asks, staring at me from across the booth we're sitting at. I met her after work in an attempt to avoid my future husband for the night, but the reality is all I've done is think about him.

I shake my head. "Sorry, you were saying?"

"I was saying you look like shit."

Get best friends, they said. It'll be fun, they said.

"You know I'd be offended if that wasn't the stone-cold truth."

She smirks, patting my arm patronisingly. "There, there. Tell me all your woes."

Narrowing my eyes, I also sigh because I need to talk to someone about this. "I look like shit because I'm not getting sex." My arms flap around me as I carry on, spilling my frustration. "And I live with a man who is arguably a walking advert for every woman's fantasy, but he's off limits and I'm—"

"Horny?"

"Fuck yes, but even that's an understatement. I'm the queen of Hornville. I live in a world where everyone but me is allowed to have it, and it sucks so fucking bad. Help. me."

Nora laughs. "Help you have sex?"

"No, I mean yes, but no. I don't even know. I'm hot all the time, I can't control it, and now it's affecting the way I look, according to you." In my mind, I probably look like that Cruella DeVil meme where she's driving the car with bright red eyes, like a mad woman. The reality probably isn't that far off, either.

Nora contemplates me for a second. "You have tried helping yourself out, right? I mean, that seems like the most obvious solution here."

I roll my eyes. Of course I've tried that and none of my self-help techniques are working because it's not what I want. "Of course, I tried that," I reply flatly.

Her brown eyes narrow in thought. "But you've not had sex before and you've been fine, so why is it so difficult now?"

I exhale loudly, hoping all my frustration can be pushed away, but it doesn't work. "I know, but this time it's like being told you aren't allowed the best doughnut in the shop, and all you really want is the best doughnut that's covered in chocolate, caramel, and muscles and... fuck's sake. See my problem?"

"That you have a weird fetish with muscley doughnuts?"

I throw my hands in the air, slumping my arms on the table in front of me with a groan. "No one who is having sex understands me," I whinge. "I can't have sex with my future fake husband because it'll complicate things, and we agreed to keep it as uncomplicated as possible. I can't have sex with anyone else because then I look like I'm cheating on my fake husband. I'm basically going to become a person who doesn't have sex ever again."

Nora chuckles beside me, and I turn my head to see her amused face. "I can't have sex with you. I can't even offer you Grayson because, weird, but I can distract you and feed you dinner right now?"

I nod solemnly. "I don't know how I get myself into these messes. I am the epitome of that Taylor Swift song, "anti-hero." I'm the problem, it's me."

Nora cackles and throws her head back. "Oh my God, that's definitely y—" She stops when I glare at her and clears her throat. "I mean, it's definitely the most extravagant Zoey thing to date."

Rolling my eyes, I pretend to ignore her, agreeing that I get older but not wiser like that bloody song says. "The worst part? He's so nice. If he could get an award for best fake husband, he deserves the Oscar because the man is wonderful."

Nora stares at me, holding back her smile. "You have a crush on your future fake husband?"

"I do not." *I definitely do.*

"You're adorable when you're in denial."

I scowl deeply at my ex-best friend. "You're fired." I'll fire everyone in my life if they continue to piss me off.

Nora laughs maniacally because she knows I'm stuck with her. "You're not firing me from being your best friend."

"I so am."

I tear the napkin in front of me for something to do with my hands, but her smug face makes my inner brat itch to scream at her and tell her she's wrong, but the truth is that she isn't. Maybe I never stopped crushing on Harrison. I had no issues bunking up with him and almost marrying the man in Vegas. *Jesus, why do I do this to myself?*

"Okay, so, important question. What are you wearing Saturday?" Nora asks as our food arrives. We ordered as soon as we sat down, and I was starving, but now my appetite is almost non-existent.

"I don't want to wear a dress," I admit because that feels like a real wedding, and I'll reserve that for my real husband in the future, if that even happens. "I have this pale pink trouser suit I might wear."

She catches the words I didn't speak because that's what she always does. Nodding pensively, she picks up her cutlery. "You know it's okay if you feel like this is all a little underwhelming."

"It's all kinds of... whelming, over, under, sideways. You name it." I sigh, picking at the rice bowl in front of me.

"And it's okay if you want to stop all this."

I nod.

"Don't think I haven't missed the fact that you've torn up two napkins whilst you've been here with me. I know you're worried," Nora says, calling me out again.

But she's right. I have my own free will, but I also know that those animals need more. I need more for them. The shelter is my responsibility, my only responsibility, and I can't let that fail. If it means tricking my parents into thinking I'm happily married to do that, then yeah, I'll do it. And I guess I won't fire my best friend either.

When I get home, it's after ten and I'm torn between wanting to torture myself more with Harrison's presence, and wishing he wasn't around so I can slink off into my bedroom unnoticed. When I open the door and spot him slumped on the sofa, laptop open, tie long discarded and a sleepy frown pulling at his brows, my entire body deflates. *Why does he have to be cute and manly?* Seriously, I can barely cope with him awake, but asleep? He looks so perfect I can hardly handle it.

I tiptoe over to him, lift the laptop from his legs and he jumps with a gruff, sleepy noise that shoots straight to my nipples. *Sweet baby Jesus, I need help.*

"Zoey, you're home," he mumbles, rubbing his eyes.

"I am. Come on, mountain man. Let's get you to bed." *With me,* my inner ho screams. At this point, she's got a crowbar and is trying desperately to get out of the cage I've put her in.

He moves and groans. I almost ask him to button it, because those damn noises... but I think better of it. He propels himself upwards, misjudging the distance between us, and suddenly our chests are touching and we connect on a gasp when he practically engulfs me with his body. It's too hot, too much, too close, too fucking tempting.

I crane my neck to stare up at him. The dim light makes him look like some sort of beautiful giant, a being that definitely doesn't belong in this world.

My throat is suddenly lined with needles, and I can't swallow. His nearness is choking me. I'm surrounded by notes of fresh clean cotton, musk and something that I've learnt is just Harrison. I'm drunk on him and my own arousal. It floods my every sense and clouds my rational thoughts, making me feel like I should lean closer and touch my lips to his.

There's a whisper of sanity somewhere here, and I should find it. But with the way Harrison's eyes are flaming with desire and him almost touching his chin to his chest to stare at me, I think I'm about to lose it.

"Zoey." The low timbre of his voice vibrates through where our bodies connect as I instinctively lean closer to him. Close enough that I can feel his hot breath only a whisper away from my lips. The whole world could be on fire right now and I'd have no clue, because all I see is him. All I feel is him.

And then I don't.

He sidesteps out of the space we've wedged ourselves in, between the sofa and the coffee table, and I'm left feeling like I've been slapped with a wet fish. That harsh dose of reality really stings when you're desperate.

He mutters a curse, but all I hear is static because I very nearly kissed my soon to be fake husband because I'm desperate and horny. And I really want to fuck him.

I snap my gaping mouth closed and manage to say the only word in my vocabulary these days. "Horny," I whimper and immediately yelp, realising my error as his eyes widen. "Oh my God, I meant Hi. Hello, Hola, anything that doesn't mean horny and means hello instead." I collapse onto the sofa, close my eyes and throw my face into my hands, wishing there was a black hole around here that I could crawl into and die inside. "Fuck," I groan.

Then I hear it; it's a low, deep tickle of a noise that stops my breathing altogether. It gets louder and deeper as he increases the tempo of his... laughter. He's laughing at me.

When our eyes connect, his laughter slows, and he tries to regain some of his usual composure by taking a deep breath and then staring up at the ceiling.

"I'm sorry." He trembles on the apology and coughs to cover up another laugh. If you ask me, it's the worst apology I've ever heard. "I'm not laughing at you."

"Funny, it feels like you are."

He shakes his head, a smile still beaming from him. "I'm not, promise. It's just... It's like you reached into my mind and plucked the one word I was thinking."

My eyes narrow. "You're horny too?"

The laughter dies in his throat. "I'm currently living with a beautiful woman who I can't touch. What do you think?"

Well, fuck. I hadn't really thought he'd be feeling the same. We agreed to sleep separately, and I assumed he would be fine with it.

"But we should probably still not... you know."

"Fuck?" I offer.

He smiles, obviously still amused. "Confuse things, I was going to say."

Right. He's right. "Stick to the plan," I confirm, standing as I inch away from him. The ache in my body has simmered down, but I can't risk being around him still and God forbid he reached for something and flexed in front of me. I need to get a handle on this. "I'm gonna head to bed."

He groans. "Zoey?"

I close my eyes, spin on the balls of my feet as I turn and open my eyes cautiously. "Hm?"

"We good?"

I nod and smile. "Of course."

When I get to my room, I realise this is going to be the longest year of my life.

Chapter 23

Harrison

This is going to be the longest year of my life.

The last twenty-eight days have been testing enough.

Seriously, being around Zoey is, in some ways, so easy. She's such a force of nature that it's impossible not to bask in her light. But it's also impossible because I think I've made a deal I can't keep. I want her in a way that a fake husband shouldn't want her. I want her in a way that our business arrangement didn't detail.

"You ready, man?" Grayson knocks on my bedroom door, breaking me out of my thoughts and peers around it before walking inside, looking dapper in a dark grey suit. Buttoning my cufflink, I look at my reflection in the mirror. *Am I ready?*

"I think so," I say, staring at my reflection. Black suit, white shirt, black tie. I fiddle with the tie again, not sure why it's not sitting right today.

"Nervous?" he asks with a laugh, gripping my shoulders and turning me before tugging out the knot and starting again.

"Thanks," I reply when he's done, shifting the loop that's oddly starting to feel like a noose around my neck. *We're doing the right thing, right?* "I didn't think I would be because it's a business arrangement, but..." I drift off, not really sure what I need to say. "Never mind."

Grayson's hand lands back on my shoulder, reassuringly squeezing. "If you're having second thoughts, I have a getaway car."

I huff a laugh because I know he'll whisk me away if I need it. That's the type of guy he is. I suck in a deep breath and remember why I'm doing this and who I'm doing it with, and the weight in my stomach settles. "Nah, I'm good. Let's go. Can't keep my bride waiting."

Bride. And even though I'm a little nervous over this whole thing, picturing Zoey in a white dress tames the swarm of bees currently flying around my stomach, giving me the reassurance I need to prove this is right.

It takes us ten minutes to drive to Chelsea Old Town Hall. The big cream building with Grecian-style pillars stares at me. This is it. The place I'm saying I do.

Grayson goes ahead of me as we walk inside the building and are directed to a room with a long cream carpet to greet the registrar. We quickly go through some pre-wedding questions before she disappears off into a side room to interview Zoey, too.

"Hey, Harrison?" I turn to face Grayson, my back now to the aisle. I don't know if I ever thought I'd be stood here, especially not with Zoey Bancroft of all people. But nothing feels out of place. I hate crowds, I wouldn't want a big wedding and this feels right. Just me, Zoey Grayson and Nora. And now, I'm overthinking it again. Am I in too deep here? Why does this feel so right? It's just an arrangement. I have to remind myself several times before it actually sinks in.

Grayson moves to adjust my tie again. I tip my chin to give him more room, grateful for the distraction. "I'm gonna need you to take a breath because you look like you might puke. And dude, these shoes are my favourite, so I'd rather not have your sick all over them."

A smile breaks over my face, and I exhale. "I won't puke, promise." I wring my hands and straighten the cuffs of my shirt again.

"Then stop fidgeting," he says, smacking my hands away and quickly straightening my sleeves. "You've got this. I believe in you. You can do it."

"You know, reeling off bad motivation quotes isn't helping. Pretty sure if you finally grow a pair and ask Nora to marry you and were this nervous, I'd be nothing but a pillar of support."

"Yeah, but my wedding would be real," he deadpans, and I narrow my eyes at him. "Besides, who's even saying I'd ask you to be my best man?"

"Fuck you, man. It's not too late for me to change my fake best man, y'know."

"Okay, sorry. I'll shut up and we'll just get you married," he retorts, just as the registrar returns to the room.

Classical music filters from the speakers around the room, and I turn to watch the doors a few feet away open to reveal Nora and Zoey and just like that, my heart thunders in my ribcage. Unlike my imagined picture of Zoey, a classy light pink trouser suit hugs her in all the right places. Her makeup is minimal, her hair is straight, brushing the tops of her shoulders. She's beautiful.

The organ in my chest creates a staccato rhythm as she walks towards me. Time stands still when she reaches me with a smile and a wink. "You ready, mountain man?" she whispers, handing her sweet smelling bouquet of wildflowers to Nora before she stands next to me, brushing her little finger against mine.

"Today marks a new beginning in two lives together. I thank you both for being here to witness their wedding vows and celebrate their marriage." The registrar nods to Grayson and Nora. "Who gives this woman to this man?"

Nora steps forward. "I do."

"Marriage is a commitment not only vested in love but friendship, mutual respect and calls for honesty, care, patience, and of course, humour. A good partner will be loving, caring and above all, a true friend..." Words slowly become a distant hum as Zoey's bright blue eyes look into mine, a small smile tugging at her lips as her pinky finger brushes against mine again. The contact is so soft, yet it feels like I've been hit by a live wire. Suddenly, I want to wrap my whole hand with hers, feel the warmth of her skin against mine, but is that even appropriate? Would she want that? Would she flinch at my touch and pull away, making it obvious that this is fake? Is marriage fraud even a thing? Shit, should we have been holding hands right from the start?

"Please take each other's hands and face one another," the registrar says, breaking into my panicked thoughts. Zoey slots her hands into mine where they fit perfectly, and I feel the questions from earlier disappear as a calm settles over me. "Harrison, will you take Zoey to be your lawful wedded wife. To share your life with her and comfort her in whatever the future may bring?"

"I will."

The remainder of the ceremony goes off without a hitch. Both of us promise our future to one another with ease, as though we've been together for years and this is a mere formality. It feels... real, and I need to remind myself that it isn't. Grayson passes us the rings we bought in Vegas. We lock eyes and an understanding passes through us. We're doing this, and we're in this together.

Fake wedding? Nailing it.

Zoey

"You may now kiss the bride."

I hesitate because I'd forgotten that we'd have to kiss. That Harrison's lips, the very ones I have been fantasising about, would be on mine.

Before I can think, Harrison takes a step towards me. His big hands cupping my face as though he's done it a million times before and the entire room fades away. The only thing I can feel is his warmth against my skin, and all I can hear is the hammering of my heart. "Hey, Mrs Clarke," he whispers before he takes my mouth in a searing kiss that forces me to grasp onto him to stay upright.

The way Harrison kisses me is feverish and confident, yet it settles something inside me that feels like it's been lost, wandering around for an eternity, looking for its way back home. His lips move against mine, but our tongues never meet. I want to push my luck because that's what I've done my whole life, and if this is the only kiss I get with my childhood crush, then you bet I'm going to go all in. Trailing my hands to the back of his neck, I hold him against me as I open my mouth, peeking my tongue out and licking his lips. When I feel a rumble in his chest at the contact, I do it again and suddenly, our tongues are duelling for dominance.

A throat clears somewhere near us, breaking us both apart too soon for my liking. Our chests heave in sync as we stare open-mouthed and ravenous at each other. The wetness left on my swollen lips from his kiss chills as the air hits it.

"Ah-hem." The sound happens again, and I turn my head to see my best friend and her boyfriend both smirking. I step away from Harrison, immediately missing the feel of his body against mine, and focus on the floor as I try to recover from that kiss.

"I hope you both have a happy life together and enjoy the rest of your day," the registrar says next to us, making it sound like this is a conveyor belt operation. Which I guess it sort of is.

Nora grabs my arm and pulls me into a hug. "Congratulations, Mrs Clarke," she says, but when she's got me close enough to whisper into my ear, she continues, "*That kiss*, Zo. We need to talk."

I pull back and smile at her, but it's forced because all I can think about is how I know that kiss won't be enough. It hasn't satiated the need that I feel for him. A need that's been ignited and grown with all the small touches and glances that's been happening more and more the longer we've spent together. And now I'm more terrified than ever to be alone with him.

Harrison hugs Grayson, but the whole time his eyes are on me. It's the kind of stare I can feel all over, the kind I crave from him daily, but right now it's torture, and I'm certain I'm not the only one suffering. I think we both know exactly where we *want* this to go. But we both know we shouldn't.

He only dips his attention to take my hand and lead me from the town hall. Walking in step with our friends, we turn to the nearest restaurant, a little pub on the corner. Seeing as though we opted for an early evening wedding, the place isn't that busy, and we find a table without fuss.

"So, when do you tell your brothers, and can I please be there?" Grayson asks, sitting down opposite me and Harrison.

Nora thwacks his chest and glares at him. "I know you think you're cute, but you're just annoying."

Grayson gleams at her. "Are you getting mad at me, shorty? Because you know I'm all for that."

"Guys," I groan as I rub my temples, not needing to hear my friends talk about their sex lives right now. "Grayson, you can tell them if you really want to be there so badly. I'm cool with not being there at all."

"Zo, you know we have to do it. Together." The word sounds so final and when Harrison takes my hand, our rings connecting, brushing the metal together, I know it's no longer me versus my family. He's got my back. Even if it is fake.

"Do we though?" I reply, dragging my gaze away from our connecting fingers to look into his dark eyes.

He pins me with a stare that tells me our first marital spat is going to end with him winning because who the fuck can say no to those eyes? I huff, conceding to the fact that he is right and we already have plans with my family tomorrow. Then we have plans with his sister the week after. It's a lot to deal with all at once, but once it's done, we can finally get what it is we both need from this agreement. But when Harrison's calloused thumb brushes over the back of my hand, I'm struggling to remember what that was again.

Chapter 24

Zoey

"I don't want to do this," I admit, turning to face Harrison, a pout playing on my lips.

"You might've mentioned that," he says, ignoring my petulance, taking my hand and striding towards my parents' house with me trailing behind. I have to practically jog to keep up with him. Damn him and his long legs.

Okay, I guess he's immune to my pouting. Noted. That still doesn't make me want to go in there and be fed to the lions.

He stops in front of the front door, taking in the multitude of door knockers and I watch as his hands shift between all four, hesitantly reaching for each of them, and I have to stifle a laugh. Then he mutters 'fuck it' and uses his knuckles to knock. My smile grows wider because that's exactly what I do.

When Owen opens the door, my body goes into flight mode, and I pull my hand away from Harrison's as a sudden rush of fear bursts through me. I'd like my husband to at least get past the threshold before he's jumped by one of my brothers.

Owen's eyes immediately narrow at the sight of us, but I launch myself at him as a distraction. His stiff arms wrap around me in a hug that makes me feel his suspicion already. "Hey, big bro. How's things?" I say, stepping into the house.

"I'm fi—wait, did you and Harrison come together?" he asks, straight to the point. Never misses a trick. That's Owen.

"We didn't," I shriek just as Harrison says, "We did."

Owen's frown deepens, his focus flicking between us as he tries to figure out who is telling the truth.

"Let's go inside, man," Harrison says calmly, slapping Owen's shoulder as he passes him.

"You're both acting weird," Owen replies, letting us pass but crossing his tattooed arms over his chest.

"We are?" I wobble, nerves getting the better of my voice.

His scowl deepens as he looks between us, then he turns and huffs in the direction of the kitchen and I deflate.

"Jesus," I mumble under my breath. I knew today would be draining, but I'm already so exhausted from keeping secrets, from the shelter stress, and getting absolutely zero sex, I need a holiday from my life right now.

"Way to play it cool, sweetheart." Harrison's deep voice makes me jump, reminding me that I'm not alone. "You okay?" He takes my hand and presses the back of it to his lips. In moments like this, when he touches me without thinking, I have to remind myself that this is temporary and it's a business arrangement. He's doing it because it's a part of our deal, the doting fake husband. And that's fine, I'm great at business deals.

So, I nod and smile. "As good as can be expected. Listen—"

My mother breezes into the hallway, interrupting me before I can say 'sorry for my fucked-up family'. "Zoey, how lovely you're on time," she snides, already getting dig number one in bright and early in the evening.

I stiffen as I lean towards her, not letting go of Harrison's hand as she does her usual air kisses. Her eyes flare with interest when she spots Harrison, and my blood runs cold at the thought of her flirting with him.

"Mother, you know Harrison."

He extends his hand with his usual cool smile and gentlemanly manner, and she doesn't hesitate to place her hand in his. "Good to see you again, Mrs Bancroft. I trust you're well?"

Oh God, kill me now. He's too perfect, killing it in the fancy pants fake husband role. Round one goes to Harrison.

"I'm well, thank you. Come, John is waiting for us in the formal area."

She turns, leaving us in an invisible cloud of her perfume, as Harrison looks at me quizzically. I lean in towards him to explain. "Formal living room is posh people talk for 'I'm a wanker with too much money and huge house.'"

He stifles a laugh, rolling his lips between his teeth, his eyes flaring with amusement. "You forget I walked these halls when we were kids," he whispers, regaining his composure.

We pass some family portraits of me and the twins when we were young and cute, and Mum could get me to pose without sticking my tongue out for pictures. That lasted until I was five, and then the family pictures became only of the boys. I'm not bitter because I hated being dressed up and told to sit still.

As we enter the living room, I'm not even going to call it what my mother calls it because it's ridiculous. My father sits in his usual high-winged brown leather chair, already a whisky in hand and a scowl in place. He stands, and his expression lessens when he sees Harrison.

"Harrison, it's good to see you again," he says, striding towards him and shaking his hand when they meet.

"Mr Bancroft, it's good to see you too."

"Please, call me John." My father has two settings, scowling and businessman. Sometimes, they overlap but I've not seen him be nice to anyone but my brothers in years, so his reaction is a bit of a shock. "Zoey," he greets me coldly, and inside I shrivel, because there's just too much distance between us for him to ever be nice to me. I grimace in response, wishing I could be anywhere but here.

"Let me get you a drink, seeing as though Zoey has forgotten all her manners." My mother grazes past Harrison, not meeting my eye but letting that second dig of the night sting just as they always do. I notice Harrison stiffen as she walks by, and he flicks his scrutinising stare around the room. *Buckle up, buddy. We've got at least a couple of hours of this.* Maybe I can convince Seren to undercook the chicken so we all have to go home early with food poisoning.

I stop as I notice my own thoughts. I'd rather risk salmonella than be in the same room as my parents. Oh, what a wonderful life.

"Zoey?" Harrison's voice brings me out of my daze of imagining throwing up instead of being here.

"I'm sorry, I spaced."

"That's okay. You've been busy working late this week." He gives me one of his genuine smiles and rubs the back of my hand in a way that makes the organ in my chest do a double beat. "Would you like a drink?"

I nod softly. "Just a soft drink or water, please." Because if I have alcohol, I'll make a scene, and I don't want to do that tonight.

"Harrison? Owen said you were here. I didn't realise you were coming tonight," Max smiles, striding over from the patio to his best friend. They shake hands and hug like they always do, and I have a pang of regret for possibly destroying their friendship over my trust fund. Max hugs me too and the guilt settles like a led weight in my stomach.

"Please don't be mad at me," I whisper into my brother's ear. He pulls back, confusion marring his face when I turn to Harrison, hoping he understands why I have to do this. "Harrison and I are married."

I'm met with silence. The kind that is suffocating because no one knows what to say or if they should be the first to say something.

"What the fuck?" Max eventually curses. "How... when..." he fumbles, running a hand through his hair.

Harrison holds my stare, reassurance gleaming in his brown eyes, and I feel myself take a cleansing deep breath. "Zoey and I have been seeing each other for a while, but we didn't want to upset anyone, but when we were in Vegas... well, we almost got married and we realised that it was what we both wanted."

Silence again. "It was planned, but it also wasn't. We wanted it to be intimate," I explain to everyone while they openly gawk at us.

"Typical," my mother snorts, and I glare at her. "Well, it is Zoey. You always were unable to follow the rules. Now, you're married. I suppose I should be grateful it's Harrison and not some charity case you felt you needed to save." Her words are bitter and hurtful and something that should chip away at my self-esteem, but I learned a long time ago to put up shields with my mother. However, that doesn't always stop my inner child from screaming.

"Congratulations would suffice, you know," I snarl, holding her disapproving glare.

"Why didn't you tell me?" Max mutters angrily, gaining both of our attention. Harrison is still holding my hand, and when Max talks, he squeezes it tighter. We both hear the hurt in his voice and now we have to deal with the consequences.

"Max, I never wanted to keep this from you, but I also know how protective you are of me—"

"For good reason, Zo. You're my little sister. I always need to keep an eye on you. I never want to see you hurt."

"You don't need to keep an eye on me, Max. I'm a grown woman and I can take care of myself. I know you love me, but I need you to respect me too, and a part of that is letting me love who I want to love," I explain, straightening my spine.

I know we don't technically love each other, but it's definitely something that my family need to hear to know I'm serious. I glance over to Owen, his brows are furrowed as he stares at Harrison and my connected hands, but he hasn't said anything yet, and I daren't look at my father.

Max looks torn between wanting to punch Harrison and giving in because I know I've struck a chord with him. "You're right. I'm sorry if I've been an overbearing arsehole." He shakes his head and holds his arms out for me. Without hesitation, I let go of Harrison's hand and run into my big brother's arms.

Relief washes over me as I think about all the ways this could've gone badly. "*If* you've been an overbearing arsehole? That's your apology? I don't know if you know the meaning of the word." I tease.

"Fine, I'm sorry."

I squeeze him harder. "Maybe I didn't give you enough credit either," I whisper into his shoulder.

"Why?"

"I thought you'd punch your best friend."

Max chuckles but doesn't let me go. "The night is still young."

When we break apart, Max moves to Harrison and hugs him, probably whispering death threats into his ear. The thought makes me laugh. Owen comes around them both and assesses me. "I knew there were heart eyes when you were pretending not to know Harrison on the plane."

I smile. "I never kiss and tell, big brother," I reply as I hug him too. Owen's hugs are so different to Max's. Max hugs you like it's the first and last time he'll ever see you when Owen is so stiff and unwelcoming. He's hugging me because society says it's what he should do in this situation and not because he wants to. "Thank you for not punching my husband."

"I've punched him enough times to know that I always come off worse, so my self preservation kicked in. You're welcome." He pulls back and I stare into his eyes, exactly the same as mine, and grin.

"You and Harrison fought?"

"All the time when we were kids. I won once, and that was the last time I ever threw a punch his way."

That makes me laugh, and for a moment, everything feels like it's okay again.

"If you are done, I'd like to speak to Zoey... alone." My father's unforgiving voice filters into the happy bubble I'm temporarily in, well and truly popping it.

No one moves an inch, which makes me feel marginally better. They don't want to leave me with him—not that he'd hurt me—he leaves all that to his words, just like my mother.

"With respect, John. Whatever you need to say to Zoey, you can say with me present." Harrison comes to my side again and takes my hand, giving me an anchor to hold me for a moment. And it hits me; I've never had that before. It's always been me against them. Just me constantly fighting my corner, but now I have Harrison with me, and it feels... really fucking good.

"As you wish. Boys, darling, please give us the room for a second," he says with enough dominance in his tone that they all leave. Max casts a weary glance over his shoulder as he exits.

Anticipation fills my lungs as I try to breathe, even though it feels like there isn't a whole lot of oxygen in this room that's breathable. Just toxic air radiating from my father.

"I'd like to say I'm surprised Zoey, but I'm actually disappointed."

Oh good. The whole I'm disappointed card. I'm familiar with this speech. I've heard it enough growing up that I'm practically immune to its effect on me now. "Are we going to pretend that's new for us?"

His nostrils flare and he opens his mouth to say something, but clamps it closed with a forceful snap. The silence between us sits heavily in the room because if I know anything, it's how my parents act right before they're about to explode. My father's murderous eyes glare into the drink in his hand.

"I'm going to assume you think I'm not stupid and give you one chance to come clean. Both of you," he spits without looking up.

I tentatively glance over to Harrison, who shifts uncomfortably for a second, then his jaw twitches and he drops my hand, stepping forwards. "John, I'm not sure what you expect us to tell you. What

Zoey and I have is real. It might be something we built in secret, but that doesn't mean it's less than if we were honest from the start."

"I thought you were smarter than this impulsive behaviour, Harrison. It's beneath you."

Harrison scoffs but stiffens. "Not that my personal life should be any of your business, but Zoey and I are not impulsive. We are two people who want to spend our lives together."

"Bullshit. You're really taking that approach?" he sneers, spinning to face us with a look of utter disdain that I can almost taste the sourness of his words.

I step next to Harrison. "Why is it so difficult for you to understand that someone could actually pick me and love me?"

"That's not—"

"That's exactly what this is. You can't fathom that anyone would pick me because you always consider me to be a complete fuck up."

"When you spend your entire existence rebelling against me and your mother, what am I supposed to think, Zoey? That you just happened to see your brothers get their trust fund and come up with a plan to get yours, too? I know you. I know your tricks. You're more like me than you realise, and if I find out that this is all for show to get your trust fund, you can kiss it goodbye."

I feel the blood drain from my body, each of my limbs becoming heavier and emptier at the same time. He can't know, and yet he's calling me out. His accusation is like two invisible hands trying to choke me, but I can't let him win. My heart thuds erratically in my chest as I break into a sweat. My head suddenly feels like it's full of cotton wool and I can't form a rational thought. Those animals, my animals, they need me; they need more help than I can give right now and if I mess this up, I'll never forgive myself.

"I'm not playing a game," I argue, with a wobble that restricts my throat.

He scoffs, and it hits me like a burn to the skin. "You're always playing a game, Zoey. You're unreliable, unpredictable and irresponsible—"

"That's enough!" Harrison erupts next to us. My eyes widen as I take in the flush of anger on his cheeks, and the fury building in his eyes. "No one talks to my wife like that." His chest heaves and my jaw drops.

"Excuse me?" My father rears back.

"She deserves respect and if you can't give that to her, then we are leaving," Harrison replies calmly but sternly.

I watch my father stew on Harrison's words, unsure if this man in front of him is serious with his outburst. And just when I think Harrison isn't the most perfect man for defending me, he continues. "If you're willing to apologise, I'll talk to Zoey and see if she's comfortable staying here. Either way, I'm giving her the decision because I respect her, and she deserves that. Your daughter is the most caring, driven and resilient person I've ever met and nothing you say or do is going to stop us from being together."

His hand grips mine as he stares down at it, like he's contemplating what he wants to say next, while I'm completely dumbstruck by the man next to me. When his eyes meet mine, everything inside my chest sparks to life because he's fighting... for me. "Yes, we kept this a secret because we weren't sure how things would pan out..." He pauses, taking in every inch of my face. It's intoxicating and... confusing. "But I can safely say that I have been in love with Zoey from the moment we reconnected and she couldn't remember who I was." He turns to look directly at my father whilst I'm left fixated on him.

But wait, that was on the plane, or the wedding. He can't be saying, surely not. I'm turned around because I don't know if even I can spot the lies between the truths now. This is all to make sure our story is straight; it has to be.

One thing I do know is that Harrison Clarke, the man I married, is officially the world's most perfect specimen. Take a bow, sir. You've just ruined me for anyone else. Fake or not, I'd want him in my corner any day.

My father runs his tongue along his teeth, snarling like the evil bastard he is as I tear my focus from Harrison to him. "You're free to leave," he sneers, and the high I felt from Harrison is replaced with a dagger to the chest from my father. A sob threatens my throat, but I swallow it down.

"Now I'm the one who is disappointed. I expected more of you, both as a father and a human being," Harrison replies, then turns to face me, his face soft and hurt, but maybe that's my own hurt mirroring back at me. I knew my parents could be cruel, but this is another level. He directs my heavy feet out of the living room and into the foyer. There's a distant chatter from the kitchen that I'm assuming is everyone else, but I tune it out.

"Zoey, I'm sorry that was... I couldn't let him talk to you like that. Are you okay?"

I nod, then shake my head as I tuck my hair behind my ears. "I just need a little air. I'll be right back."

All the air depletes from the house as I rush through the foyer and to the back room that leads to the garden patio. I fumble with the lock and when it springs open, the sliding door lets in a gush of fresh air that fills my lungs painfully. My chest expands and tears prickle at the back of my eyes. *No, I can't cry here. I can't be that weak. Not now. Not now.*

I let the cool evening air whisper around me as I try to regulate my breathing when two strong arms wrap around me from behind. His familiar soft, clean scent settles me. The tornado swirling inside is nothing but a cool breeze when he holds me and that realisation scares me because I know I'll be chasing this feeling I have with him forever, and what we have was never meant to be forever.

"It's okay, I'm here."

Four simple words that, coming from him, calm every fibre of my being because he's right, he is here; we are in this together. I need to lean on him. I want to lean on him. I've just never had a partner to rely on before. I've only ever had myself, and the thought that someone else cares enough about me to weather my chaotic life breaks something inside me.

I let one tear slide free. Harrison doesn't let me go. He presses his lips to the top of my head and breathes deeply. Minutes pass as the cool air begins to nip at my skin and an involuntary shiver travels over my body. The contrast of his warmth and the cool air makes me feel like I'm in a tropical storm. "I—" I pause, not sure what I was going to say.

He presses his lips to my temple and then softly and briefly to my lips and I'm frozen, stuck in a moment that I've been dreaming about, unsure of what's happening.

All too soon, he pulls back. My instinct is to lean towards him and silently ask for more, but I don't. He flexes his hands around my waist and hums a noise that travels around my head like a siren song. He dips his face into the crook of my neck, peppering soft kisses against my flaming skin, when he settles against my ear and whispers, "I overstepped, Zoey, and I'm sorry."

I swallow hard, still feeling the imprint of his lips against mine as I lick over them. I plead with the beating organ in my chest once more, begging it to find a calm rhythm again. "Harrison," I say, my voice breaking. I squeeze my eyes tightly and take a deep breath. "Thank you." I swallow the emotion lodging in my throat and look up at him. "He's right though. I'm the black sheep. I'll sully your name against my father. He could destroy you and your company. I'm difficult, and you—"

"—Nothing about you is difficult, Zoey." He places both his hands on my face, forcing me to look into his deep brown eyes and my body responds by softening under his touch. "There's no one else I'd rather be married to. You are important, and you are worthy of love." His words simultaneously sting and soothe me because I realise I don't think I want this to be fake. But how do I bring that up? Everything is so new and up in the air still. Tonight has just heightened my emotions, and I know I need to rein them in before I get notions of more.

I plaster a fake smile on my face for my fake husband and pretend that I'm not feeling anything other than the arrangement we made.

"I'm taking you home for a bubble bath," he tells me, and I go without an argument because I don't think I ever want to say no to him again.

Chapter 25

Harrison

"Have you ever been to Ascot before?" I ask Zoey as she sits at the dresser in her bedroom, getting ready. I spot some post-it notes with kittens on the edge and smile. I've noticed the flat becoming more and more 'Zoey'. It started with her favourite woven throw blanket that now lives on the back of the couch. And there's more post-it notes by the front door and in the kitchen. All with cute animals and very 'Zoey'. The thing is, I like it all.

It's been four days since we told her family about us. Since I shouted at her father, I refuse to let anyone make Zoey feel less than she is. She's amazing, kind and full of life and hearing someone try and tear all that from her... No, I wasn't about to let that happen. Luckily, her brothers have been okay about it all. Max hasn't cut me out and Owen, well, he's still his usual stoic self.

"Uhh, I think once, when I was younger," she replies, fluttering a brush over her cheeks.

"Okay, well, most of my team will be there, so you can meet them." I pull out my cufflinks from the box and put them on as I continue. "We're in a box, but they're connected to other companies too, Bancroft Insurance included."

I look up just in time to see the flicker of hesitation in her eyes. "So, that's why you told me there would be booze because I'll need it to survive today?"

"That and... I'm pretty sure Vanessa is going to be there," I say, wincing, waiting for her to flat out refuse to go. I wouldn't blame her. Not only will she be around her parents, but also my vindictive ex. If she's really okay with this, I'll massage her feet for the entire year as a thank you.

She shrugs. "Okay, no big deal. If I've lived my whole life with my parents, a little entitled socialite won't hurt me. It might actually be fun."

It's official. Zoey Bancroft is perfect.

Walking up behind her, I watch her in the mirror, not able to stop the smile from spreading across my face.

"What? Is my make up too much?" she asks, looking back at her reflection.

I shake my head. "No. I was just thinking about how I'm grateful for you. You make marriage seem easy."

"I make fake marriages seem easy," she replies, her blue eyes focusing on me in the mirror, sending a bolt of need spearing its way into my body. And this isn't the first time it's happened. Zoey is a very touchy feely person. I know she's told me before that physical touch is her thing, but I don't know if she realises how much each of her touches engrains into my skin and keeps me coming back for more. A graze, a brush of a fingertip. I'm an addict, and I can't stay away from her.

And now, even though she isn't touching me, her stare blankets me completely, making a warmth pool in my gut.

Considering I'm older, I should have better check on my impulses. The issue is, I can't always convince my dick he won't be going near her. He's overeager for Zoey's attention, and that's unnerving for a guy who likes to be in control.

"Stop looking at me like that," she says, breathlessly.

I smirk as I lean down behind her, caging her in between the dresser and my front. Yeah, that control is slipping for sure and I'm barely hanging on. "How am I looking at you, Zo?"

Her breasts heave with exertion from the fluttering of her rapid pulse I can see in her neck. "Like you could devour me with one bite." She swallows thickly, and I turn my head to inhale her hair. Sweet and soft, just like her.

"Is that so?" I inhale again, letting the smell of her seep into my soul and I'm rewarded when she shudders, goosebumps marring her flesh. Her head tips to the side, and her beautiful soft skin is even more exposed, enough for me to take a bite of her if I wanted to. To mark her as mine, as much as the ring on her finger tells the world. "Do you want me to devour you?" I rasp, licking my lips, imagining how sweet her skin tastes.

"Harrison," she pleas, and the sound of her begging has something inside me roaring for release.

Closing my eyes, I shift on my feet. "Sweetheart, if I'm going to devour you, I need longer than..." I lift my suit jacket to check my watch. "Twenty minutes." I straighten my stance, moving away from temptation and cock blocking myself, wishing that today wasn't the day we have somewhere to be.

Zoey holds my stare in the mirror, want, need, and desire all shining in her bright blue eyes. "You're the worst kind of tease, Mr Clarke." She spins around so her face is in direct line with my crotch, and an involuntary groan leaves my throat when she zeros in on the obvious bulge and licks her lips. *Goddamn.*

Zoey slowly widens her legs, letting the robe she's wearing fall to either side of her thighs. A peek of white lace tells me she's wearing a bra, but I have no idea if she's wearing underwear, and if I were to look too far down, I'd forget all the reasons why we shouldn't even be doing this much teasing.

She presses her hands between her legs onto the stool she's sitting on and arches her back, tipping her head backwards as she looks up at me like a goddamn seductress.

"*I'm* the worst tease?" I counter, raising my eyebrows.

She smiles slowly and sensually and my cock thickens further against my chinos. *Does she have any idea what she does to me?*

"It doesn't matter because we're not going there." The way she says it doesn't feel like fact, she's framed it like a question, and I don't know how to answer without breaking all the boundaries we've set.

"That's true, so why don't you spell out your problems for me because I know you've got something to say," I reply, need wavering my voice.

She sighs long and deep, breaking our eye contact for a second before bringing it right back with enough fierceness it could set me on my backside. "I can't control these urges I get around you and they're making me crazy." She shifts, pressing her fingertips into her thighs and dragging them up to the edge of her robe, gripping enough to see the pull of the material around her neck. "Phallic objects everywhere.

Sex crazed animals follow me around at work, and it's..." Her wild eyes lock onto mine as she exhales throatily. "It's driving me insane."

I tilt my head, watching her pant with need, staring at the marks she left on her thighs, wishing they were my marks. I watch her eyes fall to my lips like she wants me to kiss her. *Fuck, I want to kiss her.*

"You want to know real insanity, Zoey?" I ask, crowding her again, leaning into her, needing to be close enough so my words cement themselves into her skin. "It's watching you but not being able to touch you. It's seeing you be this force of nature that I can't tame. It's *wanting* to kiss you, have you, claim you, but being unable to because we agreed not to complicate things." I brush my nose against hers, relishing the heat blasting from her and the hitch in her breath. "But what drives me over the edge is every time you wear a dress, I have to stop myself from wanting to flip it up and taste you." My heart thrums loudly in my ears as I stand to my full height again, looking down at the beautiful woman with yearning in her eyes. "*You*, Zoey Clarke, drive me certifiably insane."

I run the pad of my thumb over her plump bottom lip, and her eyes flutter closed. "Now get dressed before I do something I shouldn't."

"Like what?" she asks in a breathy whisper.

"Like bend you over and fuck you on your dresser."

Chapter 26

Zoey

H *oly fuck.*
Holy fuck.
Holy fucking fuck.

My blood feels like it's on fire, racing through my body, making me hotter than I've ever been before. My husband turns me on something fierce and then leaves me high and dry. I'm partly impressed with his restraint but severely disappointed by it, too. My skin is humming with the memory of his words washing over me and my body is hellbent on giving up on this arrangement. Desperation claws at me like a living, breathing thing, dying to be set free, but I hold it all back because today I'm going to Ascot to impress my husband's clients and be a good wife. The possibility that I might see my parents instantly cools me like I've been dunked in a vat of ice water. I really don't want to see them, but I'm sure as hell not going to let Harrison know how much I'm bothered by that. I'm going to be there for him today.

Standing on wobbly legs, I make my way to my wardrobe and pull out the dress I'd planned to wear today. It's navy and makes me feel like I'm getting ready for church. I hate it. Pushing it back into my wardrobe, where I hope it gets eaten by moths, I flick over the other options I have that aren't just dresses.

"Too pink, too slutty, too many sequins... pfff, I take that back you can never have too many." I continue flicking until I reach one that could work. When I pull it out, I know it'll work. "Bingo."

I quickly dress and grab the fascinator that's actually better with this outfit than the last, anyway. As I step out into the hallway, Harrison is there, staring at his phone, looking even more delicious than he did a minute ago because he's added a dark tan blazer that I already know will make his brown eyes pop.

When he focuses on me, his whole face darkens just like it did when he was behind me in my bedroom. He lets his heated gaze sear right through the black jumpsuit I picked. I know I look good. The material clings to every curve and dip of my body until it flares out at my hips. This particular jumpsuit is my favourite and I feel amazing in it.

"You look stunning, Zoey," he says, tucking away his phone, giving me his full attention.

"You don't look so bad yourself," I reply, walking towards him, heat filling my veins again. I take him in with his perfectly fitted navy chinos, and a light blue shirt that compliments the whole outfit. That damn blazer, that yep, I knew it, is just the right shade to bring out the colour in his eyes. Ugh, even his shoes are sexy on him. God, I should've had a cold shower. "Let's get going before I do something *I* shouldn't now."

Harrison hums a laugh and we both turn to walk towards the door.

It takes us about an hour to get to Ascot from Chelsea and being in the car with Harrison smelling so good I could eat him and looking so good... well, I'd also eat him. The last hour has felt like an eternity.

When we park up, Jess, Liam, Nora and Grayson are all getting out of their car at the same time. Jess spots us and marches over to Harrison and me.

"Zoey," she yells as she stomps over to me. The scowl she's wearing tells me I'm in for a Jess dressing down, and I'm betting it has something to do with my nuptials. "How the hell did I have to find out you got married from my own husband?"

I wince and offer her a half smile. "I know. I'm the worst friend ever. It just needed to be low key."

Jess' eyes flash with hurt for a second and the pang of guilt I feel for doing this entire sham hits me square in the ribs. God, I really am the worst kind of friend.

"I didn't even realise you were seeing anyone." She glances at Harrison and smiles. "Hi, I'm Jess. I don't know if Zoey mentioned me because she seems to have forgotten we're friends."

"Scotty, put your claws away." Liam approaches his wife, towering behind her, and she turns her glare to him, but it's swiftly removed when he leans in and kisses her. When he releases her and looks up at us, he smiles. "Congratulations is what my wife has neglected to say. We're really happy for you both." His hand extends to shake Harrison's and Nora and Grayson join us too, as we all head to our box.

I link arms with Jess and lean my head on her shoulder, needing to make amends. "Don't be mad at me," I pout.

Jess huffs. "I'm... not mad. I just wanted to be there for my friend."

"I know. I'm sorry, I wasn't thinking," I lie because the fewer people who know this is all a rouse, the better. It feels bitter on my tongue. I hate the fact that I have to lie to my closest friend, but it's the only option right now. I hope they'll all still be there for me when they have to pick up the pieces from this arrangement ending because I already know it's going to hurt like hell.

When we're settled inside the box, Harrison's hand lands on my lower back and I almost jolt because I still haven't managed to completely calm down from our conversation earlier. "Would you like a drink?"

I nod. "Champagne, please." I exhale as I watch him walk away. It's only when I feel Nora poke me that I realise that I'm staring and daydreaming. "Hm? Sorry, I—"

"Was staring after your hot as hell husband?"

"Yes. I mean, no. I mean, duh, of course, he's hot and mine and…" *Jesus, stop rambling, woman.* "Anyway, what were we saying?"

"The sex must be really good if he's got you rambling," Jess muses.

I swallow all the words I want to say like, 'I wouldn't know because as badly as I want to jump my husband's bones, we decided not to do that'. I'm equal parts stupid and smart for agreeing to that arrangement. I'm also equal parts turned on and affected by my *husband*, which is something I need to address. But not today.

"Out of this world," I say, hating that my usual excitement has up and left my body. Jess tilts her head and opens her mouth to say something—probably to call me out on lying to her face—when Harrison approaches me with a glass of cold champagne. I eagerly take it from him and take a big sip. The bubbles burn slightly with the bitterness from that first taste and it serves as a good distraction from… well, everything right now.

"Thirsty, sweetheart?" Harrison's gruff voice shouldn't make me tremble, but it does, and I do. *Yeah, I'm the most parched I've ever been in my life, thanks to you, dear husband.*

"Very thirsty," I reply, sounding a little too desperate. But when Harrison's eyes darken, I have to fight a shiver, wondering if maybe sex isn't off the table as he seems to be as needy as I clearly am. Maybe we could come to an arrangement. *Oh good, another arrangement.* Yeah, that won't work.

The men all chat business, which I'm not really listening to. Harrison's big, warm hand finds its way around my hip, stoking the fire inside me. I'm barely able to stay upright when he squeezes against me every now and again. I'm dizzy from holding my breath and from his proximity. Frankly, I'm surprised I haven't passed out.

After twenty minutes of touching, I'm ready to tap out because unless he's going to *devour me* like he suggested earlier, I need a break. Or a shot. Or to be fucked against my dresser. I'm not picky. Well, I am, and I want him, but I know that won't happen. So, I excuse myself to the ladies' room to take a breath.

I take care of business and just as I'm about to flush the toilet, I hear a name I'm all too familiar with. Two women walk in, talking about Harrison.

"But did you see how he's practically begging for my attention?"

"Absolutely, he wants you back."

"Am I going backwards if I take him back, though?"

I listen with my breath stalling behind the closed bathroom door. I can't see the women, but it's clear that one of them is his ex. How dare she think he'd want her attention. I'm about to burst out when I hear another one mutter.

"You'll have to get that blonde hussy away from him first."

"Please, have you seen me? She doesn't stand a chance. Besides, I know how to play Harrison."

Blonde hussy. Those little... I don't care if it's true for my past self. No one gets to assume they know me and have the audacity to try and steal a man right from under my nose. Rage bubbles in my chest as I flush the toilet and fling the door to my stall open so abruptly the thwack of wood-on-wood echoes around the small space and as I step out, heels clacking on the marbled floor, two sets of eyes assess me.

I slowly walk towards the sink, knowing the moment they realise I heard everything they said and I'm the one who is with Harrison because they practically stop breathing. It takes all of my energy not to bitch slap them, but if I've learned anything from my vindictive mother, it's how to piss people off.

The spray of the tap stops, and silence fills the room like a threat as I turn to face both women. One is tall and brunette, the other red haired and around my height. Both dressed in boring office attire style dresses. Both staring at me like I have two heads. Both stupid for messing with me.

"This particular blonde hussy won't be going anywhere except home with Harrison Clarke tonight," I hiss, letting my eyes lazily trawl over them with disgust. "Enjoy your day, ladies." I smile, but it's laced with venom because if anyone wants to try to get between me and my fake husband, I'd love nothing more than to see them try.

Walking back to the box, I barely hear someone calling my name. When I do, I turn to see Aaron approaching me. All wild blonde hair, charm, and bronzed skin. "Hey there, baby girl," he says, pulling me into a hug. "I thought you were running from me for a second."

I hug him back. It's good to see him. I haven't in over a month. "Run from you? Never," I mumble into his chest.

"Your brothers told me something that might just mean my heart has broken." His green eyes gauge my reaction. "But I know you wouldn't do me dirty like that."

"I hate to tell you…" I reply, biting my lip.

His hand clasps dramatically over his chest and he staggers back. "No! Say it isn't so. My girl is off the market for real?"

I laugh lightly. "Afraid so." I flash him the ring, and he gasps.

"He got you a Tiffany diamond? I could never compete. Not on the peanuts your brothers pay me."

"My brothers do not pay you peanuts."

"You're right, they don't. I just have expensive taste." He pulls me in for another hug, and just as he lets me go, the two women from the bathroom walk past and throw a sneer my way. I hear one of them mutter something under their breath, but I brush it off and smile at Aaron instead.

"I have to go rescue Nate, but I'm coming to find you later."

I tilt my head. "Nate okay?"

I see fear and something else in Aaron's eyes for a moment, but it's gone once he blinks. "It's… complicated. I'll come find you later."

"I need to find my hubby anyway." I kiss his cheek and walk towards the box again.

Chapter 27

Harrison

How long is it acceptable to stay at these things? I've forgotten all my manners when talking to clients. My eyes keep searching for a particular bombshell who's under my skin. The champagne I've been nursing is warm and bitter now, and all I'm doing is ignoring people and actively not drinking.

A small female hand travels up my arm from behind, and I warm. Just as I turn, thinking it's Zoey, I see two cold brown eyes, not the baby blues I'm used to seeing. *Vanessa.* My face hardens and the ease I felt in my bones moments ago dissipates and leaves me a statue, staring at the woman who fucked me over.

"Harrison, honey, how are you?" Her leathery voice isn't anything like Zoey's soft rasp, and it makes me shudder. She leans towards me to peck my cheek, but I don't want her near me. Stepping backwards, she drops her hand from my arm and I watch as her fake happy face morphs into hard edges as she scowls at me.

"Vanessa," I greet her coldly, not interested in keeping eye contact.

When I scan the room, I spot Zoey coming back in through the entrance. The light from her emanates like a beacon, her hair haloed around her delicate face, the bright pink fascinator peacocking from the headband on her head, fanning around her, makes me smile. When she spots me, she smiles so widely I can't help but return my own as heat creeps into my cheeks. Vanessa turns her head abruptly to find out who has made my cheeks flame, and when she spots Zoey, she hisses under her breath.

Zoey's focus flicks to Vanessa, and she stiffens but advances confidently towards us. Something shifts inside me and a weight lifts as she approaches. I take a full inhale that feels like the first day of spring is filling my lungs. With each step she takes, I can breathe easier see clearer.

"Harrison, baby." She sidles up to my side, fitting perfectly against me, and rests her palm effortlessly on my chest. "I'm sorry that took me so long." She lifts to her tiptoes and presses soft, warm kisses across my jaw, along my cheek and once to my neck and my entire body comes alive. I wrap my arm around her waist and hold her against me, silently telling her that I need her.

She stops kissing me all too soon and turns to Vanessa, holding her eye contact and keeping her hand on me possessively. "Oh, we don't need any more drinks, thanks."

Vanessa's mouth gapes as she stares at my wife. Snapping her mouth closed, her jaw ticks and she folds her arms over her chest. "I'm not the help. I'm Vanessa. Harrison can tell you exactly who I am."

Zoey thrums her fingers against my chest but doesn't look at me. "Ohhh, Vanessa, I forgot we met in the bathroom. I know who you are, and oh," Zoey gasps, lowering her hand from my chest and extending it to Vanessa. "I'm so rude. I didn't introduce myself. I'm Zoey, Harrison's wife."

Vanessa's head draws backwards. "I'm sorry, what?"

Zoey smiles, lacing her words with cruel and purposeful intention. "Zoey Clarke, it's *so* nice to meet you."

Vanessa looks past Zoey, ignoring her handshake offer, and shakes her head. "What the f—"

I step forward, interrupting Vanessa and pulling Zoey against me. "I'd be very careful about what you say next."

Vanessa rears back, searches the room and then clears her throat. "Harrison, can we talk somewhere, privately?"

"No. Anything you need to say to me can be said in front of my wife. *We* don't keep secrets from each other."

Anger flares Vanessa's nostrils as she looks away and then back to me. The chill from her eyes always made me uneasy and now, seeing it differently, I can't believe I ever wasted time with someone who clearly never cared about me. "I had no idea you were serious with anyone, I thought. I assumed we would—"

I hold my hand up between us. "Let me stop you right there. In no uncertain terms would I ever accept you back into my life. It's been eight months, Vanessa. You call my office, you harass my staff, you are unwelcome in my life," I seethe, shaking my head at my own stupid past mistakes. "The moment you cheated on me, you lost all rights to ever speak to me again. And now, that includes my wife, so if you'll excuse us."

I turn to Zoey to walk away when Vanessa's hand lands on my bicep. "Wait."

Zoey flies into action, her hand pushing against Vanessa's on my arm, setting me free of her claws. "Get your hands off my husband."

Vanessa's brown eyes fill with tears, fake tears because she was always good at that. "Harrison, you're going to let her talk to me like that?"

I sure as hell am. Before I can answer, Zoey steps closer to Vanessa.

"Did you miss the part where he told you he doesn't want to speak to you again? Or do you need help understanding?" Zoey's head cocks to the side, disdain dripping from each word.

"But—"

"—But nothing. You fucked up and lost him. He's mine now, and there is absolutely nothing you can do about that."

Zoey takes my hand and drags me to the back of the box behind the bar. Meanwhile, my brain is stuck on a loop where Zoey called me hers. That primal part of it has sparked to life at the word and how openly she claimed me. Logically, I know she did it because of what we're doing, but logic isn't ruling my brain right now. She is.

She spins to face me, her breath rapid and her eyes lit up. "Harrison, I'm sorry if—"

"—No one has ever fought for me like that." I lift my hand, brush her cheek and let my palm settle at the base of her neck, my fingers intertwined with her hair, pressed to her soft skin. Her gaze flicks from my eyes to my lips and her breathing shallows. Uncertainty gleams in her gaze, but I also see a want there. Leaning in closer, I kiss her forehead softly. "Thank you," I breathe against her.

The memory of kissing her on our wedding day comes to the forefront of my mind. Her soft lips, her sweet taste, the way she melted against me. Memories I haven't been able to forget.

Her hands snake around my sides and grip onto my blazer, her touch firm and pleading. "Harrison, I—"

"Oh God, sorry." An employee barrels into the small space we're sharing, and their eyes ping pong between us, realisation dawning that they're interrupting something. "I needed to get something, but I'll come back." They spin around and Zoey deflates. I drop my hand and stare at her. Cataloguing the freckles she tries to hide under make up, the perfect shade of ocean blue in her eyes, the cute little scar she has near her eyebrow. I want to touch her and memorise everything. *Fuck, I think I might like my wife.*

"We should probably..." she says, her hot breath dusting across my beard, sneaking through the gaps to reach my skin.

I clear my throat and sigh. "We should."

And just like that, the moment has gone, and all I wanted to do was kiss my wife.

For real.

Chapter 28

Zoey

You know that ache you get in your feet from being on them all day? The kind that snakes up your heels, into your lower back and then gives you a tension headache too?

I feel like I have one of those, but it's not because of being on my feet, it's the lack of being on my back, or my knees, or any position that might relieve this sexual tension in my body.

Harrison almost kissed me. I almost bitch slapped his ex, and he almost kissed me. If I'd known that it would be that easy to get him to give in, I would've invited her over for tea way sooner.

I've played the role of wife incredibly well today, given that I've never had any experience in being a long term girlfriend, let alone a wife. But Harrison has been smiling at me like I hung the moon all afternoon since our almost kiss and I'd be lying if I said it didn't make me preen every time. Having that man's attention is like being bathed in direct sunlight, and I'm becoming obsessed.

"Zo?" Max gets my attention, nudging my shoulder with his.

"Yeah?"

"Harrison said you've had some issues with the shelter?"

He did? Damn, why would he do that? Surely, the topic is off limits because it's an obvious reason why I need my trust fund early. What if he suspects? What if Dad asked him to spy on me? *Oh God, breathe, Zoey*. Somehow, I manage to school my face despite my inner turmoil.

"Nothing. Headache is all," I lie because apparently, that's all I do with my brothers now. "We had a plumbing issue with the new building." Then I think back to the fact that the very insurance company my name is connected to is trying to fob me off and frustration thrums in my ears. "Actually, it's annoying because I'm trying to claim through the insurance and I'm getting the runaround. Is that how Dad stays so rich? He never pays out on claims."

Max's brows slope. "I'll talk to customer claims and expedite yours. Send me your claim number." He stares at me again. "Why didn't you tell me you had issues with insurance?"

I shrug. "I don't know. Pride, probably."

"Zoey," he sighs. "I wasn't kidding when I said I've got your back."

"I know. But I'm also capable of sorting my own mess. Please don't say anything to Dad about the shelter."

He slowly nods. "I won't. But you have to promise me no more lies, okay?"

God, way to guilt a girl. "Okay," I agree, forcing a smile. "No more lies." At least no more beyond the ones you're already believing.

A warm hand finds my back and makes me jolt, my husband catches me and wraps my arms around his waist, holding me to him. "Sorry, sweetheart. I didn't mean to make you jump. Are you ready to go?" My pulse evens out from his proximity and there's that damn smile again.

I rest my chin on his chest and look up at him, exhaling a long breath. "I'm ready. Take me home, husband."

Max chuckles behind us. "That's my cue to leave. I do not need any other details." He slaps Harrison's shoulder and disappears.

My stomach flutters with holding him like this, out in the open. If only I could do it in private too. "Let's go," I say. "I'll text Nora and Jess from the car."

"Don't you want to say goodbye to your friends?"

I shake my head, leading him out the door. "I'll text them." They'll probably be mad at me, but this isn't the first time I've disappeared, and it probably won't be the last.

In the car, tiredness overcomes me, and I slip into a sleepy haze of soft touches and warm kisses from Harrison. Even my subconscious can't stop thinking about him. When my eyes open again, we're at the flat and I realise that Harrison's hand never left my thigh. *No wonder I was dreaming about him.*

Walking through the front door, I kick off my heels, place my light jacket on the hall hooks and flick the light on, a low glow casting its way across the space. Harrison closes the door behind me and removes his jacket too.

"Do you want a cup of tea?" I ask, turning to face him but walking backwards towards the kitchen. "I feel like tea is mandatory after a busy day."

He chuckles, deep and smooth. "Sure, sounds good."

Now I'm awake again, my body is a hive of energy and pent up sexual frustration. I don't blame the champagne because I only ended up having one glass. I blame myself for the public claiming I performed of Harrison, who has shown me his gratitude in heated stares, soft touches and forehead kisses. My skin is branded with him at this point, so unless he's going to ravish me, I'm going to busy myself by making tea, and then I'm going to pray to the vibrator God's that my vibe is charged.

I reach up and pull out two mugs from the cupboard and place them on the worktop. "You know, today was actually fun," I tell him as I flick on the kettle. "I wish you'd let me bitch slap your ex, but the look on her face when I said I was your wife… Priceless." Harrison follows me, unfastening the cuffs of his sleeve and placing the cufflinks on the worktop.

He watches me for a moment, and something ignites in his eyes. A fire, a passion, a need. He stalks towards me, stealing a breath of air with each measured step. I turn my body slowly, gripping the edges of the worktop to stop me from reaching out and grabbing him, pushing my heaving chest outwards.

*Touch me, m*y body begs silently.

He stops in front of me, our feet close but not enough to touch as his stare slowly roams all over me and I feel every single caress of his gaze. "You were amazing today." His voice is gravelly and low.

I bask in him being so close. "Just being a good wife…" I say in a breathy whisper. *God, why is he this close?*

He pushes forward until his hips are grazing mine, but it's not nearly enough; it's just a whisper that sets me alight.

"Zoey…" he groans softly, ghosting his thumb over my bottom lip. His warm breath fans over my willing lips as his strong hands snake around me and settle at the back of my neck, holding me in place. "Tell me to stop."

I gently shake my head. "Please," I beg with every fibre of my being.

His hands tighten in my hair, and he pulls me closer, taking control. Before I can think, his mouth devours mine in a frenzy, fuelled by weeks and weeks of desperate need. Our lips collide, and I can barely breathe with the way he's consuming me. It's taking me higher and higher with every stroke of his tongue against mine.

He shifts one of his legs to rest between my thighs and I want to grind against him to find the friction that my body craves. But all too soon, he breaks the kiss as he hoists me onto the worktop, my legs immediately widening in invitation. He moves to stand between them so we're at the perfect height for more kissing and touching.

I pull him the last inch and seal us together. His beard tickles my skin in the most delicious way. He groans into my mouth, his hands sliding behind me to grip my arse, his hands squeezing, caressing, and claiming my skin. He's everywhere, and it's still not enough.

My nipples ache as they brush against my jumpsuit, and I inwardly curse for not wearing something easier to get off in a hurry. I break our kiss, breathless and aching with need. "Harrison," I whimper, tilting my head to the side as he continues to kiss down my neck, nipping, sucking, owning. I'm so drunk on him that I can barely see straight.

"God, you make me so fucking hard, Zoey," he purrs into my neck, making everywhere clench with need. When he straightens and looks at me, his eyes are like swirling pools of lava, full of lust and raw energy that he can barely contain. I run my fingers through his hair, loving the softness of the strands as he groans, the sound so primal and needy that it makes me moan too.

His hands tighten against my arse and he pushes forwards just as I do, our centres crashing together with white hot heat. A gasp escapes when I feel how hard he is. He's thick, mouth-wateringly perfect and I want nothing more than to taste him. "Let me see," I purr, giving him a squeeze with my thighs before releasing him and pushing against his chest.

He steps back, his broad shoulders straining against the fabric of his shirt. One by one, torturously slowly, he undoes each button, never breaking eye contact and never fully revealing everything that I want. Every movement he makes is hyper masculine and controlled, and I hope that extends to the bedroom because whilst I'm grateful for his softness with me, I want nothing more than for him to be the one in control. When he reaches his belt, I interrupt his movements, jumping down to take over, but he grasps my wrists, his body heat burning into my skin. "Sweetheart, you need to learn patience. Sit back on the worktop."

My bottom lip automatically protests and he laughs. "That pouty lip will be mine soon. Don't you worry," he says, as I jump back onto the surface, thanking my lucky stars that my prayers have been answered.

Demanding Harrison is a complete turn on.

I watch with wide eyes because I can't look away as he uncovers every tight, sculpted muscle of his chest and reveals his defined stomach. *God, his muscles.* His body isn't for show, it's a temple, and I want to drop to my knees and worship every inch of him.

When he smirks and lowers his chinos, taking his socks with him, he's left in his pale blue shirt, opened for my eyes only, and his black boxers that are not hiding what he's packing. Instinctively I look at all of him, licking my lips as I take in every curve, edge and mouthwatering part of him.

"Do you want me, Harrison?" I ask, needing to hear his voice.

He exhales, but it's rough, needy, desperate, and the sound travels south at warp speed, hitting my clit with a zap. His head lolls backwards, exposing his throat, half covered in his beard. I want to lick him, mark him and—*Oh, Jesus*. I watch as he palms himself over his boxers, his hardness pushing against his hand. All man. *All mine.*

"Sweetheart, I don't just want you. I fucking *need* you. Do you know how many times I've dreamed about this? About you ... How you'd taste, how you'd feel ... how you'd fuck." He moans, and it's the most erotic sound I've ever heard. "I'm feral for you, Zoey." I swallow, a thickness coating my throat.

Arousal pumping my heartbeat ten to the dozen. "I want to touch you," I moan softly.

Harrison drops his hands to his sides and looks me dead in the eyes. "Take me out, Zoey. See how much I want that too." He steps closer and I lower myself to my feet.

Slowly, I let my fingertips trail over his abs, down the happy trail leading to where he wants me most. His hips push forward, searching for my hand, but I take my time as he curses under his breath. When I finally reach the seam of his boxers, I dip my finger inside gently, slowly and tease him some more, brushing the tip of his cock with my forefinger.

He grips my wrist, shooting a fiery energy through his touch. "Zoey," he warns.

A smirk lifts the corners of my mouth. "Patience, mountain man. Isn't that what you said?" I dip my whole hand into his boxers and push them down as he groans loudly.

I continue pushing them down past his hips, and his thick cock springs free as I move down with his underwear until he steps out of them. His hard length stands proud and leaking as I stare up at it, licking my lips, anticipation filling my veins.

His fingers wrap around himself, and he pumps twice, throwing his head backwards again. "Jesus, the sight of you on your knees," he growls. "It's enough to send me over the edge."

"Hmm," I tease. "I probably shouldn't do this then." I lean in, licking the underside of his dick all the way to the head and lap up his salty taste, humming around his head. His whole body shudders and he falls forwards gripping the worktop.

"Fuuuuuuuuck," he hisses.

I take more of his hard length into my mouth, and his hips thrust forward gently. He's holding back. I can feel it. So, I place my hands behind his thighs and swallow him deeper until he hits the back of my throat.

His eyes connect with mine in silent question, and I nod my head. His pace picks up as he pushes in and out of my mouth with more force. I groan with pleasure as he hits the back of my throat again and again, and he curses above me. "Your mouth," he mumbles.

I take him deeper, hollowing my cheeks and sucking harder. He becomes frantic, his cock hitting the back of my throat and water escapes my eyes. I love seeing this side of him. He's normally so controlled, but seeing him losing it unravelling because of me. It's addicting.

His hands come to hold my face as the threads of his control snap one by one. The salty taste of his precum tickles my tastebuds and I hum around him, pressing my thighs together to satisfy the ache deep in my pussy.

"Fuck, Zoey." The gruff neediness of his voice making me whimper. And then he pulls out of my mouth, hauls me upright and claims my lips so fiercely I have to grasp his shirt to stay standing. He consumes me like he's starved and when he stops, every nerve ending I have protests. "There's plenty of time for playing, but right now, I need to fuck you."

Well, okay then.

Chapter 29

Harrison

I take Zoey's hand and stride through the living room into my bedroom, wearing only my shirt and Zoey's saliva on my cock.

I turn to face her and claim her mouth again. *Fuck, I'll never get enough of her lips.*

"Take your clothes off, Mrs Clarke."

She smiles against my mouth, taking measured steps away from me and I let her go because I like watching her. "Mrs Clarke? You like roleplay, *Mr Clarke*?" she whispers sultrily as she shrugs her slender arms out of the sleeves on her jumpsuit and shimmies the whole thing down to the floor, leaving her topless and in bright pink lace underwear.

It's so Zoey. I'd laugh if I wasn't stupidly turned on.

Running my hand over my beard, my cock pulses at the sight of her, precum leaking from me and she tracks my reaction, smirking. "I'm into fucking my wife," I rumble deep in my throat. Stalking towards her and hauling her body up so her legs wrap around my waist, I smash our mouths together, walking until her back hits the wall with a light thud. She groans as we devour each other, our teeth clashing. My rock hard length is trapped between us, dragging against the lace of her underwear as she moves her hips. "Fuck, you're soaking and I've barely touched you," I pant against her mouth, grinding against her as my fingers dig into her thighs.

Her lips part on a whimper. "More," she begs desperately. I stare at her swollen lips, her flushed face and God, she looks beautiful. She tilts her hips to rub against me again, the soft lace sliding along my shaft as she moves and my head throws back on a groan before we lock eyes again.

"I'm going to fucking worship you, sweetheart. You'll be ruined for anyone else because now..." I pause to lick a trail up her neck until I get to her ear. "You're fucking mine," I growl.

Her hands tighten around the back of my neck as she seeks my mouth again, pushing her tongue inside. I move us away from the wall, towards the bed, and bend forward slightly before throwing her onto the mattress. Her tits bounce as she hits the mattress with a soft squeal, but she quickly settles, lust shimmering in her eyes as she moves her hand to touch her clit.

Possession lights up my veins as I dive forward, my hand wrapping around her ankle as I drag her across the bed to me until our noses bump. "Did I not make myself clear when I said you're mine?"

Zoey grins, a spark of wild energy lighting up her blue eyes. "But I need to come," she pouts defiantly, showing me a glimpse of that brat inside her.

"And I'll be the one to make you come," I suck her bottom lip into my mouth and pull hard until she whimpers, her nails digging into my shoulders before I let her go. I want to claim her. I need to.

Running my tongue along her lips, I move to her jaw and across her collarbone, nipping at her skin and loving the little flushes of red I'm leaving behind. My mouth moves south and when I get to her nipples, I suck one into my mouth, lightly biting the rosy peak. Looking up, her head is thrown back as her hands tangle in my hair. She tries to push me further down her body and I can't help but smirk because I'm in charge tonight.

"Are you aching for me, sweetheart? Like you'll die if I don't touch you..." I pause to cup her pussy over her underwear, and she moans. "Right here?" I press a featherlight touch against her clit with the heel of my hand, she arches back, baring herself for me to take. I suck a nipple into my mouth again.

"Yes, yes. God, yes," she whimpers.

Pulling the lace of her underwear to one side, her bare pussy glistens. My mouth waters as I tease her soft lips, parting them with my fingers but not letting myself slip inside her yet. "What do you want, Zoey?" I ask, my voice deep and thirst filled.

"I want you all over me," she begs, and my mind buzzes with adrenaline that I'm going to deliver that to her.

I drag my fingers through her folds again and find that pulsing clit waiting, begging for my touch. A growl builds in my throat as I press against it, loving the noises of pleasure leaving her mouth. I tease her for a moment before I trail my fingers down to her entrance and push two inside her. Fuuuuuck, she is so tight, my breath hitches. Her walls clamp around my fingers as she cries out incoherent words. I move them slowly, twisting and pushing them in and out, the sound of her arousal echoing in the bedroom until her thighs tighten around me, and she rises slightly to take me deeper.

"Fuuuuuck," she hisses in a whisper.

"You like my fingers inside you?" I ask before I bite her shoulder and lick the spot to soothe it.

She cries out, "So fucking much."

Increasing my pace, I press the heel of my hand against her clit as she starts to ride my hand, rocking and taking her pleasure. "So. Fucking. Sexy," I growl, pulling her to me in a burning kiss, taking her mouth without apology because I *need* to taste her.

We kiss until we're both breathless and she's close. I can feel it in the way her walls pulse around my fingers and her nails scrape through my hair and send shocks of pleasure down my spine. "Harrison, I can't... I'm gonna..." She slams down onto my fingers, and I grind against her clit, forcing a husky groan to fall from her lips, watching with awe as she rides the high I'm giving her.

Her body sags against the mattress, her head dropping to the side, her warm breath shooting out in short, sharp bursts. My cock still stands proud, leaking between us, desperate for her sweet heat.

I line myself up to rest over her pussy and rub myself over her sensitive clit a few times.

"Oh god, Harrison. Please." Her voice breaks on the last word as her hands reach out to grab me, but I pull back slightly out of reach.

"Patience, sweetheart," I murmur, needing a minute to calm down, or I'll blow my load the minute she touches me. I force myself to sit up, reach into my bedside drawer, and pull out a condom. Zoey watches me with rapt attention, her chest heaving and eyes hazy. I roll it over my length and watch as she palms her breast, paying attention to her nipples. Diving forward, I push her hand away and replace it with my mouth. Sucking and swirling my tongue over her peak.

I line myself up again with her entrance and push until the head of me is resting just inside her. She clenches around my tip, my arms wobble and I almost lose it because finally, fucking finally, I get the girl.

With a deep breath, I slowly sink in, inch by inch, feeling every gasp and ripple her body makes. "You feel so fucking good," I groan, barely recognising my own voice. Squeezing my eyes closed, overcome with sensation and elation of being here with her, I bottom out. As our eyes connect, she pulls me to her lips and pauses.

"Fuck me, Harrison," she whimpers. "I need to feel you move."

So, I do. I pull out and slam back into her as her back arches, opening more for me as I thrust back in again and again.

The sound of our connection echoes around the room, each grunt more feverish than the last.

I push up to look at her body. Her face flushed and glowing from her orgasm. Her perfect, perky nipples, so round and begging for my touch. Reaching down, I twist one between my fingers as I move inside her, loving the hum of satisfaction she gives me.

Her hands reach out to touch my abs, stroking down until she reaches her clit. I slap it away immediately. "Mine," I growl. Then I place a light slap on her pussy.

"Ohhh fuck," she groans. "Yes, that. Do that again." I pull back and as I push inside her, I slap her clit again and she jolts forwards. "Fuck *yes*," she screams.

"You like that? I can't wait to get you on your knees next time and mark that sweet peachy arse of yours too."

She makes those breathy, blissed out noises that I'm beginning to learn is her getting close and goddamn, she makes me wild. I push myself balls deep inside again and again, eliciting all her pleasure.

"Harrison, I can't hold on. I'm... oh, God." She trembles, jaw slack and eyes shining, as I feel her flutter around the length of me and

I watch with awe at her falling apart beneath me. Seeing her flush, blissed out expression makes me even harder, and I realise I never want this to end. I lean down, brushing our slick bodies together as I claim her mouth. She holds me to her, hands tugging the strands of my hair as she tangles our tongues. My body burns for her, and as much as I want to savour this, my spine tingles uncontrollably with my impending release.

"Oh, fuck," I manage to force out, increasing my speed just as my balls draw up and white hot heat races through me as I come harder than I ever have in my life. A wave of satisfaction washes over me, my chest tightening because that was fucking sensational. She is sensational. And all mine. *Or at least she is for now.* Something inside me shatters at the thought of this ending. I know now, I'm never going to get enough of her.

Our breathing is shallow and fast but in sync, as I roll off her and immediately, I miss her heat.

"Well, I guess we broke that rule," she pants with amusement in her voice.

I chuckle, pushing away thoughts of more as I discard the condom. "I guess we did." Then I pull her naked body closer to mine and inhale her scent. It's mixed with sweat and sex, but I fucking love it. I've never been much of a cuddly guy, another thing Vanessa hated about me, but with Zoey, it feels so natural to be near her and more than that, I want it.

"Should I go back to my room?" she asks, hesitation lacing her voice.

I squeeze her against me. "No fucking way I'm letting you leave this bed."

"Ever?"

"Ever."

Chapter 30

Zoey

Everything is going to be fine. Harrison and I had sex and now I'm meeting his family. The same family I've been avoiding for the last month of us living together. The same family that knows we got married because he couldn't keep it from his sister any longer and blurted it out when she called yesterday. His dad is out of the country but wants to meet me as soon as he's back, apparently. And now, I'm worrying my bottom lip again over his sister liking me.

Well, technically, I've already met his sister when I was younger, but now, I'm sleeping with her brother and we're fake married—everything's fine. *God, I hope I don't blurt out the part about sleeping with her brother.*

His sister's house is a beautiful cottage style bungalow in Richmond. There are wildflowers decorating the front of the property, lining the path to the door. My fingers itch to pick them because wildflowers are my favourite.

Harrison's big hand eclipses mine as we walk towards the front door. He knocks but doesn't wait for them to answer. He just walks straight inside, like this is his house. Oh, to have that kind of familiarity. The only people I'd do that with would've been Jess and Nora, but since they coupled up, I refuse to barge in and catch a glimpse of something that would need erasing from my memory.

The bungalow looks cute and tiny from the outside, but it stretches back so far that I can barely focus on the bi-fold doors at the back of the hallway. The hum of children laughing and squabbling filters through the space, making this house really feel like a home. There are no pointless hallway tables with flowers, there are shoes left strewn across the floor, folded clothes on the stairs, coats hanging on the banister, and toys everywhere.

"Katie!" Harrison shouts through the house. A leggy brunette peeks her head around the hallway doors, which I'm assuming is the kitchen. When she spots us, she smiles and I'm instantly reminded of the time she babysat me when I was younger. Her smile hasn't changed, and her brown eyes are exactly like Harrison's. "Girls, come here," she shouts as she approaches us.

"Baby Bancroft, you're all grown up. I haven't seen you since you were a pre-teen." She stops in front of us and Harrison pulls her in for a side hug, letting my hand go.

"Oh, pre-teen Zoey was a handful," I agree. "But then again, not much has changed." We both laugh and I smile a genuine smile at my now sister-in-law. "Good to see you though, Katie."

"Where are my girls?" Harrison asks his sister as she narrows her eyes at me again. Okay, I guess I have something to prove here; that I'm not the little brat she once looked after.

"In the garden. Girls! Uncle Harrison is here."

The swarm of shrieks, squeals and giggles get closer and closer as two little curly haired tornados run down the hallway and throw themselves at a waiting Harrison. Two slightly taller girls follow and do the same. My heart does a little flippy dance, seeing Harrison overpowered by these little munchkins.

They harass him, peppering kisses and love all over him, and he's never looked happier. "They're always like this with him." Katie nudges me, awakening me from my thoughts of him being so perfect.

"He told me he spoils them," I tell her.

She nods and smiles warmly. "I mean, yeah, he does spoil them, but not just with gifts. Harrison is the kind of guy who likes to spend time with people and makes sure they know they're loved."

I read between the lines because it definitely feels like she's telling me her brother is a good man, and I need to treat him right. Guilt settles into my stomach like a weight, but I smile through it. Even though Harrison ended up telling his sister beforehand, she said he would have to be the one to break the girls' hearts that we had a wedding without them, which now feels a lot harder. "I'm getting that," I reply because she believes this is real, and I'm not about to blurt out *'Oh, don't worry. I'll take good care of your big brother, especially when our arrangement ends and we divorce.'* But I can't deny that I feel bad for lying to all these tiny Clarke children.

"Okay, okay, girls. I need you to meet someone. Let me up." The four girls scramble off him, but the twin with the wildest brown curls grips his hand and looks up at me with wide eyes, using Harrison's hand as a shield.

Instinctively, I bend down to be more at their level. "Hi, it's so nice to meet you all."

"Who are you?" the tallest one, which I'm guessing is Cassie, asks. I open my mouth but am immediately interrupted.

"Are you Uncle Harrison's girlfriend?" the little one gripping Harrison's hand questions with a frown. I swallow thickly, all the blood draining from my face as I look at Harrison. He chuckles, looking totally at ease. Bending down to his niece, he strokes a wayward curl from her face.

"Ophelia, bubs. This is Zoey. She's my wife."

"Your wife?" her twin yelps from beside her. They're not identical. Ellie has bright blue eyes, whereas Ophelia has brown soulful ones.

"You had a wedding without us?!" The one with straight brown hair and a missing tooth squeals.

"I know. I'm sorry, Alanna. We just had a quick wedding."

"You sure did," his sister remarks. Inwardly, my body cringes.

"Will you have another wedding so we can be your flower girls?" asks Cassie, eyeing me. She's actually pretty tall and I have to look up at her from where I'm crouched. And she's beautiful, her hair somewhere between wavy and straight and her eyes a deep brown like her mum.

Harrison doesn't get a chance to answer before Alanna interrupts. "Wait, we should ask Zoey. She's the bride. What's your perfect wedding day? Does it include flower girls?" Her missing tooth causes a little lisp on her S's, and I stifle a grin because it's the sweetest thing.

"Oh, umm..." Four pairs of big round eyes stare back at me with anticipation. Damn, I really need to nail this answer. What do I want for a wedding? I guess it wasn't the shotgun wedding we had. "If I could have anything I wanted, I would want to get married on a beach somewhere hot, with a white flowy dress, four beautiful flower girls and no one would have shoes on."

"No shoes?" Ellie and Ophelia giggle.

Ophelia steps forward, surprising me. "You have pretty hair, and I like your pink jacket," she says, letting Harrison's hand go as she smooths her hand over my cord jacket. "Pink is my favourite colour in the whole wide world. My bedroom is pink, wanna see?"

"I'd love to. Pink is my favourite colour, too."

I look up at Harrison, and he winks. "Welcome to the madhouse," he whispers as I pass him, being dragged by a little pocket rocket. "They'll never let you go now."

My heartbeat increases because the thought of being a part of this family doesn't feel scary. It feels right and if he's serious, then if anything, I'm more afraid of losing them once I love them. And right now, the way Ophelia's tiny little hand wraps around my fingers, I think I'm already in love.

So, it turns out, when little girls ask you to come see their room, what they really mean is, 'You're going to play with me, and I'll put a plethora of hair clips in your hair, dress you up and make you play Barbies with me'. Am I mad? Not so much. I could happily live in any of the girls' rooms. I love pink. I could take or leave the Barbies, though. I used to cut all their hair off if my mother brought me one. But being here with the girls is nice. It's just me and the twins now; the other girls stayed in their rooms once I got the tour.

Harrison appears around thirty minutes later, leaning against the doorframe of the twin's room with his arms crossed over his body, showing me those sexy forearms of his. His lips twitch in a smirk when he looks me over. "Having fun?"

"So much fun," I reply. "Come, join us."

He doesn't hesitate. He walks right in and plonks himself down next to me, where Ellie and Ophelia jump on him, covering him with hair clips and putting pretend make up on him as well.

"You're so pretty, Uncle Harrison," Ellie coos, snapping another clip in place. I chuckle as he winces from the impact.

"Not half as pretty as you girls." He nudges my arms with his elbow. "All three of you."

My little abandoned heart jumpstarts in my chest—his words, seeing him so at home and at ease with these girls, how much he adores them. I openly admit I never wanted children, but watching him with these girls... his girls, makes me want to have a whole *Von Trapp* family with him.

What the ever loving fuck is happening to me? To my brain? It's turning to mush.

I don't dwell on that because it must just be some sort of biological reaction, or pheromones or chemistry. *Something scientific* – that I'm not willing to get into when I look like I've robbed a hair accessory store.

"Uncle Harrison, we want Zoey to stay here forever. Can she? Can she?" Ellie asks, tucking her tiny hands under her chin. Who knew that almost four-year-olds have such skill in guilting someone already?

Harrison's face falls for a second and he swallows and clears his throat, avoiding my eyes. "We have to go downstairs for dinner now. Can we make a plan to keep her after dinner?"

My heart squeezes at his words. Keep me. Damn, if that doesn't give me hope.

I swallow hard.

"Uh, girls? A little help?" I say, gesturing to the hair clips they put on me.

"But you look so pretty," Ophelia pouts.

"Honey, I love your pout, never lose it but I'm gonna take these out because..." I pull one out and about a million strands of my hair with it. "Ouch, yeah, this part isn't so fun."

We head downstairs and there's a tall blonde guy in the kitchen. He grins when he sees me and walks over, his hand extended. "Hey, I'm Jake. You're Zoey, right? Congrats on the wedding." I smile and shake his hand. Wow, none of his girls take after him, except maybe Cassie. Those Clarke genes are really strong.

"Thank you."

"We're going to make them have a do-over wedding," Cassie announces confidently.

"Oh, are we now?" teases Harrison. "I don't remember agreeing to that, do you, sweetheart?" he muses, looking at me mischievously.

"I don't think I should come between you and your nieces. I'm way smarter than that." I reach up to peck his cheek and watch a slight blush creep across his face. "I'd also probably end up siding with them. Sorry, not sorry."

Dinner is easy. There's no animosity or bitter words. Everyone smiles and talks about what they're excited about for their upcoming week. When I say I'm looking after some kittens, all the girls squeal and we promise they can visit the shelter as long as they help us feed the animals. Which, of course, they love the idea of. Little girls are super excitable.

Harrison and I offer to clean up and everyone sits outside on the huge sofas as the girls play in the late summer sunshine.

Alone in the kitchen, Harrison whips the tea towel over my bum, and I yelp. He instantly soothes it with his hand, coming to stand behind me. His beard tickles the sensitive part of my neck as he leans down and brushes kisses across my skin. He surrounds me with his broad shoulders, pushing my hipbones against the worktop as he squeezes my bum with a growl. "I miss you," he whispers.

"I'm right here."

More kisses. More goosebumps. "You know what I mean. I feel like sharing you isn't my strong suit."

"Are you feeling needy, Mr Clarke?"

"Always for you, sweetheart." He spins me around and captures my mouth in a kiss that is perfectly soft and claiming. "Come on, let's mingle for a while so I can take you home and eat you up."

When we open the door to our flat, my eyes are barely open. Tiredness weighs heavy on my bones, I could fall asleep standing. "Come on sleepyhead, let's get you to bed," Harrison encourages me, one hand behind my back, ushering me through the hall to our bedroom.

"Your sister and her family are amazing, but I'm bone tired." I yawn.

"Yeah, they're a lot." I hear the smile in his voice, even though he's behind me.

"When Ellie asked if she could keep me, I think I melted a little," I reply, taking my shoes off at the bedroom door.

"They all loved you. Thank you for playing with them. It means... it means a lot," he says with equal parts happiness and sadness in his voice. I turn to face him, wrapping my arms around his neck.

"What are you not saying?"

He sighs, running his hands up and down my arms with rapt attention. "Vanessa and I were together for a few years, and I never took her to meet the girls. Deep down, I think I felt like something wasn't right and I'm glad they never met her because they know you."

My belly floods with warmth, which then hardens like ice because I'm scared that I'll break those little girls' hearts when I leave. But I don't want to. Hell, I don't even think I want to leave the man in front of me, let alone his family. Familiarity is a funny thing. It's not something I'm used to with relationships. I have people who I care about and love. My brothers, Jess, Nora and Seren, my old housekeeper. But to have someone who's constantly at your side because they want to be is something I always assumed wouldn't happen for me. That deep seated familiarity, it's nice. And maybe I want that.

Maybe this doesn't have to be an agreement, maybe it could just be... us.

Chapter 31

Zoey

"Why do you look so happy?" Sam's eyes narrow, assessing me. Then he steps into my office fully and shrieks. "Oh my God, did I win the bet? Did you sleep with your husband?" I've managed to go all of thirty seconds without thinking about the sex Harrison and I have been having every night for the last several nights and mornings too. But Sam just brought it back to the forefront of my mind.

Oh, who am I kidding? It was always at the forefront of my mind.

"I have no idea what you're talking about," I reply, ignoring his accusations.

"You totally did," he smirks. "Is this what it feels like to win? Gosh, it's addictive. I feel like I'm floating." He muses smugness marring his tone.

I look up from my desk. "Look, it's none of your business. Now go feed some kittens, save a pig or something. I'm busy." I shoo him away with my hand and go back to my work. My incredibly interesting work that I'm absolutely concentrating on.

He crosses his arms over his broad chest and narrows his brows, pausing. "Ohhh... you like him."

My cheeks immediately heat, and I tear my gaze from the laptop I was pretending to pay attention to. "I wish everyone would stop assuming that. First Nora, now you. I'm capable of sex without feelings. I've been doing it for years."

"Right, except *that* was random strangers. *This* is your husband. You know him, and now... you like him."

"Sure, I like him as much as I used to like you. As a friend. Which you no longer qualify as because you're harassing me."

"You love me and don't even try to deny it." He rolls his eyes.

"Maybe I used to love you when you didn't make bets with your husband about how long it would take for me to fuck my fake husband."

He smiles, widely. "A bet I'm winning, by the way."

I scoff, waving him off, but of course, Sam doesn't take the hint. "You know, that fake husband of yours is at the front desk being flirted with by Lloyd. Said something about updating your software." I jump up from my seat, ignoring the smug smirk still playing on Sam's face. "Is that a euphemism for fucking in your office?"

I stomp over to the doorway and bump hips with him as I pass. "I'm going to pretend you didn't say that." Sam's chuckle follows me as I walk down the hallway where eventually, another voice overtakes it. One that is deeper and full of gruff tones. The closer I get, the more my body begins to perk up, knowing I'll be near him in a matter of seconds. I feel tingly when I hear him. The deep timbre of his laugh, the memory of the way his eyes crinkle when he really lets out a loud laugh. The way—

Ohhhh balls.

Maybe I *do* like my husband.

No, it's all the orgasms, that's it. Just sex crazed. Except the way he held me last night was so tender. I've never been cuddled like that before, and I liked it. And the fact his family are the most accepting people I've met in my life also put a tick in his column. They even added me to a group chat called 'Operation Wedding do-over'. My heart immediately warmed when I saw it, a sense of belonging filling my chest; the idea that they really care was almost too much. Harrison said they won't give up either, and I don't know what that means (nor am I pushing for answers) but I saw his smiles when Cassie sent links for beach wedding venues.

Opening the door, I see Lloyd leaning over the desk, cackling at something Harrison has said as Harrison casually stands against the front desk, both hands in his grey suit trousers, white shirt rolled up, showing me those veins I traced with my fingers last night. Damn, he looks fine. He's looking at his shoes, smiling because I know the way his face crinkles when he smiles and when he looks up, those brown eyes deepen, and my stomach takes flight.

Yep—I definitely like my husband.

Damn it. I hate it when Sam's right.

I take small steps because ogling Harrison's fine form might go against any objectification rules in society but I. Do. Not. Care. The man is hot.

He removes his hands from his pockets and stalks towards me, eating up the space I was trying to keep so I could objectify my husband, but the pace at which he's making his way to me, I might...

oh no, I'm definitely swooning. My stomach swoops to my feet, and when I catch the scent of his aftershave—fresh and clean—I may as well be drooling.

"Hey, sweetheart," he coos with devastating suave as he bends and kisses me, but that isn't what he's doing, he savouring me. Kissing me slowly, deeply. His big, warm hands land on my hips as he pulls me closer, pressing the kiss so deep into my lips that I know that this one will stick with me all freaking day. I daren't put my hands on him because I know I'll drag him to my office to 'update my software'.

When we break apart, he stares at me with a tenderness that I'm not used to and my heart niggles in my chest. "Mmm, I missed you," he grumbles.

I smile because I can't stop it even if I try. "You're cute when you're needy for me."

His chest rumbles with a small laugh. "I'm one hundred per cent okay with that."

Of course he is because he's so self-assured. It's one of his most attractive qualities.

"Harrison was just telling me he's here to update your office software and honestly, I'm glad to be rid of this." Lloyd gestures to the computer at the front desk, reminding me that he's there because I definitely forgot we had company.

"I'm also going to get you some new monitors and I need to check out your workspace to make sure you're using ergonomic office supplies."

"Oooo, ergonomic office supplies," I mock and lower my voice to a sultry whisper. "Talk dirty to me, mountain man."

I smile up at him as he winks, and an unfamiliar feeling of contentment ignites deep in my bones. "Can I show you around first?" I ask, wanting him to see what I've worked so hard for.

"I'd love that."

Taking his hand, I lead him through the hallway and to the double doors. The telltale sounds of the pups yelping and barking excitedly behind the door filter through into the hallway. "Ready?"

He nods, and I open the doors, revealing pens with various dogs; big, small, tall, short, brown, blonde. You name it, we've got it. "Wow, Zoey. This is incredible." His eyes scan over the space, and I can't help but smile proudly, taking in the state of the art pens each dog has to themselves. Except for Pete and Peggy, who arrived together and are our resident old married couple, they share.

"It's pretty amazing, right?"

"You did all this?"

"I did," I reply, walking over to one of the pens with a golden lab, Jelly, inside. Leaning down, I unlock her door and let her say hello to me with big, sloppy licks and paws that have no coordination. "Hey there, beautiful girl. Did you miss me? I missed you." I rub her ears, watching her eyes close in happiness. "You're the sweetest girl here, huh? Yes, you are."

Harrison joins me on the floor, and Jelly's attention immediately shifts to him as she sniffs all around his neck, barking her approval.

"I know he smells so good, right, girlie?" I agree and she barks again.

Harrison laughs, as we both lower to the floor to pet her and Jelly takes this as an invitation for her to sit in his lap. "She's beautiful," he says, stroking her thick fur. "Was she abandoned too?"

I nod. "All the animals here have been found either on the streets, their owners passed, or maybe someone just doesn't want them."

Emotion lodges in my chest as I stroke Jelly. "It breaks my heart because they just need someone to love them."

He nods, his hands moving rhythmically down Jelly's back, too and her eyes close again, that same goofy puppy smile on her face.

"She likes you," I smile.

We sit fussing over Jelly for a little while longer, and then we stand to walk to the new section of the shelter.

"This part is where I get my daily serotonin." I swing open the doors and am greeted with a concerto of meows, my heart instantly melting.

"I probably should have told you, I'm allergic to cats," Harrison announces and my head swings to face him, mouth gaping.

"Noooo. You can't be. I'll have to divorce you. Please tell me you're lying," I plead.

His face transforms into a smirk. "I'm kidding. No need to divorce me."

I sag dramatically, wiping my brow. "Phew, for a second there I thought I'd found a flaw."

"Hmm, besides," he rumbles and pulls my back to his front, his arms snaking around my middle as his head dips to my ear, making my whole body tingle again. "You can't divorce me because I'm not nearly done with you yet, Mrs Clarke."

Putty. I am putty in his hands when he says things like that. My poor heart can barely keep up with the excitement. Especially, when he's near, it starts thumping like it's trying to escape from my ribs. I move my hands to cover his around my waist and I bask in his warmth for a second. My mind wanders, and somewhere deep inside whispers...

Please don't ever be done with me.

Chapter 32

Harrison

"What's her name?" I ask with both eyes trained on the little ball of white fluff in my arms. She's so small I'm genuinely scared I'll break her. I'm about as on edge as I would be if someone handed me a grenade.

"I don't know yet, she hasn't told me. We're not on a first name basis, but I'm confident she'll talk any day now." She blinks at me sarcastically.

I lean over to whisper in her ear. "Giving me snarky answers only makes me want to turn your arse red, Zoey."

She smiles smugly, but I don't miss the little shiver that rakes through her body. "Ooo, incentive. My inner brat is preening." She wiggles her brows and then focuses back on the cat. "I haven't named her yet."

"Why not? Her siblings have names."

"Well yeah, because Lloyd and Sam named them," she sighs, petting the kitten in my hand. "I don't want to get attached. She's my favourite."

"It sounds like you already are attached, sweetheart."

"Hmm, I thought maybe a human name, but I feel like every other person has a cat called Gary or Kevin and this kitty is just too pretty to become a statistic like that," she murmurs dreamily, taking the kitten from my arms who then climbs into the crook of Zoey's neck and relaxes immediately.

"Well, that and she's a girl. Calling her Gary might confuse all the boy cats when you call her. They'll assume she's a cat in drag."

Zoey laughs and snorts, it's just as adorable as the kitten on her shoulder. "Oh, she has the drama for drag. She hissed at her own reflection in the mirror for twenty minutes last week. Highly entertaining this cat business. Oh, how about Mrs Ru Paul?" she shrieks.

I pause. "Veto. It's not her. Grizabella?"

Her nose scrunches. "Veto. Cindy Clawford?"

I stifle a bubble of laughter. "That's good."

"This cat naming business is tough, right?"

I nod just as the white ball of fluff yawns on Zoey's shoulder, I smile. "She's a little mouse, not a kitten. That's why. We can't give her a cat name when she's part mouse. Look at her."

"Huh..." she hums, tapping her fingers on her chin.

"What?"

"Mouse. I like it. Good job, mountain man, I knew you were useful for something," Zoey chirps as she stands from the floor, moving to fill three big water bowls from the cat pens before she scoops Mouse from my palm all too fast and places her back with her siblings.

"Oh, she was keeping me warm."

"I thought that was my job?" She winks over her shoulder before locking the kittens away securely.

I go to stand, but instead, I reach up and grab Zoey's hips and pull her into my lap.

The breathy noise that leaves her lips in shock reminds me of the ones she was making last night, and my dick thickens in my trousers.

I drag my fingertips roughly up her jean clad thighs and, yep, her sharp inhale goes straight to my cock that's now leaking in my boxers. I hum satisfaction into her neck, and she bares her perfect skin for me. "Harrison," she breathes as my mouth connects with soft skin behind her ear.

"Yeah, sweetheart?" I continue my kisses along the slope of her neck, relishing each roll of her hips and the little gasp she lets out.

"I think I'm ready for you to update my software now," she rasps, and I pause my mouth on her.

"I-I'm... confused."

She chuckles lightly and turns in my arms, straddling my lap, wrapping her arms around my neck and grinding down onto my hard length. "Sam used it as a euphemism earlier for you fucking me in my office. He said you were here to..." She puts on her best 'Sam voice'. "Update the software."

She pushes down and rotates her hips against me again, and I succumb to the friction for a second, my eyes closing and jaw clenching shut. When I open my eyes again, two bright blue ones are staring at me, waiting to devour me. "You want me to fuck you in your office?"

Her face turns sheepish for a minute, and then she grins and nods. "I want you to fuck me in my office."

I groan. "You're killing me, Zoey."

She leans into my lips and places featherlight kisses on my mouth, the tip of my nose, on my chin, between my eyebrows. "I'll make sure the guys are taking Jelly and some other dogs for a walk if that makes you feel better?"

Moving my hands to her hips, I dig my fingers into her sides and hold her down on my cock. "You know what would make me feel better?"

She bites her bottom lip. "Me?"

"Yeah, sweetheart, but also, being able to fuck you with no one listening in so I can hear every sinful noise that falls from your perfect mouth." I kiss her, and she responds by wrapping her hands in my hair. *Fuck it all. I can't resist this woman anymore.* I deepen our kiss, thrusting my tongue into her mouth, which she strokes with her own. She tastes delicious, like mint and strawberries.

I've been kissed by enough women who were wrong for me to know that what I'm experiencing now with Zoey feels completely right. It's like the world has been in black and white and she's the vibrant rainbow of colour beaming through the grey clouds.

Zoey pulls away, reaches into her back pocket and types out a group text to Sam and Lloyd, telling them that Jelly needs a walk, stat. I laugh at Sam's reply. *"Sure, is it time for that system update?"*

"He's such a cheeky shit," Zoey chuckles, pocketing her phone. "Come on, mountain man. You've got thirty minutes to make me scream."

"I'll only need ten."

Zoey

His hot mouth on me is the best kind of foreplay. I'll never get enough of his lips pressed against mine. Or the feel of the hard muscles of his chest against my breasts as he backs me up to my desk.

"Take off your jeans and get on the desk, sweetheart," he demands against my mouth. The shiver of him telling me and not asking whirls through my body, and I can't help but wonder, where the fuck did this man come from? My fucking dreams? His strong, confident, patient exterior is juxtaposed by this demanding alpha male in front of me.

This side of him brings out the brat in me and damn, do I love it when she gets to play, too.

"What if I say no?" I raise an eyebrow, dragging my fingers over his buttoned shirt.

His head tilts. "Why would you do that when we both know you're dying to suck my dick?"

I wet my lips and clench my thighs, unable to hide my need. He's right, of course he is but I have this need to push him, provoke his inner alpha to play with me. "Oh, yeah?"

"Yeah," he says with a drawl and depth that my mouth waters at the thought of taking him in my mouth. He steps closer, the back of my legs hitting the desk. "See, I was going to make you come first, but I think that bratty little mouth of yours deserves to be fucked now, purely for even thinking you'd be able to deny or resist me."

A breath escapes my lips as they tilt to a smile. *There he is.* "So fucking cocky."

He gleams. "Cocky enough to know that you'll sink to your knees and take everything I give you, sweetheart." He reaches his hand up to push a strand of hair from my face, his cool fingers brushing against my heated skin makes me lean into his touch. His thumb ghosts my lower lip, and my mouth opens automatically as he pushes the pad inside with a "Fuuuuck". I suck his thumb deeper and let my tongue swirl around it before letting it pop out, watching his eyes darken. "How about we feed the brat instead? I know she's hungry. I can see it in your eyes." The side of his mouth lifts to a half smirk as he smears his wet thumb over my chin, holding me in place, his eyes never leaving mine. "Kneel."

Said brat inside me whimpers and is already begging me to get on my knees for him. When I bend, and my knees hit the rough floor, Harrison looks down at me with so much lust and adoration that my pulse flutters. "There you go," he praises and my insides peacock with pleasure. "Open that pretty mouth for me."

"Take off your shirt first," I demand, pushing back on him, running my hands slowly up his trousers-clad thighs. He hesitates but smiles and rids himself of his shirt, undoes his trousers and pushes them down to reveal his body and cock to me.

And hot damn, what a sight he is.

He looks like some sort of Greek god, with sculpted, hard earned muscles, a dusting of chest hair, long, thick hard cock standing proud. People could paint him and never capture his beauty. My pussy throbs, dying for attention, but I don't touch myself because I need to taste him. I lick the underside of his length, dragging my tongue along the protruding veins, and when I get to the tip, I smear his precum over my lips, painting myself in him as we lock eyes and I slowly lick them clean. "Mmm, you taste good," I purr, dragging in a rough breath before I take all of him to the back of my throat in one motion.

"Fuck!"

His strong thighs contract as his cock twitches in my throat. I hold him there and swallow around him, noting his knees wobbling again. "Zoey, sweetheart. This is going to be over really fast if you keep doing that," he splutters, his voice uneven. The sound of him unravelling has me internally smiling.

I draw back slowly, using my spit as lube, stroking him firmly and look up. His hand comes into my hair and his thumb caresses my cheek. "God, you're beautiful." The lust that made his irises come to life has softened into something *more*, something I can't name.

I smile up at him before I take the head of him in my mouth, fisting my hand around his base and up his shaft. He hums as I watch from my knees, his eyes closing and his head rolling backwards. His abs flexing beneath his open shirt.

Then he shudders and pushes me back, popping himself out of my mouth. "Get up here," he commands, his voice heavy with need. "I've changed my mind. I need your lips on mine." He hauls me upwards, setting me on the desk again, and takes my mouth without apology. I reach between us and stroke him as he fucks my mouth with his tongue. His hips move in sequence with his kisses. It's messy and frantic, and when I reach my other hand between us to touch his balls, he bites my lip and heat floods between my thighs, a wetness coating my underwear.

Breaking the kiss, he whispers throatily. "Lay back and take off your top. I'm going to paint you with my cum whilst you play with your perfect nipples."

The speed this man gets me to comply should be concerning, but I will always listen to him because he knows exactly how to make me feel like I'm everything to him. I quickly remove my jeans, top and underwear and throw them to the side, lying back as I watch him stroke himself. His arm veins pop, and his eyes are so dark I can barely tell his iris from his pupil.

The heat from his gaze washes over me like lava, and I move my hands to play with my nipples, sending shockwaves over my skin.

"I want you to get yourself off without touching your pussy."

I pause. "I don't know if—"

"You can and you will." He groans with a hard squeeze of his leaking cock. "Play with those perky tits for me."

My hands move back to my nipples, and he's right, the sight of him, the low sparks of pleasure travelling from my where my fingers twist my rosy flesh all the way down to my clit. I am going to come like this. Especially if I have a front row seat to Harrison touching himself too.

"Fuck, you turn me on so much. I've never wanted anyone as much as I want you, Zoey."

The way he says my name with so much heat gives me a push I need to come. My body pulses as I squeeze my breast, and his hot mouth lands on it a second later, his hand still frantically working his cock.

My head throws back at the sensation, then he lifts slightly and his jaw goes slack, when he stands just as ropes of his hot cum hit my stomach. My body no longer belongs to me, it's like I have no choice in what happens next, I unravel at the sight of my husband marking me as his.

"Harrison," I pant, unable to stop the breathlessness.

We're barely out of our orgasms when he sinks to his knees, spreading my thighs apart. "You want my tongue or my fingers?"

"God, both. Now," I say, edging myself to the lip of the desk, my body begging for anything he'll give me and still trembling from my first orgasm. He surges forward on a growl and licks me with a flat tongue from back to front. My trembling arms that are holding me up almost give way at the first touch.

I moan when he inserts a thick finger and curls it around, reaching that spot that makes me see stars. "Oh, my God." My eyes roll and I let myself fall back onto my desk, thankful it's not cluttered today.

Harrison kisses, sucks and laps at my sex, humming and eating me like he's starved. "You're fucking delicious, Zoey."

"Mmm, I'm even sweeter when I come, and I'm so fucking close again. Don't stop," I demand.

I'm careening over the edge when he inserts two fingers, as I pant from the stretched feeling burning through me, but I need more. He pumps his fingers expertly and when he grazes his teeth against my clit, I detonate. "Ohhhh, Harrison, I-I'm coming," I cry, throwing my hand over my mouth to stifle my scream. A burst of white-hot heat explodes in every nerve in my body. My skin feels too hot, my head feels fuzzy as I fall apart on his face.

I'm floating, I'm flotsam and jetsam in the ocean with nowhere to go as I drown in the orgasm high. Harrison peppers kisses along my inner thigh and when he reaches his cum that's still coating my stomach, he pauses, then smirks devilishly, admiring his work. I expect him to stop and move away, but when he dips his head, and his tongue peaks out to collect the cum, my clit throbs at the sight of him tasting himself from me. "Ohhhh, fuck," I drawl, feeling his hot tongue licking against my skin, knowing he's tasting himself heightens my arousal again.

He moves up to my mouth, eyes hooded as he presses our lips together. When he pushes his tongue inside, the mixture of me and him explodes on my taste buds. Sweet and salty. I hum, relishing the need building again inside me.

When he breaks the kiss, I try to chase after his lips, but his chuckle stops me. "Thirty minutes are up, sweetheart."

I deflate back onto my desk. "I think I lost brain cells after that one."

He laughs deeply and bends to kiss me once more. "Me too. Now get dressed before Sam and Lloyd come back. I'm the only one who gets to see you naked."

"Yes, sir." I mock salute, but he groans and I remember to use that again the next time we're blowing each other's minds.

Chapter 33

Harrison

"You have a lot of post it notes."

"I love post it notes. I leave them everywhere." She beams, puffing her chest out a little.

Smiling, I try to focus on the updates I'm doing for her office software and not on how she smells like me and sex or how she looked painted in my cum ten minutes ago. "I know. I found one with turtles on it attached to my suit jacket the other day."

"Oops." She lifts one side of her mouth but shrugs. "At least you were thinking of me at work."

I stop what I'm doing and turn to face her. "I am thinking about you. All the time lately."

Her bottom lip gets trapped between her teeth and several emotions flicker across her face. I know her well enough by now to know they are fear, anticipation and happiness. And that last one in particular sticks as she leans in and pecks my mouth. "I'll get you your own little stack of post it's. In fact." She spins, opens a drawer and gives me a pack with Labradors on them. "Here, these are yours."

I take them, unable to keep the stupidly goofy grin from my face. "They're perfect." *You're perfect.*

I break away from the computer and kiss and her eyes close as she hums a satisfied noise from the back of her throat.

Then suddenly, the whole place goes dark.

Zoey's eyes spring open. "I know I had my eyes closed, but did the lights just go off?"

"They did. Do you have a back up generator?"

She groans, and it's not the good kind. "Out back, it should kick in, but it's really old and I'm not sure if it's been used since I've been here." Luckily, it's not that dark because it's the middle of the afternoon. "I'm going to check the fuse box."

"I'll come too."

Zoey leads me to the back storage rooms, and when I spot the giant old fashioned style fuse box with a horrible smoky smell coming from it, I know it's not going to be good.

"Is that smell coming from the box?" I ask, covering my nose and mouth with my sleeve.

Zoey coughs. "Fuck."

"How old is this place?" I ask as Zoey goes to touch the box, but I stop her by grabbing her wrist and hold it against my chest. "Zoey, leave it. What if you get hurt?"

She sighs low and long. "You're right. That would really end my year with a bang. Literally." Emotion clogs her voice, as I take her hand, leading her out of the smoky room.

"I know a guy who can help. Let me make a call."

She stares at the floor, nodding to herself. "Okay, maybe I can afford a call out and hopefully, he can fix it within my budget."

I ignore Zoey's comment because I think she was mostly talking to herself anyway. Annoyance bubbles in my chest at the fact her father still hasn't given her the trust fund. If she were pissing away the money I could understand, but this... Not cool. She's such a good person, and he's too far up his own entitlement to see that.

I'm already texting my friend from school. We don't talk often, but he's always the guy my family uses for electrical issues.

"Grant will be here in an hour."

An hour and a half later, Zoey has chewed through all her nails while pacing back and forth.

Grant, the electrician I called, manages to stop the smell from the box, but I have no idea how. When he comes back to the office, he's shaking his head. "I've had to keep the electrics off for now. And I hate to tell you this..." He tries to offer a reassuring smile, but it's not reassuring enough. "Your fuse box is out of date, which means your wiring is out of date. I had a quick sneak behind the wall in the storage room, and you also have asbestos."

A rush of air leaves Zoey's mouth as she plummets into her office chair wearing a vacant expression. I hate seeing her like this. "What... h-how." She clears her throat and swallows thickly. "That sounds really expensive..."

"Wiring could be anything from three to five grand. Asbestos, I'd hazard a guess that it could cost anywhere between five to ten grand."

Zoey's expression doesn't change. She stares at Grant but doesn't really look at him. "And that would take a long time?"

Grant nods. "It might not be in the whole building, but considering the age of it, it might be everywhere. I know a guy if you want his details."

Zoey nods mindlessly, so I take the lead.

"Thanks, man," I say, offering my hand. I lower my voice as I lead him out of Zoey's office. "I'm booking you to do the wiring but send me the bill. You have my office email."

"Sure thing. Let me know when the asbestos is sorted, and I'll get it done in a few days. I'll send you the asbestos guy's details. I'm sorry it's not better news."

Grant leaves, and when I go back into the office to see Zoey, she hasn't moved. Walking over, I lower myself to my knees so I'm face to face with her. She flinches, and her glassy blue eyes flick to me.

"Sweetheart, are you—" I don't get to finish my sentence because Zoey has flung herself into my arms and buries her head into my neck, sobs wracking her body. Her petite frame lost in my chest. "Shhh, it's okay."

She mumbles something that I don't hear and when she pulls back, her eyes are red, and her face is wet. I use my thumb to wipe away her tears. She sniffs and tries to compose herself. "It's not okay, I have to figure out where to put over fifty animals for the next what? Three weeks, maybe more, and on top of that my arsehole father won't give me my trust fund. Why are we even doing this if he doesn't give it to me? I've worked so fucking hard on this place, and it keeps testing me." Her watery eyes connect with mine as they darken with sadness. "Jesus, I've dragged you into such a mess."

"Hey, don't think like that. We can figure this out." She slumps back onto my chest as I stroke the back of her head, holding her close to me with my other hand, and I brush my lips against her forehead.

That maybe isn't the right thing to say because Zoey plunges into me again and starts crying, her delicate hands clinging onto my shirt for dear life.

After a while, Zoey eventually relaxes and sits back in her office chair and I stand too, stretching my legs.

"Shit," she says, slumping her head into her hands. She sniffs and then sits upright, pushing her shoulders back. "I ruined your shirt."

I look down to see wet patches on my chest. "It doesn't matter, it's a shirt. Are you okay? Can I get you anything?"

She nods. "I need to make some calls to other shelters to get the animals looked after." She pauses and then looks at me, puffy eyed and red nosed. "Can you find Lloyd and Sam and update them? They should be back now. I think the animals will be fine for the next few days whilst we sort things, but I need them to know."

"Of course, I'll find them."

I find the guys just as they're coming back from a walk and I explain everything. They both want to help Zoey figure things out, so I find myself hovering a lot. Grant has emailed me the details for the company he recommends for the asbestos, so I figure I may as well call them too. If nothing else, I can get an idea of the cost for Zoey to work with.

Chapter 34

Zoey

I t's midnight. Harrison and I went to bed hours ago, but I couldn't sleep. I'm plagued by what happened today at the shelter. The post-it notes surrounding me in the living room are covered with scenarios and costs that I've managed to get from the internet. None of which are probably accurate because the asbestos isn't in my house, it's in my business. And the wiring in the shelter dates back to the Jurassic period, it seems. *How am I meant to fix all this?*

"Fuck," I whisper to myself, running my hand through my unruly hair.

I glance over the rough cost of the asbestos. Even if I can get it covered with insurance—which I don't think is possible judging by the policy I scanned through an hour ago—there's a good chance I'd have to pay upfront again, and until my dad decides I'm not lying, even though I am, about my marriage, he's stubborn enough to withhold my trust fund, and I'm left without any cash.

I swallow thickly because that's just not an option.

Max emailed me yesterday saying the claim has been approved for the plumbing works and I should get the money back in the next week. That would give me five grand, which might cover some of the asbestos cost, but the wiring? Unless I'm planning on selling my body and all my organs on the black market, I think I'm going to struggle to come up with anything.

What I thought was my answer to getting more money has just turned out to be me, dragging Harrison into my mess, sleeping with him, and feeling guilty about it all because nothing is resolved. Fun times.

I decide looking at numbers is making me too antsy, and all the numbers are starting to look like hieroglyphics. So, I open my phone to find the list of other London shelters. I know a few of the managers by name, but I write down each number on more post it notes, and when I have a decent stack to call tomorrow, I lean back on the soft sofa and exhale roughly.

You've got this, Zoey.

Fighting for this shelter is, without a doubt, the hardest and most rewarding thing I've ever done in my life. But I know it's something I could never live without.

My eyes grow heavy and I close them for a second when I hear padding feet behind me.

"Sweetheart?"

"In here," I reply, my voice flat and weary.

The padding gets closer and two large hands thread into my hair, tipping my head backwards against the sofa; his soft lips land on mine. My fingers instantly thread into his hair too, holding him against me, taking the kiss like it's the only air in the room. He moves his hands to glide over my throat and down my pyjama top, aka his t-shirt, and cups one of my breasts, awakening a deep yearning in my sex.

"Come to bed," he whispers against my mouth, breaking our kiss. His hair is tousled, and his eyes are still half asleep.

"I can't. Not yet. I have to... figure all this out. My brain is on a carousel," I reply, gesturing to the stacks of post it notes decorating his coffee table.

"All the more reason to rest and reassess tomorrow," he states, matter of fact, as he walks around the sofa to stand in front of me with his hand out, wearing only his soft pyjama bottoms. "Come with me."

Can someone please tell me how I'm meant to deny this man when his perfect, strong chest is on display? He looks so fucking good all the time, even when he's sleepy. In fact, especially when he's sleepy.

My hand twitches. I want to take his, but I know that I won't be able to settle until I've got some sense of control over this. "I have to sort this. I can't make these numbers match and it's driving me insane."

A frown passes his lips before he sits next to me and eclipses my kneecap with his hand, squeezing. "Walk me through it. We'll get a solution, and then I'm taking you to bed."

"You don't have to do this."

"I do." He turns to face me, determination blazing in his tired eyes. "I want to. You're my wife, and I'm not letting you face this alone."

My pulse thunders, my fingers tingle and all of a sudden, I really feel the weight of my wedding ring on my finger. I do have him, and even if I'm being selfish, I want him to help me. I want him to want to help me. Even if I can't accept his money, this I can do. "Okay," I say, nodding my head and placing my hand on top of his.

He scans over my notes with his other hand while not letting me go, looking at the costs I found on Google. "What funds do you have available?"

I chew my bottom lip, my cheeks heating at the fact that I have to admit it's not much. "Around eight grand, total. But that would clear me out. I could sell my car too, I thought about doing that anyway. That could give me an extra few grand."

He nods slowly, then continues staring at the post-it notes, flicking through each one before he pauses. "Let me help you, Zoey."

My skin bubbles with a coolness that has nothing to do with the temperature of the room. "No," I say resolutely and when he turns to face me, I stumble at the hurt on his face. "I'm sorry. I mean, no, thank you. I can't accept anything."

His head shakes slightly. "I don't understand why not. We agreed this is a partnership, no?"

"A business agreement," I correct him a little too harshly than I mean to and my stomach plummets at my words.

He goes rigid for a second and his eyes flash with more hurt. *Great. Good one, Zoey.* "Right, fine. So. if it's a business agreement, I want to amend the terms. Let me give you the money for this, and when you get your trust fund, you can give it back to me."

I consider what he's saying, and it does make sense to a degree, except... "And what if my father never gives me the money? I can't drag you into this without being able to pay you back. It's bad enough that you married me, and we aren't any closer to me getting my trust fund."

"Zoey, you're not dragging me into anything—"

"But I am. I'm fucking all this up and I don't know what to do." I exhale roughly, looking down at all the useless numbers I've written down. "I'm just frustrated because not everything will be covered by the insurance, and at the moment, nothing is lining up. If I use my savings, I don't have enough, and what do I do with all the animals long term if I can't get it fixed soon?" My brain sabotages me, and my pride can't take a hit again. I'm constantly battling with the soul crushing feeling that I've been ignoring for the last year. That whispers in the back of my mind, telling me I'll never be good enough, not just for me, but for anyone. My shelter is the place that makes me feel at home. It's the one place where I feel enough because all those animals look at me like I saved them. I did that. I made them feel safe, and I can't give that up.

"Sweetheart." His voice brings me out of my spiral. "You need to let me help," he says gently.

Shaking my head, my eyes burn. "I-I can't. I want to do this. I have to." My voice cracks on the last word and I see the moment he gives in.

He nods solemnly. "I understand." Blowing out a long breath, he briefly looks down but quickly focuses back on me. "But come to bed. Nothing is going to be solved tonight. You need sleep. We'll figure it out tomorrow."

I lean into him, resting my head on his shoulder and inhaling his freshly washed skin. He always smells so good, sweet but masculine. I take one more inhale, and the wave of exhaustion from earlier hits me full force again, along with a realisation. "I need to see my dad again."

He strokes my hair and everything whirling around in my head immediately settles with his touch. "I think that's a good idea. I can come with you."

"I think I need to do this myself."

"Okay, whatever you need. But I'm here. I'll support you and help you in any way I can, Zoey. But I need you to rest. Will you come to bed with me?"

A sigh escapes my lips and my eyes close as I softly nod my head. We both stand, he wraps himself to my side, splaying his hand across my waist, tattooing his warmth onto my skin.

We climb into bed, him in his pyjama trousers, me in his t-shirt, and as soon as I pull the covers up, he stares at me with a frown. "What?" I ask.

"Why are you all the way over there?"

I try to think of an answer but come up blank. Then he grabs me by the waist and hauls me backwards into his front, nuzzling his nose into the crook of my neck. The goosebumps that cover my body are laced with lust and comfort. He makes me feel safe. Here in his arms, he makes my mind less noisy, and I feel stupid for ever thinking I wasn't in 'like' with my fake husband because the truth is, I am.

"Mmm, that's better," he hums into my skin, moving his hands over my stomach, igniting that spark deep in my core. I lace my fingers with his and feel something long and thick resting against my arse. I wiggle slightly, and he groans, gripping my hand tighter. "Careful, sweetheart, I'm trying to be a gentleman here and make sure you sleep."

I suppress a laugh. "It seems like *he* has other ideas."

The scruff of his beard tickles my neck as he laughs. "He always has bad ideas where you're concerned. But it's not about him tonight. Sleep." He kisses the back of my shoulder and rests his head back on the pillow.

I could sleep so easily, too. My body is tired, and so is my mind, but having him near me like this, making me feel warm, it sparks another need, and my body definitely has other ideas. I turn and hike a leg over his, pulling him closer to me, his erection straining between us.

"Suddenly, I'm not so tired," I whisper, stroking his abs, the fever inside building. I ache for him, for everything about him; the way he soothes me, the way he touches me, the way he fucks me. I know right now I'm not going to want to give him up when this fake marriage arrangement is over.

"What do you need, Zoey?" he whispers, eyes fixated on my mouth.

My stomach flutters at a euphoric speed.

"Everything."

Chapter 35

Harrison

I need to take Zoey away. I want to help her, but I understand that she feels she has something to prove, especially after witnessing that spectacular display of *affection* from her parents not long ago.

We'll sort the shelter and get the animals temporarily into other shelters, and then I'm taking her camping. I know she joked that she'd hate it, but I have a feeling she needs to completely switch off, and this is the perfect way to do it.

I tap my pen on my desk. Work this morning has gone slowly, and exhaustion has begun to creep into my vision. The late night with Zoey ended up being a *very* late night after she and I did things that aren't considered resting.

Last night, the defeat in her eyes nearly killed me. I want to fix this for her; I want to save her from any hurt, to protect her, to make all her fears disappear and seeing her look so small and fragile... that was when I realised that I have feelings for her I've never had for any other woman. The tightness in my chest when I'm not around her seems to be a permanent thing now. So, when she threw the whole 'business arrangement' at me again, I tried not to let it show, but that stung... a lot. Truth is, this hasn't been a business arrangement since the moment I kissed her. I'm being fully led by my emotions here, but I have no idea if she's on the same page.

"Knock knock, brother." Max's voice wakes me from my daydream of Zoey as he walks into my office.

I sit up straighter and drop my pen on my desk as I stand. "Shit, I forgot you were coming over."

We do our bro-hug that we've always done since we were kids, slapping each other's backs. Yeah, we're a cliché, but it's weirder if we don't do it now.

"Don't dent my ego any more than you already have. I'm adjusting to being the second most important Bancroft in your life now." He huffs as he sits in the chair opposite me, stretching out his long legs. "Speaking of. How is my little sister?"

"She's good. Busy, some shit is going on at the shelter again. She's stressed," I admit and immediately wince. I need to tread carefully here. I know Zoey hasn't spoken to her brothers much lately. She even left a post-it with a cartoon hedgehog on the coffee table last week with '*Don't forget to call Max and Owen*' written on it.

Max's head tilts. "Again? That place is a liability, I swear. She needs to cut her losses. Not that I'll ever tell her that."

"I wouldn't either. She's more attached to that place than ever." I rub my hand through my beard, avoiding his stare as best I can while trying not to blurt out that Bancroft Snr is a complete arsehole.

I feel the weight of Max's stare because that's the thing about being friends with someone for most of your life; They can tell when you're keeping something from them. "What's up with you?"

"Didn't get a lot of sleep last night," I tell him honestly.

"It doesn't take a genius to know why, but it does take a brother not to tell me the details, please. Considering that'll be my sister's doing, I'm sure." He shudders dramatically. "Is that all though?"

I twirl the wedding band on my finger, still not looking up.

"I'm good, man. Honestly." *Just figuring out my feelings for your sister, but I can't talk to you about that because you think we've been dating in secret for ages. God, this is complicated.*

"Okay, well, the offer is there if you need an ear." He stands, running his hands down the front of his chinos as he does. "Ready for lunch? Owen is meeting us there."

I stand, too. "Sure."

Max stops me before I advance past him. "Dude, seriously, you're acting weird."

I blow out a breath, wracking my brain for what I can say. "I want to take Zoey camping, and I don't want her to hate it. I feel anxious about it, okay?" It's not a total lie, so I go with it.

Max bursts out laughing, and just when I think he's stopped, he starts again. "I'm sorry," he splutters, not sounding apologetic at all. "Zoey and wilderness don't mix, man. We went to Canada when we were kids and she had a panic attack when a fly landed on her arm as we were walking around Lake Louise." He shakes his head and grips my shoulder, looking me dead in the eyes. "Good luck with that, mate."

I shrug his arm off, huffing incredulously. "Pff. She works with animals, man. She's changed. I'm telling you, she won't be scared of a fly."

"No, but she's a handful and a princess."

"Do you even know your sister, man? She's a fucking warrior, not a princess." I scoff. Zoey isn't actually what her brothers think of her.

They see parts of her now, not her whole self and that makes my heart twinge a little for her. "You should call her. She misses you and Owen."

Trepidation mars his face. "Yeah, I will. I miss her too."

Lunch came and went. Owen ribbed me too, telling me I was making a mistake and Zoey would way prefer luxury, but I think they're wrong. They don't know her as well as I do. They might live their lavish lifestyle every day, but she doesn't, and I appreciate that.

I call the shelter, hoping that one of the guys will pick up and not Zoey.

"Hello, Paw Prints shelter. How can I help?"

"Hey, Lloyd, it's Harrison."

"Hey man, want me to get Zoey?"

"Actually, I wanted to talk to you."

"Oh, really?" he says with a smile in his voice. "Decided you wanted a husband instead? Look, I'm flattered, but I'm also married to Sam. I hate to break your heart, but..."

I laugh. "You really are breaking my heart. But I wanted to ask how long until you think the animals will be settled in other shelters?"

"Oh, uh, I'm pretty sure they're all being moved tomorrow morning. We managed to find one that could take them all, which is so much easier. And they agreed to let Sam and I do their up keep still, so hopefully no one will be anxious."

I nod, even though he can't see me. "That's good. Great even. And the contractors haven't been booked yet, right?"

"I think Zoey might have been talking to someone about that today. She was scowling a lot at numbers."

"Yeah, we had a lot of that last night."

"Lloyd, I need another set of eyes on this. I can't look at numbers any longer." Zoey's raspy voice echoes in the distance.

"Boss needs me. Sorry, Mr Zoey. Gotta run."

"Wait, just really fast. I want to take Zoey away. If we get things booked before the weekend, can you both handle the contractors if she isn't there?"

Lloyd hesitates. "We can, and we did when she was in Vegas, but…"

"…but?" I prompt.

"I'm not sure she'll let us take the reins on this one. The woman is a fierce mama bear with this place."

"I'm not giving her a choice. She needs a break."

"Well, alrighty then," he chuckles. "I can see why Zoey likes you. Don't worry about this place. We've been with her since the beginning. We can handle it."

"Great," I sigh in relief. "Oh, and Lloyd?"

"Uhuh."

"Don't tell her. It's a surprise."

Chapter 36

Zoey

Harrison has been acting strange.

How do I know this? He's fidgeting. And the man does not fidget. Ever. He's so calm and collected all the time, but it's been going on for a couple of hours now, and he's putting me on edge.

Take now, for example. He's tapping his thigh in a rhythm that sounds a lot like a Katy Perry song. I'm sure he's never listened to her in his life, but all I can hear is "California Girls". But my point is that he's never done that before. It could be because I've got a tub of ice cream in bed, and he has an adamant no food in the bed rule. However, he didn't challenge me earlier when I waltzed in here with two spoons.

Sure, it could be because I sent all my babies off to another shelter today. Sure, it could be because when he picked me up from work all I did was sob into his shoulder for twenty minutes about how Jelly might get sad, or how I should probably go with them because what if someone feeds Mouse wrong?

I told him I shouldn't have named that bloody kitten, and now I'm attached.

But I'm a breath away from purposefully dropping ice cream on the sheets and seeing what happens just to make him explode and stop bloody fidgeting. I really am considering it, but I decide to abandon the tub and focus on my husband. "Hey, Harrison?"

"Hmm?" He doesn't look up, still with the tapping.

"Can you take a look at my nipple?" I say, hoping that will get his attention. When his head snaps up to look at my boobs, laughter escapes my throat in a chortle. "Men are all the same. Boob, ass, pussy, any of those get your attention."

He finally stops the tapping and smiles. "I'm sorry, I've been—"

"—ignoring your wife?" I flutter my eyelashes.

"I was going to say distracted, but since you think I'm not giving you enough attention, I think I should rectify that."

He settles his head on his arm, which is propped up, and his free hand (the tapping hand) is now coasting gently up my leg, leaving a trail of heat behind. "Hmm," I groan, feeling like I might sink into the mattress. "As nice as this is, and I have no doubt it would be. I want to know what had your hand tapping that Katy Perry song a second ago."

His brow scrunches together, looking at me blankly. "I couldn't name one of her songs."

"Ugh, why did I marry you?"

"For my charm and quick wit?"

I pat his cheek. "Oh, I was going to say for your monster cock, but sure, we'll go with your answer."

He shakes his head with a smile. "You're a cheeky shit sometimes. You know?"

"Oh, I've always known that. It's taken you a while to catch on, though," I say with a wink.

He rolls on top of me, completely covering my body under his six foot four frame. "I kissed a girl, and I liked it," he whispers into my ear.

"Huh?" I ask, distracted.

"Katy Perry."

"Oh yeah, sorry you climbed on top of me, and I forget almost everything when that happens." I'm not joking. I feel every hard inch of him against me and I love it. As I roll my hips up to feel his other hardness push against my sex.

"Nrgh," he groans.

I giggle like I've just been passed a love note in school. "You incoherent? That's a first."

He rolls his own hips down this time, eliciting a moan from my mouth, too. "What was that you were saying, sweetheart?"

"I have no idea, but do that again, please."

He does making the friction between us delicious and heady. My body responds by shivering and heating up at the same time. The perfect mix of hot and cold running in my veins. I'm surrounded by the fog of lust that always overtakes me when he touches me. It's like my body is an instrument, and he's the only one who knows how to play it.

My nipples are wildly sensitive, straining against the cotton of my—actually his t-shirt. "If I dip my finger inside you right now, I bet you'd be soaked for me."

He'd absolutely be right, and he knows it, judging by the cocky smirk on his face as he rolls into me again, earning another breathy noise from me. But somewhere in my mind. Way, way back in the depths where I don't focus on Harrison's hot breath against my skin or his huge dick trying to fight past our clothes right now. I know I have a more pressing matter to deal with. A previously fidgeting husband who had something on his mind that I want to help with, and he absolutely cannot distract me with sex. *And breathe.*

"Wait," I say weakly. Although he's not fidgeting anymore, so should I stop?

"What is it?" He doesn't stop.

"I was trying to figure out why you were—okay, I'm gonna need you to stay still for a second because I cannot think when my pussy is shouting at me." A chuckle rakes his whole body as he shudders laughter above me. "It's not funny. I can't think straight."

He laughs again, but it's more controlled now and under his breath as he lifts his head to look into my eyes. "I think I want you to not think straight. Isn't that the point of sex?" he says, rolling into me again.

"Baby," I plead for him to continue or to stop so I can figure out what was wrong. I have no idea, but I rarely call him that during sex, so he pauses.

"Don't ask me why I was fidgeting. Just know that I'm taking you somewhere this weekend. But that's all you're getting from me." He pins me with a stare that says, 'No arguments. "Now, if you don't mind, I want to make my wife come so I can fuck her into the mattress."

My mind is still stuck on the little bit of information he gave me about going away this weekend, and I feel the blood draining from my limbs. How can I go away when the shelter is so up in the air? What if something goes wrong? One of the animals needs me?

"Did you hear me, sweetheart?" His deep voice breaks my spiral.

"I did."

He doesn't buy it. "I don't think you did, so I'm going to say it again. I need to make my wife come and fuck her into this mattress." He pauses, making sure I'm paying attention. "Did you get all that, or do you need to have another internal freak out? I can guarantee my way is more fun."

My breath hitches when he moves his hand slowly underneath my t-shirt and I forget all those worries when he brushes skin on skin. "Your way, definitely your way." I close my eyes and just feel his big hands moving against me, awakening every inch of me as he moves north. When he grazes the underside of my boob, I clench my thighs as his hips roll forward again.

"I want you so fucking badly. The thought of me sinking my dick inside that tight little pussy makes me want to blow right now." He growls, my hands drifts to his arse as I push him into me again. "What I'd do to fuck you bare and feel every single muscle spasm as you come." He picks up the pace, our hips meeting with such pleasure and friction that I'm writhing beneath him.

"Do it. I want you," I pant.

He stops and kisses the tip of my nose. "Soon, sweetheart, but not tonight. I need to take my time when it happens and tonight, I'm running out of patience." The intensity in his eyes makes me burn from the inside out. "Lose the t-shirt," he demands, his words going straight to my needy clit.

I do as he says, and he's ripping open a condom with his teeth and rolling it onto his length. God, the man has the Ferrari of dicks. It's perfectly thick, not painfully big, but plenty big enough to reach your g-spot, which I'm hoping is about to happen.

He leans over me, imposing and sexy like some sort of dark god, the flecks of grey in his beard catching the low light in the room. Lining himself up to my sex, he only dips the tip inside as my greedy walls contract, needing more. "Harrison, I need you inside me like right fucking now," I whimper, my eyes rolling closed with frustration.

When I open them, he keeps me trapped in his gaze, and it's clear he wants my attention because when I don't waver, he slowly and purposefully sinks inside me. Rippling inch after rippling inch.

I try to roll my hips to meet his when he bottoms out, but he stops me by pinning my hips to the bed. "I'm pretty sure I'm the one doing the fucking here, sweetheart."

Just as I nod and think he's going to pound into me for punishment, he slowly draws back and eases back in with the most sensual noise I've ever heard.

"Fuck, Zoey. You were made for me."

My body begs him for more, but he doesn't relent in his slow and devious torture of me. My clit pulses between us, my nipples ache for his mouth. "Harrison, baby, you're killing me."

I'm close to the point of insanity as a fog drifts over me. I clench my sex around him and he stutters. "Ohhh, fuck me." His eyes close and open with a new flame burning behind them. "You think you can top from the bottom, sweetheart?"

I smile wickedly, clenching again, and I feel him pulse inside me. "I think I c—"

My words are interrupted by the force of him pushing into me wildly. He's sinking, growling, claiming, and I'm so fucking here for it. "Yes, more."

He slows and immediately the intensity goes from a roaring need to a deep throbbing again, I all but whimper. Dipping his head next to my ear, he whispers. "You can try to top from the bottom all you want, but I'm the one in control here. I get to say when you come and how hard you come."

My mouth is dry, my pussy is soaked, and my body is on fire. "Make me come then, mountain man."

He smirks and pumps into me enough that each connection of our bodies sends a slap to my clit, making me desperate and breathless. When he sucks on my nipple, my orgasm hits me out of nowhere, making me cry out. "Oh, my God!" I scream. "Fuck, fuck, fuck, fuuuuuuuuuuck."

I come so fucking hard I couldn't tell you what year it is. "Fuck, I can feel you coming," he whispers into my neck, and he gives one final thrust as he comes too.

Chapter 37

Harrison

She looks beautiful this morning, lying naked on our bed, with just the covers over her lower half. She looks especially beautiful when she looks at me like she wants to kill me after what I just told her.

"You're taking me camping?" she mutters with a tone that implies she wants me to say 'jokes, we're going to a spa'. I'm not joking though.

"I'm taking you camping," I repeat, my fingers swirling over her shoulder.

Her eyes close, and she twists her mouth. "I hate bugs."

"I've got bug spray."

Her eyes open and narrow on me. "I hate being cold."

"Good job you've got me, your human radiator."

Her lips twinge unamused. "I can't leave the animals."

"Already taken care of with Lloyd and Sam."

She pauses, her beady eyes trying to find a weakness. "What if I say no?"

"You won't." *She could, but I'm hoping she doesn't.* I'm very aware of how much she hates camping. Max and Owen filled me in on their little trip as kids when she was eaten alive by mosquitos and got lost in the woods near the campsite. But she was younger and now she deals with animals for a living. I mean, how traumatised can she be?

"Oh, won't I?" She juts her chin towards me, and I pull her to me in a blistering kiss. Stealing her taste and inhaling her sweet scent.

We break apart and she's already softened. I can see it in the way her eyes are now glossy and not harsh. "No, you won't. Because this weekend is important for you, and that means it's important to me, too."

She softens further, wrapping her arms around my middle and putting her head on my chest, inhaling and exhaling deeply. "Fine, you win."

Three of my favourite words.

"Do you need all that stuff?" I ask Zoey as she carries a full suitcase to the front door of the flat.

She pins me with a glare. "Of course I need this, and it's not stuff. It's my clothes."

"You realise we're going for two nights, and you'll spend most of it in *my* clothes or your birthday suit," I remind her, picking up her case and then putting it down again, groaning from the weight. "Seriously, Zoey, go get rid of whatever fancy shit you've got in here and put *some* of it in the backpack in my wardrobe. If it doesn't fit in that bag, you don't need it."

She pouts, widening those big blue eyes. "But—"

"That princess pout doesn't work on me. Go," I instruct, pointing to our bedroom.

She huffs and the little scowl that makes her nose wrinkle appears. "My pout works on everyone, even Owen, who is emotionally stubborn. I swear that man doesn't understand affection and even *he* gives in to me." Her foot stomps a little as a last-ditch effort to get her own way.

Stepping forward, I place my thumb and index finger on her chin and tip her head back until she's staring into my eyes. "I guess that makes me special, then. I might not be able to resist you in many other ways, but I'm not budging on this." I place a soft kiss on her mouth, as she sighs. "Go," I urge.

"Camping Harrison is strict," she says, twirling around with her suitcase. "Maybe if I'm bad enough, he'll spank me later."

I chuckle. "I heard that."

"I know," she shouts back.

An hour later, we're finally on our way. Zoey did listen to me about her clothes and managed to fit what she wanted into my backpack without much fuss. I'm glad because the car is filled with camping gear, so fitting that suitcase in would've meant sacrificing the tent and as much as I might've got Zoey to agree to the weekend of camping, sleeping without the tent wouldn't have been the way to ease her into this trip.

The drive to the New Forest isn't too far, and we should be there in about two and a half hours. As we leave London, Zoey finally looks up from her phone with an apologetic look on her face.

"Mouse and Jelly settling in the new shelter, okay?" I ask, knowing that she would've been messaging Lloyd and Sam.

She nods. "I've been told to politely 'fuck off'," she laughs. "Honestly, the balls on them. I'd fire them if I didn't love them so much."

I extend my hand over the centre console. "There is one rule this weekend. No phones," I say, glancing at her to see her reaction.

"But you have your phone," she protests.

"Because that's our map and music. Hand it over, sweetheart."

She slaps the phone into my hand begrudgingly. "I hate that I can't guilt you into anything with my pouting."

Smiling, I place her phone in the compartment between us. "No, you don't. You like me taking control."

"In the bedroom, sure, but I'll have you know I'm an independent woman," she retorts, crossing her arms over her chest, pushing her breast upwards. I can't focus on them like I want to, but I can't stop a quick glance, either.

"Oh, believe me, I know. You're also stubborn and have to do everything yourself." I side eye her, as I move my hand to cover her knee. "But you're also kind, smart, resilient, and you have a talent for sucking my cock like you were born to do it."

Zoey barks laughter, throwing her head back into the headrest. "Nice save there, mountain man."

She picks the music, and when I see she's chosen a Katy Perry compilation, I have to laugh. "It's so you can learn her backlist," she coos, batting her eyelashes at me. This woman is going to be the death of me, I swear. Either that or two hours of Katy Perry will do it.

The drive is easy, even with the music, and the conversation flows between us. We laugh about the message we both received from Cassie in our group chat last night, with a list of beach destinations we should do our 'wedding do over' at. Turns out, Cassie inherited my sister's art of being subtle. I don't even want to think about how invested the girls are in all this because that means I'd have to think about this ending, and I... I don't want to do that.

I don't want this to end. Truth be told, this is the most fun I've had in years. Zoey brings out something in me I thought I'd left behind when I became the corporate version of Harrison Clarke, but it turns out all I need is her. I'm more emotionally invested in Zoey in the few months we've been around each other than I ever was with Vanessa. I know Zoey, and I said we would let this run its course once her trust fund is secured, so is it bad that a part of me hopes her dad turns her down? I mean, of course I don't want him to treat her badly. That night at her parent's house almost broke her, and I hated seeing her unhappy, but I wish she'd accept my help instead sometimes.

"Oh hey, did you call your dad? I saw Max and Owen this week and they mentioned he's being a bigger arsehole than normal." I flick my eyes over to her to gauge her reaction.

I don't miss the shift in her mood from me mentioning him. I shouldn't bring him up because this weekend is meant to be a relaxing one, but it slipped out without thinking too much about it.

"I emailed him. He said he'd make time for me Monday afternoon," she says quietly, and I hate the way her voice is small. Zoey might be short in height but usually she's larger than life in every other way.

"I'm sorry. Let's forget about that. I shouldn't have said anything. I just know how stressed you've been."

"It's fine," she replies. "I have to believe this is all going to work out. Otherwise, I might have a full on snotty, screaming, crying, throwing up, honest to God meltdown."

"It *will* work out," I tell her confidently because no matter what, Zoey will not lose that shelter. I won't ever let that happen.

Zoey nods, but I fear I've made the mood more solemn than I meant to. We travel in silence for a few minutes, when she grabs my hand and hugs it to her chest before bringing it to her lips and kissing my knuckles.

"Hey." She taps our connected hands with her free one. I glance over at her, flicking my gaze between the road and her. "I was thinking. You know what rhymes with camping?" she asks, and I shake my head in reply. "Alcohol."

I chortle. "I have everything covered, sweetheart. But we are not having alcohol before the tent is up."

She hmphs. "You really are so strict. Maybe I like this version of you."

Maybe I like you.

Chapter 38

Zoey

Camping is not some kind of retreat to be relaxed at. How can anyone be relaxed when you're sleeping on dirt and there are bugs? I don't care what notions my *husband* has about this weekend being for me. It's one hundred per cent for him.

Although I did melt a little when he said this trip is important for me, and so it's important to him. I mean, emotions are big and scary, but this man feels them so easily and makes me feel them too.

To his credit, he's put the tent up in record time. We've been here for thirty minutes, and somehow, we have a little cosy corner of the campsite all to ourselves, complete with tent, blankets, firepit and self-inflating mattresses. *Who knew they were a thing?*

When Harrison ducks into the boot of his car again and appears with strawberries and my favourite chocolate, I actually swoon out loud. "Oh my God, you have to stop being nice to me. Are you kidding with that?"

He laughs as he walks towards me, the low afternoon light glistening in his brown eyes. "I'll never stop being nice to you, Zoey."

See? The man wears his emotions like he wears a t-shirt. Or maybe that's just with me. I remember him saying he never actually felt connected to his ex, and honestly, I could see why when I met her. The woman was an ice queen.

He's so warm and honest, I can't picture them together at all. But that whole encounter did make me think that I guess I haven't invested much time in relationships the last few years to notice that I missed that connection with someone. I always thought physical touch was my love language, but maybe it *became* that when I was only getting physical with people. I mean, one night stands don't really lend themselves to meaningful words of affirmation, aside from the occasional dirty talk. Harrison, fortunately for me, provides all love languages. Seriously, the man is a fucking god.

The way he swipes his hand over his beard when he's thinking about something near enough makes me combust every time. Watching him advance towards me with the bloody strawberries, my favourite chocolate and a smile that's becoming my favourite thing to see every morning tells me one thing... I'm in trouuuuuuuuuuuuble.

Eh, I happen to like trouble.

"So, now that we're here, in your mountain man domain." I wait for him to sit on the camping chair next to me, brushing his arm against mine as he shuffles closer. "Am I finally gonna see you chop that wood for me, baby?" I say seductively.

He smirks devilishly, and my body definitely appreciates it. "Play your cards right tomorrow and I just might." His voice is low and gravelly as he leans in to peck my cheek. "But just for tonight, I've got pre-chopped wood because I wanted this to be efficient so I can fuck you under the stars later."

"Be still my beating vagina," I say, cupping my sex over my leggings.

Hearing him laugh floods me with a warmth I'm beginning to crave. It's something only he does to me and has been doing to me since the moment he kissed me on our wedding day. Being around him is so... easy. I wasn't lying the other week when I said I don't think I'll want to let him go. It's becoming a problem, but one that I'm not going to dissect this weekend. I've been ordered to relax, and that's what I'll do.

He sets up the firepit and lights the fire, whilst I sit on a camp chair with a blanket and the biggest smile on my face.

"You know your brothers told me I was making the wrong decision bringing you here," he says, tapping my legs, gesturing for me to turn and put my feet in his lap.

"They told you about Canada, right?"

He nods, turning to face me. "Did I make the wrong decision?"

I sit forward to be closer to him. "Too soon to tell." I widen my grin, teasing him. "I will say that, so far I'm impressed, and I haven't been eaten alive by bugs so it's already better than Canada. Plus, you're here and not my stupid big brothers and you got me *Magic Stars*." I wiggle the bag of chocolate in front of him.

He rumbles a laugh, deep and low. "It still baffles me why they're your favourite."

"Magic Stars are amazing. The little faces on them are the cutest thing. But you can't eat the baby faces first. They have to be saved until last."

He hides his smirk behind his hand, pretending to brush his beard down, but I see it. "There's an order you eat them?"

"Obviously," I deadpan.

He assesses me for a second, then quirks an eyebrow. "You're serious about this."

"I'm always serious about chocolate."

First night camping, done. I did get bitten by a bug, but I didn't lose my shit like I did when I was a kid. Honestly, it hurts my feelings a little that my brothers think so little of me as an adult.

Harrison, as promised, has bug spray and has been my human hot water bottle. I might never go back to London at this rate. The fresh air, the peace and quiet, no dramas from my crumbling shelter, no judgemental parents who refuse to give me the rest of my trust fund. The only thing is, I could never leave my animals, so if they could come here, that would be great.

"You ready?" Harrison asks, popping his head in the tent where I'm tying my shoelaces.

"As I'll ever be."

He extends his hand to help me up and when I'm upright, his strong arm wraps around my waist, holding me to him. "You look good enough to eat in those shorts. Maybe going on a walk is a bad idea."

"I'll make sure you work up an appetite then by making you walk behind me the whooooooooole time."

"Such a tease," he grumbles with a smile.

I don't think he understands the meaning of tease. He's wearing a sleeveless t-shirt today *and* a backwards cap. He is the definition of tease.

"Come on, mountain man. Let's go."

I go to walk off and then realise that I have no idea where I'm going. Harrison's smirking face realises that too, as he points in the opposite direction I'm walking.

My feet thud on the dusty, muddy ground as we walk for another 'five minutes' as he keeps saying. He's lying because he told me that ten minutes ago. I'm not complaining though, the views here of the beautiful tall trees, the lush green landscapes, the occasional stream, and oh, wild horses. It's like being in a fairyland and I love it.

Harrison might have been right that this escape from the city is exactly what I need.

"Turn right up here," he says behind me.

I stop to assess the area. It's all woodland and there's no clearing to indicate where I should turn. "Um, where?" I look around again in case I missed something.

"Come." He takes my hand and drags me into the woods, past some giant green bush thingy and wildflowers that I'd kill to pick.

The smell of the mossy grass and the oak trees waft towards me as we walk deeper into the woods, and then all of a sudden, there's a clearing and a stream that stretches around the side of the wooded area. It's completely secluded.

The sunshine glistens on the dark water, and my body tingles with excitement. "Wow, can we go in?" I turn to face Harrison as he strips off his t-shirt and shorts, leaving him in his boxers. "I'll take that as a firm yes," I say, losing my clothes except my underwear, like him.

When he wades into the water without fear, I hesitate. "Wait, what if there are fish?" I worry, leaving my toes touching the water's edge.

Harrison turns around when the water reaches mid-thigh and grins at me. "It's water, sweetheart. Of course there's fish. Probably lots of other creatures, too. All waiting to take a bite out of Zoey Clarke."

"You're not funny," I huff, edging closer. "I'm *very* tasty."

"Oh, I know that already," he says darkly, dipping his head forward into the water. *Holyfuckballs.* The world goes into slow motion, I'm pretty sure *Barry White* is playing somewhere in my head when he flips his head back, and water explodes like a fan over him. Droplets cover his shoulders, chest, stomach as his hands run over his face and into his hair. *Hello there.*

"Damn, my husband is sexy," I groan, braving the water, gasping from the chill as it encases my body all the way up to the top of my hips.

He shakes his hair out and laughs. "Damn, my wife is sexy," he retorts, and when I reach him, I run a finger down his abs, across his chiselled muscles, and bring it to my mouth to suck.

"Mmm," I moan, tasting the saltiness from his skin mixed with the fresh water.

His eyes zone in on my mouth, and they darken to the same colour as the stream, but those flecks of gold that I love to see blaze at me with such heat I could melt. His gaze wanders from my lips to meet my hungry eyes and then he continues to let them drift all over my face, as if he's cataloguing me. I feel exposed by the way he's looking at me. The intensity has disappeared, replaced with an intimacy that I've never experienced firsthand. It's like he's seeing me, all of me, even the parts that are broken that I hide from the world.

"You're perfect, Zoey," he says quietly, his tone laced with a softness that hits me square in my chest. Water drips from the tip of his nose and onto my heaving chest; the chilled droplet sizzles when it hits my heated skin.

I don't want to talk because I like the way he's looking at me, seeing me, and more importantly, not looking away. I run my fingers through his hair, looking up at him as his mouth opens on a moan when my nails scrape his scalp lightly. Then I pull him into a kiss.

His hands grip my hips, squeezing tightly. Our mouths move against each other in sync, lips touching, teasing, and when his tongue meets mine, my body trembles. He plunges it inside my mouth as one hand wanders up my back until it reaches the back of my neck, the other curving at the top of my bum, and even though I'm pressed against him, I'm now glued to him, our bodies mixing sweat and stream water when his hands urge me closer.

My nipples ache for more attention, peaking under my sports bra.

He breaks the kiss and stares at me with something I can't place, and my heart does a little flip. I grip the back of his head and he moves to cup my jaw. "I could kiss you for the rest of my life."

My heart that was flipping, suddenly tightens and I really, truly believes he means that. I'm not sure at what point our arrangement became so complicated, but one thing that seems really simple… I'd let him kiss me forever.

Chapter 39

Harrison

It's a miracle I didn't just fuck Zoey in the stream. There was hardly any clothing between us, and it would've been so easy to slip inside her, but it definitely would've been extreme sports, trying to balance on slippery stream rocks whilst fucking her.

When she went quiet after I said I could kiss her forever, I wasn't sure what to make of her silence, so we ended up having a water fight. I may have worried for a second that she would tell me that can't happen. And I wasn't sure I wanted to hear that.

Our underwear is gone, but we're in our clothes again, walking back to the campsite when I spot an opportunity. And since she decided to torture me by walking in front again, I catch up to her, placing my front to her back.

"Harrison, what are you doing?" The way her head falls back into my chest, I can see her nipples immediately harden under her top. *Fuck, she's beautiful.* She doesn't fight me at all when my hand dips between her legs and I push her back to meet my hard length.

"It was painful watching you walk up here, but now knowing that you aren't wearing underwear." I groan into her neck. "It's fucking with my head in a big way. I need you."

She whimpers softly when I move my hand against her sex. "We're in the woods."

"And?" I say, biting her flesh on her shoulder, and she near collapses, but I move my other hand around her stomach to hold her up.

"And… you're gonna have to work fast because someone might catch us," she replies, jiggling her peachy arse into my crotch.

I grip her hips, holding her still. "Fuck, Zoey. Don't do that," I protest weakly, trying to actively not come in my shorts.

She giggles as she does it again and I push against her clit, making the laughter die on a strained moan. "Fuck, okay. I'll stop teasing."

Looking around the wooded area, I pick a spot. The shading from the tall trees around us should provide us some privacy, but she's not wrong; even though this path isn't on the popular route, it's not like we're invisible.

"Are you going to be quiet for me?"

"Am I ever?" She moans, shamelessly grinding into my hand.

"How badly do you want my fingers right now?"

"So. Fucking. Badly."

I let my hand drift slowly up the seam of her shorts until I reach the waistband. When I don't increase the pace, Zoey shifts on her feet and arches her back towards me.

"Shh, patience," I whisper, letting my hand dip down lower until I reach the top of her sex and I move to the left to stroke her inner thigh.

"Uhhhh, Harrison. I said be quick."

I tap her thigh under her shorts, but it doesn't give me the friction I want to give her on impact. "And I said, have patience. I never agreed to being fast."

"You're such a—"

Her words are cut off when I quickly thrust a finger inside her and, fuck me, she's dripping. I pepper kisses across her shoulder and leisurely move my finger in and out of her, dragging her arousal up to her clit and back inside.

Zoey trembles against me and I laugh into her fiery skin.

"Something funny?" she asks, tilting her head back to see my face.

"You need to trust me. I always give you what you want, don't I?"

Her scowl deepens but quickly dissipates on a moan and a nod. Her eyes flutter closed as I increase the pace, circling her clit as I angle her head to meet mine and capture her mouth in a kiss.

When she pulls away, her jaw is slack. "I need you inside me now."

"I need you to come now," I growl in response.

She shakes her head. "Get inside me. I'll come on your cock and don't even think about getting a condom from your wallet. Ever since you said you wanted to fuck me raw, it's all I can think about. I have an IUD, we've both been tested. You're clean. I'm clean. So, like I said... Get inside me."

Who am I to argue with her?

I remove my hands and lead her towards the tree I spotted earlier. "Put your hands up and stick your arse out. This is going to be fast and hard."

"God, yes," she groans.

I yank down her shorts, enjoying the view of her perky arse jutted out for me. I jiggle it and go weak in the knees when it ripples, and her legs spread wider. "Fucking hell, Zoey. You have the most biteable arse."

"Harrison," she whines and damn if my cock doesn't jump at the sound.

"Tell me again."

Her blue eyes peek over her shoulder. "Fuck me raw, baby."

I take myself out of my shorts, line up to her entrance and take a breath before slapping the bare skin of her arse, loving the redness that immediately flushes there. The sound of my palm against her skin and her soft and breathy gasp echoes in the woods, disturbing a few birds in the trees, but I don't stop. I give her one more slap and soothe the area with my palm. I plunge inside her full force. The feeling of her sweet cunt milking me on impact makes me see stars.

"Jesus," I hiss, blinking to clear my foggy vision. "You feel amazing, Zoey." Every ripple of her creates the most perfection skin on skin friction that I never knew I craved from someone.

She pushes back, obviously needing more from me. I pull out and drive back into her again and again. Sweat runs down my spine as my balls draw upwards.

Zoey's soft whimpers make me want to hold her. So, I pull her until she's flush with my front and wrap my fingers around her neck, letting my other hand travel down to her clit. I circle her sensitive nub a few times and she trembles. "Oh God, Harrison." She moans, her pulse fluttering under my fingers.

"Come for me, sweetheart. Show me what a perfect fucking girl you are."

She screams, and I move my hand to cover her mouth as I push into her over and over, letting her take and ride the high. Every thrust into her tight heat makes my blood hotter. I'm never going to last with the feeling of her wetness coating the sensitive skin of my cock and dripping down my balls.

Her walls clamp around my length as she cries out and the raw, vice like grip around me triggers my own release.

"Ohhhh, fuck yes," I groan as I spill inside her.

My entire body tingles, and when I slowly pull out of her, I bend her towards the tree again. "I want to see my cum drip out of you."

I hear her laugh breathlessly and she wiggles her bum, causing my arousal to dribble out of her pussy and coat her thighs. "Fuuuuuuuck, that's one hell of a sight."

"That was one hell of a fuck," she replies, her voice croaky and sated.

She pulls up her shorts and I tuck myself away. We walk back hand in hand to the campsite, satisfied and smiling.

Forty minutes later and we've both showered the sex and stream off us and are lying inside our tent, just staring at each other.

"So, tell me, Mrs Clarke, do you feel better? This trip was about getting you out of your head so you feel clearer when you talk to your dad on Monday. It was about getting you out of the city and breathing some fresh air too. Is it helping?"

"More than you know." She moves towards me, resting her head on my chest, and sighs contently.

It's afternoon, but that doesn't stop us from falling asleep, and as I drift off, all I can think about is how I'd want to do this again and again with her.

Make her happy. Take her away. Keep her as mine.

Chapter 40

Zoey

The drive back to London is quick, and Harrison's hand hasn't left my leg the entire time. I think I might need a girl's night soon because, for the first time I think I've got feelings—no I know I've got them—and if anyone can relate it's my two best friends, the queens of monogamy, Jess and Nora.

When we walk into his flat, my body relaxes, and that's when I realise, I haven't been back to my place since the day I moved in here. I haven't missed it, haven't even thought about it and we're two months later now. I should probably check in, at least. I grab a post it from the entrance side table, it's the ones with the cute little turtles, and I write: *Check my flat hasn't been ransacked.*

Harrison passes by me, but not before kissing my forehead, making my tummy flutter.

Yeah, I need to text the girls.

"Oh, do you still have my phone?"

He stops and pulls it from his pocket. "I charged it on the way home too."

Ugh, why is he so perfect?

I smile a thank you and he tells me he's going to shower. Something I should definitely do too.

Lifting my phone, I see lots of pictures sent from Lloyd and Sam with the message. *We know you aren't allowed your phone, but here are some pictures for when you're home.* I immediately coo over shots of Mouse eating actual food and not just milk, and my chest swells. This litter was found in a shoebox outside the shelter. A shoebox and now they're eating, thriving and healthy all because of my little shelter.

I flick through the few messages from Nora and Jess, too, and quickly reply with a '*Need a girls' night, stat*'.

Then when I open the wedding do-over group chat, I can't help but bark out a laugh.

> **Cassie**: I think you should wear this dress *sends link to strapless bodice dress*
> **Cassie**: But Alanna and Ophelia think you'd like one that's more like this *sends another link to a big poufy dress*

My nose scrunches at the size of the skirt alone. That one is a veto, for sure.

> **Cassie**: And just so you know, Ellie thinks this one... *sends another link*

When it opens, my mouth drops to the floor. This dress is exactly one I would pick. The flowing skirt and small puddle train, the pale pink colour and the drape of material on the bodice, it's... perfect.

> **Katie**: Girls, will you stop hassling the poor woman. It's bad enough that she has to put up with Uncle Harrison every day.

I laugh to myself. Yeah, because putting up with Harrison means him constantly worshiping my body and giving me countless orgasms. It's such a hardship.

> **Cassie**: Well, I want to know which dress she likes the most, and so do the girls. They told me.

These messages were sent yesterday, so I think I've kept them waiting long enough. I begin to type my reply, knowing that Harrison will also see the message.

> **Me**: They're all good choices, but Ellie's would be the winner.

A minute later, a reply comes in.

> **Cassie**: It's because it's pink, right?
> **Me**: Sure is.
> **Cassie**: Fine, but I get to pick the flowers.

I smile because I don't know how I've got here, with people who care about me so much that they want to plan a wedding for a fake marriage that won't ever last.

That familiar guilt I felt around them last week slams into my stomach again. My eyes burn with regret. Not for marrying Harrison but for not realising the effect it could have on these girls he adores so much. Had I known, I may not have gone through with it.

Maybe we'll just have to stay together, you know, for the kids.

Marching to my father's office isn't as cathartic as I'd like it to be. I'd hoped the walk from the tube station would expel any nervous energy, but if anything, I'm more keyed up than ever as I step in through the familiar spinning doors to his empire.

Approaching the reception desk, I spot Frank, who's been my father's head of security for years. "Hey Frank," I announce, startling him from his crossword book.

"Do my eyes deceive me? Little Zoey Bancroft?" His warm eyes smile at me as he stands to his full six foot height. I remember when I was little, I used to think Frank was a giant and then my brothers had to go and put all that into perspective by both growing to over six foot.

I flash him a genuine smile. "I'm a married woman now, Frank. Mrs Clarke, I'll have you know."

He pretends to stumble backwards, hand on his heart. "I think my heart just broke."

"Oh, don't be so silly." I wave him off. "How is Betty?"

"She's good. Annoying me as usual." Betty and Frank have been married for thirty years and it astounds me that two people can still be so in love after all that time. He jokes about her being a pain, but I've seen them together at parties when I was younger and he worships her.

"Send her my love, won't you?" I ask, and he nods. "Can I get a visitor pass? I've got a meeting with my father."

He clicks away on the keyboard and passes me a credit card sized key to swipe. "Give him hell, Zoey, love."

"I always do, don't I?" I say with a wink.

Walking through the building, my boots stomping on the flooring brings back so many memories of being young and coming here. After school, I'd often have to come and wait with Frank until my dad was ready to leave, especially if my mother was socialising at home. I was not allowed to interrupt that.

When I get to my father's floor, the lift doors open, and I straighten my shoulders and strut to his PA's desk. I don't know this one. I swear he scares them off.

Approaching the petite blonde at her desk, she eyes me as I stop in front of her. "Here to see my father."

She doesn't talk, just picks up the phone and tells him I've arrived.

"You can go right in," she informs me before going back to whatever she was doing.

I approach his door, my hands slightly shaking. *God, why am I nervous about seeing my own dad?* I take a deep breath and clench my unsteady hands.

Pushing the door open, his huge office is sprawled out in front of me. It's mostly an empty room with his desk facing the door, a private bathroom, and a black leather sofa with a drinks table next to it. I memorised this place because I was so rarely allowed in here. I used to marvel every time I got past the door.

"Zoey." My father stands to greet me, buttoning his suit jacket as he rounds his desk to perch on the edge.

His face remains expressionless. A smile would be considered affection from this man, and I'm not entirely sure he's even capable of doing that.

I sit in the chair he gestures to, even though every inch of that bratty little girl inside me wants to pick the other chair. I'll let him have that one.

"I assume you're here to talk about your trust fund. There wasn't an agenda for this meeting."

My face flattens. An agenda? No, this is a daughter coming to her dad because she needs some fucking help, but God forbid I see him without prior knowledge of what I'll say. I clear my throat. "Not entirely." His expression doesn't change, he just waits. "I do need to ask for something though." A bead of sweat runs down my spine. My father always had the approach when we were growing up that if you stay silent, the truth will come out eventually. And it works because I'm a second away from spilling everything, the pressure cracking my chest wide open. "There's a problem at the shelter," I blurt out, my pulse thundering.

"Hmm."

"I need a loan to help fix the building. Apparently, we need new electrics, and we have asbestos." I can't sugarcoat it. If anything, my dad will want the truth, so I'm giving it to him.

"And how much will that be?"

"I think in total I'm looking at a maximum of twenty-five thousand."

He nods. "And your trust fund has been spent on that place? All half a million?"

My throat dries. When he puts it like that, he makes it sound like I've squandered it on pointless things, but I haven't. It's been years of using that money sparingly, along with donations to keep it afloat. I purchased a building, for Christ's sake; I have staff; I have animals that need food, bedding. I want to yell, but I don't. Instead, I force all those negative feelings down.

"Correct."

He sighs deeply. "And how am I meant to give you a loan knowing that I won't get a return on it since your *business* is not for profit?"

My teeth clench at the way he says business. Okay, I may not be making millions like him, but I do okay, usually, when the universe doesn't have me on its shit list, that is. We usually have enough money to throw a ball to raise more money. We usually have more people adopting pets, but the last six months have been tricky because of all the repairs, the new building and how overrun we are with animals. Costs have risen, but donations haven't.

"I suppose you can't. However, I thought you could take it from my trust."

"The remainder that you don't have?"

"If that makes it easier for you."

"Look, Zoey." He runs his hand over his mahogany desk before looking at me. "I can't say that I'm surprised, but I will help you."

I take the backhanded insult on the chin, ignoring the fury bubbling in my chest as I flick my eyes around the room, almost waiting for the hidden camera to pop out and shout, 'Ha – you've been punk'd,' but it doesn't come. *Did my dad just agree to help me? Surely not.*

"Um, thank you," I say, resisting the urge to ask him to repeat the part where he said he'd help me. "I'd really appreciate the help." Relief mixes with confusion in my belly as my father casually writes me a cheque for thirty thousand pounds and passes it to me.

I tentatively take it and stare at the numbers. That was too easy and now my mind buzzes with another thought. *What's the catch?* I can't ask that though. He might take the money back, and I need it too much, besides the fact it's technically mine, as in from my trust fund anyway. So, I say nothing.

"Is that everything?" he asks, breaking my focus on the cheque.

"Why are you helping me?"

He scoffs, standing to walk back to his chair. "Zoey, I'm capable of a kind gesture."

Debatable, my mind screams. Especially as he just basically called me a fuck up but still lent me the money anyway. But still, I find myself standing and getting ready to leave his office with exactly what I came in here to get. And still, I hesitate for a second, disappointment swarming my tight chest. A part of me hoped he would treat me with respect or at least give me a hug. The little girl inside me craves that, but the adult in me knows I'll never get it.

Chapter 41

Harrison

"So, the app is showing there's another bug, but it's linked to the new code, which is easily fixed. I'm confident this time it's a much smaller one and I can resolve it by the end of the day," my employee, David, announces to the rest of the team sitting around the conference table.

We've been having consistent problems with this app since it launched before I went to Vegas. The annoying thing is, there's no obvious reason why it keeps happening or how. We've tried tracing the bugs, but there's never a source. It's one of the few things that keeps me up at night.

"That's great, David. Thank you. If everyone is in agreement, I say we all take a break and grab some coffee." I stand to signal everyone can leave. "Great work, everyone."

Selfishly, I let everyone take a break so I could have a quiet ten minutes in my office. Sitting at my desk, I take a deep breath and relax my head back on my leather chair. Zoey and I have had many a late night lately, and I need to get better at balancing my time with her and sleep. Unfortunately, she makes sleep impossible when we're in bed.

I pick up my phone and send the boy's group chat a text. I've also been bad at socialising, but they know that when work and life get busy for me, I tend to drop in and out. Still, it doesn't stop the guilty feeling when Aaron texts back.

> **Aaron**: He's alive!
>
> **Me**: Yeah, yeah. Things have been busy.
>
> **Aaron**: Excuses, man. We need a boys' night.
>
> **Owen**: Pass.
>
> **Aaron**: Why you gotta play me like that, boo? I thought you and Maxxie would be on my side.
>
> **Max**: No chance.
>
> **Owen**: What he said.
>
> **Aaron**: So, being lame must be a twin thing?
>
> **Nate**: Why are you all blowing up my phone?
>
> **Aaron**: There's my boy. He never lets me down. Nate. Boys' night. You're in, yes?
>
> **Nate**: I think I'm washing my hair.
>
> **Me**: Didn't you get a buzz cut after Vegas?
>
> **Aaron**: I'm hurt. When did you all get so boring?
>
> **Owen**: I've never claimed to be anything else.
>
> **Max**: He's right, we party way less than we did last year. Fuck, are we old now?
>
> **Me**: Thirty-five isn't old, dickhead.
>
> **Aaron**: I'm getting new friends. Ones that want to party with me.
>
> **Nate**: Good luck finding someone to put up with

your arse.

Max: Fuck it. I'm down for beers. Next weekend though.

Aaron: Max, I could kiss you.

Max: Please don't.

Aaron: Anyone else in? Don't be bitches about it.

Me: I'm a maybe, gtg guys. Talk later.

I exit from the group chat, but my phone still pings with notifications from them, so I silence it. It'd be good to see them. We haven't been together since Vegas, which isn't unusual for us because we're all busy working.

I try to turn my focus back to work, and around eleven, I get a text from Zoey.

She sends me a picture of the post-it note I slipped into her bag this morning before she left. She's attached it to her corkboard in her office, and I couldn't stop the smile from widening my lips if I tried.

Zoey: You're the cutest ever. Are you busy today? Can I stop by?
Me: Never too busy for you, sweetheart.
Zoey: Sweet talker. See you around 2 x

Smiling, I open my computer and log in to check on the app, then check in with a client, and before I know it, an hour has passed and my stomach grumbles for lunch.

Someone knocks on my office door, which isn't closed, but when I look up, I see the last person I thought I'd see. Vanessa. Her dark hair is scraped into her usual sleek ponytail, and she's wearing bright red lipstick and a black pencil dress. My mind flashes back to a time at the beginning of our relationship when I'd look forward to seeing her waiting at my office door. But now, I just feel... nothing.

Still, my nostrils flare as I exhale at the fact she's here at all. "Vanessa, how did you get up here?"

She steps forward in her stiletto heels, smugness marring her face. "I still have clearance. You haven't gotten rid of it."

Clenching my jaw, I internally berate myself for forgetting to remove her from the visitors list. "I can rectify that. You should leave."

She steps forward again. "Harrison, I—"

I hold my hand up. "I don't want to hear it, Vanessa. We're over. We've been over for almost a year. I've moved on. I'm married and I'm happy."

"But I'm still in love with you." Her eyes fill with tears. But if there's one thing I remember, it's how easily she could turn the waterworks on.

"That's rich, considering you never were when we were together. Not enough to be faithful," I retort, unable to keep the sharpness from my tone.

Anger flares in her watery eyes. "I made a mistake."

"At least we both agree that's what we were."

This time, *her* nostrils flare. "Harrison, please." She advances towards me and comes to stand next to my chair, resting her red manicured fingers on my shoulder. "Maybe we both made mistakes. But I'm willing—"

"—No." I bark, shrugging her hand off me. "I don't want to hear it."

Vanessa's face contorts as she silently seethes at my rejection of her. "That *wife* of yours has made you a fucking arsehole."

I snap my focus to her, giving her a stern stare. "That wife of mine is none of your fucking business."

"You know," she sneers. "My father has enough connections that he could ruin you and your pathetic little company. All it would take is one phone call from me, and you'd be buried." My pulse picks up briefly because, like Zoey with her shelter, I have built this place with my own sweat and tears. When people threaten my company, it's personal. But then I remind myself that her threats are old and worn. She's desperately trying to cling to something that was never even there.

The laugh that leaves my mouth is bitter. "Vanessa." I pin her with a cold stare, my hands steepling on my chest. "My company makes millions of pounds a year. The last time I checked, your father's company..." I suck in a sharp breath through my teeth. "Wasn't doing so well. So, getting into a big showdown with me probably won't help his bank balance."

Her face reddens. She opens her mouth to say something, but I beat her to it.

"If I were you, Vanessa. I'd leave whilst you still have a sliver of your dignity left," I say, my voice low and commanding. Standing, I walk towards the door and gesture for her to leave.

She reluctantly stomps her feet as she moves, fury marring her features. Pausing in the threshold, she hisses. "Don't come crawling back to me when she divorces you."

I laugh obnoxiously loud, my chest fluttering at the absurdity of her. "Never gonna happen."

"Keep telling yourself that," she snaps as she walks out of my life for good.

"Oh, Vanessa?" She turns to face me from across the office floor. "If you bother me or my wife again, you'll be slapped with a restraining order." I smile, showing all my teeth, when I see her jaw clench. "Have a *great* day."

I sit back in my chair, my hands stretching behind my head. The office is quiet now, with everyone at lunch. I check my watch. It's almost two. *God, it's been a day.*

A wolf whistle echoes from the doorway into my office. "Fancy place you've got here," Zoey says, seductively swaying her hips as she walks towards my desk. When she slips into the chair opposite me, I'm immediately disappointed she didn't pick my lap as her seat.

"How was seeing your dad?" I ask, blatantly checking out my wife.

"Weird." She leans forward, crossing her legs and leaning her elbow on her knee, surveying the items on my desk. "He gave me the money for the shelter. Took it out of my trust fund."

My head tilts. "That's... good?"

"I don't know. I've never had to ask him for help before, so I have no idea if it's good or bad. But I guess we'll find out soon enough. How's your day been?"

"Vanessa came by." I smile, victorious.

"And I missed it?" She looks genuinely disappointed, but then narrows her eyes. "Why are you smiling?"

"She's gone. For good." I say it with finality because I know she wouldn't dare come after me again. I've never threatened her with legal action before, but I'm done with her, with all this.

"Ah, so you're smiling because you called security to drag her filthy self out of here?"

My smile widens. "I threatened her with a restraining order from both of us. Well, technically, she threatened me first, and then I had the final say."

Zoey beams. "Is it weird that you being a sexy boss-man turns me on just as much as you being a sexy mountain man?"

My eyes grow heavy with desire as I slowly drag my finger over my lower lip, watching her. The air crackles between us. The distance feels too much, too wide. I need to touch her. And judging by the way she's licking her lips lazily, I think she needs me too.

"Get over here," I demand huskily.

She stands without hesitation and walks slowly around my desk, dragging her delicate fingers over the wood as she moves, her eyes never leaving mine. When she reaches me, our knees knock, and electricity sparks my desire to life even more.

God, I'll never get enough of her.

"Hi, husband," she purrs, the raspy sound of her voice going straight to my cock.

"Hi, wife," I reply, quirking my eyebrow.

She leans down, placing both hands on the arms of my chair, giving me a perfect view of her cleavage as her top falls forward. Her scent, sweet and summery, surrounds me and pleasure shoots up my spine when she whispers, "Kiss me."

I do without hesitation. My hands haul her petite body onto my lap, where she settles on my already rock hard cock. Her tongue in my mouth and her pussy grinding on me is exactly what I'm wanting. I kiss her like a starved animal, and she kisses me right back. Her hands thread into my hair, and she drags her nails over my shoulders as we fuck each other's mouths.

The sound of chatter begins to filter into the air around us, and my consciousness snaps back. I'm at work. I'm the boss. I can't fuck my wife for the whole of my company to see. I break the kiss, relishing the needy, lust-filled look in her beautiful blue eyes. Kissing her quickly once more, I rub my nose against hers and lean into her ear. "When we get home, I'm going to fuck you with my tongue, and you're going to come on my face and my fingers. Then, when you ride my cock, I'm going to make you fall apart all over again until you're screaming my name, and your cunt is dripping with my cum."

The breathy moan and her hands tightening in my hair send a jolt of white-hot heat straight to my balls. I move my lips to her neck, and she grips my hair even tighter, yanking my head back to meet her eyes. "If you kiss my neck right now, Harrison, I will not be responsible for what happens next."

I smirk. The desire inside me pulsing like a living, breathing entity. *Fuck, do I want to push her limits so badly.* But I have no doubt that she'd have my zip down and my cock out and inside her within a matter of seconds. Audience be damned.

The chatter around us gets louder, telling me my team are closer now, probably coming back from lunch and going back to work, and any moment, they'll see Zoey on my lap, but fuck, if her words don't make me want her more. "Patience, sweetheart," I murmur, kissing her once more before tapping her legs, signalling for her to stand.

"I don't like you right now."

"I'll make sure my tongue apologises to you later when you're sitting on my face." I wink, and she blushes.

Unable to hold in her smile, the side of her mouth twitches. "Fine. Fuck you later, husband."

Chapter 42

Zoey

"You need to tell me everything," Nora demands from next to me whilst we wait for Jess at the trendy little bistro for brunch.

I bite the inside of my mouth, cursing myself for telling her I'm having lots of feelings towards Harrison. "I like him," I admit, shrugging, trying to play it cool when, in reality, I've got a constant swarm of butterflies in my belly.

Nora slaps my arm. "There's more and you don't want to say."

I look at her stern brown eyes and deflate, knowing I won't win this game of avoidance with her. "Fine, I'm feeling... *things*. Things I've not really ever felt with anyone before."

She softens and her hand covers her chest. "Is my girl in love?"

I close my eyes and scrunch my face up. "Eww, don't even say that." Opening my eyes, I see pride shining in Nora's eyes and I chuckle. "But let me tell you, there might be a million words in the English language, but for some inconceivable reason, I can't find any that describe how he makes me feel."

"Oh my God, I'm going to cry." Nora fans her face, her eyes actually welling up.

"God, please don't. Not in public."

She smiles, but her watery eyes don't go away immediately. "I'm not going to put words in your mouth, but I think you love him."

I roll my eyes but deep down this feeling, like I'm somehow homesick when I'm not with him, tells me that I'm kinda, maybe, sorta, in love with my fake husband, which wasn't ever part of the plan.

And you know when I realised it? When he slipped a post-it note with a cute little puppy in the corner in my handbag yesterday that said, 'Stay pawsitive, sweetheart.' My first thought was, 'Fuck, I love him.' And when I saw him at his office later that day, my chest nearly exploded.

Jess arrives and thankfully we talk more about work. When the waiter pops by, we order food and more drinks too. This was meant to be a quick brunch, but I think we've all missed each other, so fuck it. We're in no rush.

"How are the renovations going?" Jess and Liam are in the middle of renovating a new hotel in Kent together, so they're splitting their time between here and the coast.

"Stressful, but they're going. We've had to pause the extension for now and focus on getting the building modernised. The heating was using oil, so that's been a massive pain to change to central heating. But it'll be fine."

"It'll be so worth it. The location of that place alone is going to sell it for you."

Our food arrives, and we eat in comfortable silence for a while.

"Did you get the asbestos fixed at the shelter?" Nora asks.

I nod, swallowing my mouthful. "The work is being done now. I went there this morning to give the guys the keys. Lloyd and Sam are splitting their time between the animals and the shelter, which helps. Electrics are being sorted next week, too."

I hadn't realised how much of a weight it had been on me lately. But knowing that things are finally getting on track, I feel like I can breathe again. Even if I do still have that niggly feeling that my father put there the last time I saw him. I try to tell myself that I got what I needed and I should stop worrying about him, but something won't let me.

An hour later, we're all saying our goodbyes. Nora is headed home, and Jess is going back to the coast for the night. Me? I'm going home to find my husband. But when I walk in the door of the flat, I quickly realise that he isn't home. I slump and sulk for a second because I miss him, and I only saw him this morning. *Am I pathetic? Eh, I don't care if I am.*

I put my keys in the pot by the door. Take off my shoes when I hear my phone ring in my bag. My hands frantically search for it, hoping it'll be my husband, but when I see the caller ID, I frown. *Why is one of my charity trustee board members calling me? They never call me.*

"Hello?"

"Zoey, it's Lance Milton."

I blink, trying to work out when the last time I spoke to Lance was. Probably last year. "Hi Lance, how are you?"

"I'm good. Listen, I got the proposal and I love it. I think making the shelter into a profitable business is a great step forward. I just wanted to call you and say we're on board with the idea."

Adrenaline shoots through my veins as his words buzz in my head. *Profitable business.* What is he talking about?

Shaking my head, I say, "I'm sorry, Lance, I'm confused…"

"You sent an email today with a proposal to turn the charity into a business instead."

My chest tightens. *Shit, where's all the air gone?* "Lance—"

"—We think it'll be great. Me and Maggie are on board with the idea."

What. The. Fuck. Is. Happening?

Nausea rolls in the pit of my stomach as I try to think about who would've sent an email and I only have one answer: *My dad.*

"Lance, I'm going to call you back."

I don't give him a chance to answer before I hang up and immediately blink away the blurriness in my eyes and pull up my emails.

I see it immediately, my eyes drawn to it like a moth to a flame. An email from my father with a full business proposal stating he recently invested in the charity. Disdain coats my tastebuds as I scoff a noise to myself.

He even goes on to say that he is my father, and this will be a family business.

Family business.

Family fucking business.

I'm not sure at what point I sunk to the floor, but I'm here, slumped in a pile. The pounding in my ears is the only thing I hear as rage courses through my blood at warp speed.

"That fucking conniving, motherfucking arsehole!" I scream loudly and abrasively. Letting all the years of their fuckery out of my system. Well, at least that's what I thought. It turns out my body and brain have their own ideas.

Propelling myself from the floor, I grab my keys again and race out the door with only one destination in mind.

I don't remember the journey here. I flagged a taxi, and everything is a blur until right now as I'm standing in front of my parents' obnoxious, stupid fucking door with four stupid fucking knockers.

My vision tunnels at their display of wealth and superiority, and my rage floats right back to the surface again, heating my skin and making my pulse roar. "Fuck this," I hiss as I push the door open, flying inside. *Hurricane Zoey is in the fucking house.*

I'm met with silence, and *God,* I should've checked to see if they were even home. I didn't even think before I flew out of the house. I quickly realise it's also Seren's day off. Now I'm here, it all feels incredibly anticlimactic if I have to traipse back to London and I don't think I'll hold on to all this rage.

I'm about to turn around when I hear laughter coming from my father's office down the hall. Fury echoes off the walls with the force my feet are stomping on the marble flooring. When I get closer, I realise the voices I can hear are my father and brothers.

Brilliant. Just what I needed. To have a breakdown in front of everyone.

I don't knock because he doesn't deserve the courtesy of that. So, when I fling the heavy wooden door open, all three Bancroft men turn to face me with wide eyes.

Max immediately stands, a pinch forming between his eyebrows. Whilst Owen and Dad stay seated on opposite sides of my father's desk. "Zoey, what are you doing here?" he asks as Owen says, "Woah, where's the fire, Tink?"

My eyes ping pong between him and my dad, and when my father's lips lilt ever so slightly at the sides, I almost hurl my five-foot-three self over his desk and throttle him. "Why don't you ask *him*?" I nod my head towards our father, seething.

Max turns to face him. "Dad? What's going on?"

Owen turns his head expectantly too. But my father stays silent, slipping his mask of indifference and disregard that he always wears for me. Never mind that minutes ago he was chatting and *laughing* with my brothers—No, he could never show me any sort of respect or emotion.

"Fine. If he won't explain, maybe I can elaborate," I hiss, taking one more step into the room. "I got a call this morning from one of my trustee board members for Paw Prints. They told me how they *love* the idea of my business proposal." I pause, waiting to see if my father will show any kind of remorse but when he doesn't react, I want to scream again. My eyebrows raise in question. "Well? Do you have anything you'd like to add, *Dad?*"

He pins me with a look that's not new to me but is full of disappointment and I bristle further. "I made an executive decision based on the fact that you are struggling at the shelter. If you're looking for an apology—"

"An apology?" I shriek, interrupting him. My throat dries with the force of the air, leaving my lungs so rapidly. "I don't want a fucking apology. I want a parade or a carnival of you telling me how wrong this is. Because you do see that, right?"

"Hold on, what's happened?" Max interjects, holding his hands out to placate the conversation, but nothing can tame the fury bubbling in my chest. "Zoey, you're clearly upset. But I need to know what's gone on."

My father sighs again, as though I'm keeping him from a game of golf with his buddies and not trying to understand why he's making moves on *my business* without my consent. "I made a business proposal to the board of Zoey's charity, suggesting that the charity be turned into a profitable business, and it would be a family run centre," he explains with absolutely no emotion in his voice.

"Fuck, Dad." Owen groans, shaking his head where he shits in his chair. "Even I know not to fuck with Zoey's shelter."

"I'm not *fucking* with it, Owen, I'm—"

"—You absolutely *are* fucking with it. You have no right to try and sabotage me like that. You have an issue with me? That's fine, but how fucking dare you come after something I've spent my whole adult life building and fighting for." Tears burn my eyes but I force them back because there's no way I'm going to let him see me cry right now. The sadistic bastard would probably laugh. And then I really would kill him. "You couldn't just let me have this, could you?"

"I invested in your charity, Zoey. *You* came to *me* for help this week, remember?" His voice is laced with venom as it booms across the space between us.

"Of course, I fucking remember," I howl. "I told you to take it out of my trust fund. Which, by the way, you *still* haven't given me, despite me agreeing to all of your ridiculously outdated notions of eligibility."

I see the fury build in his eyes. "That's because I know you're both lying to me," he shouts, slamming his fist into his desk as he stands.

I barely flinch from his outburst. This isn't my first rodeo with him. But what does make me see red is the fact that he's right, we are lying to him. But nothing about Harrison and I feel like a lie anymore. It might've started out that way, but he's wormed his way into my heart, and as much as it didn't mean to happen, it has. But I shouldn't have brought it up because this is about something else.

"No, this isn't about him and me. This is about what you did behind my back," I fume through gritted teeth.

"I wouldn't have had to resort to such measures if you were capable of running that place, Zoey, and fixing your own issues. And now, you've managed to bring your brothers' best friend into it too. In true Zoey fashion, you really have made a big mess. I simply put the proposal in the hands of the right people who would choose *me* to fix your money problems."

"But I don't want you to fix my problems!" I roar, arms sweeping around in front of me.

"It didn't seem that way when you came to my office. You asked me for money."

I march forward, meeting his desk and slam my finger into the wood. "Okay, you're right. I asked my father to help me because I thought that *maybe, fucking maybe,* he'd help his one and only daughter. But you couldn't even get through the meeting without a shitty comment about being disappointed in me, and now this?" I retort, swallowing the bitterness.

My chest heaves as I stare at my father's empty blue eyes. The disdain he's holding for me like flame for his own entitled arseholery (yes, that is a word) is never going to change. The weight of our failed relationship permeates the air like a bad smell. I hate it. I hate the disapproval. I'm so fucking tired of feeling like I'll never be the perfect daughter for them. The fight and fury leaves my body with a rough exhale as I mutter, "I'm so fucking done."

Max shifts on his feet. "Zo," he says, with pain lacing his voice. I ignore him.

All the previously muttered digs, disappointment, and failed attempts at reconciliation wash over me as my gaze flicks around the room. An avalanche of bitter memories in this house threatens to bury me alive. I can taste the resentment of my very existence here, and I hate it. "I'm so fucking done," I repeat in a whisper.

"Excuse me?" my father asks incredulously.

"You heard me. I'm done with you. With letting you think you can treat me like I mean less than anyone else. I hated fitting into your perfect daughter role, so I gave that up, but what I did after that is so much worse." Emotion clogs my throat, but I swallow it down. I need him to hear me because this is the last thing I'll ever say to him.

"I made myself smaller for you. I made myself less, and no one deserves that. It kills you that I want to help others. Those animals in that shelter have no one. I am their person, but you wouldn't understand that," I sneer, stepping backwards. "And you can't understand that I want to be loved for who I am, not what my bank balance is. Fuck, I deserve to be loved like that. I don't care if you know that Harrison and I had a business deal. I don't care if you set your lawyers on me to get your money back because the truth is, I've got something in my life that makes me feel like I'm important." My chest heaves, my heart heavy in my chest. "I'll never be enough for you. I'll never get it right, and I am done trying."

I pause, looking at my brother's sending them a silent apology that I've lied to them with their best friend. "Harrison and I might've started as a deal, but he has chosen me every goddamn day since we began this." I turn back to my father. "And that is something you've never done."

The first tear falls from my eye. This is the first time in my adult life that I've cried in front of him, and as I stare at his stoic face, unchanging and completely detached, I know I've done the right thing. Max stands, opening his mouth, "Don't. Please, just don't," I plead, not wanting to hear what he has to say right now.

Rushing out of his office, I find my mother sitting on the chair in the hallway, legs crossed, hands planted on her knees, as though she's waiting for a train to come. There's no way she didn't hear my outburst and yet, when her eyes flick to mine, she looks... pissed. The little girl inside me is screaming, causing my heart to beat wildly in its cage because this person, my mother, has never been maternal a day in her life. So, why am I hoping that today is the day she opens her arms and I run into them? Why do I keep holding on for something neither of them will give?

The final piece of my childhood crashes to the floor with a splintering smash. I can't do this anymore. I can't pretend to be fine when nothing about this is fine.

If they can't accept who I am, then they don't deserve to be a part of my future.

I turn on my heels and walk out the door. Not even looking back.

Chapter 43

Harrison

My phone rings through the speakers in my car as I drive home. I'm about to answer when I'm interrupted as soon as the call connects.

"Harrison?" Max's urgent voice makes the hair on my arms stand on end.

"Max? What's wrong?"

"Is Zoey with you?" he rushes out.

"No, she was with friends for lunch, but I haven't heard from her since around three, maybe." I check the time on my car dash and the red glowing numbers tell me it's almost seven. My pulse thrashes wildly in my neck at whatever he isn't telling me. "Max, what's going on? Where's Zoey?"

He exhales, the sound choppy down the phone. "She and dad got into a massive row and..."

His pause makes my temper snap. "Max," I shout.

"I-I don't know where she is. She isn't picking up her phone. She's not at her flat."

My right foot presses heavier on the accelerator and my car takes off ten miles an hour faster. "I'm two minutes from home. I'll let you know if she's there." She's probably wrapped up in my bed eating ice cream, or at least that's what I'm praying I'll find at home.

I hang up, my knuckles white as I grip the steering wheel and focus on driving, ignoring my rapidly increasing heart rate. Flying in to park my car, I rush out to the lift, not feeling the cooler air of the underground carpark trying to bite at my skin. What the fuck happened between lunch and now? *What if she's done lying about what we are?* I could lose her. I could lose everything.

Anxiety trickles down my throat like razor blades as I swallow and push my thoughts away. My first priority has to be finding her.

When I finally get upstairs, I tear through each room, only to find every one empty. "Fuck," I curse, running my hand through my hair.

I try her phone again but it goes straight to voicemail. A line of sweat dribbles down my spine. "Where the fuck are you, Zoey?" I mutter to myself.

I text Max to tell him she isn't here, but I'm going to keep looking for her.

I pace the kitchen as useless thoughts swirl around my brain until one sticks, and I call the one person who might know where she is.

"Hey, man." Grayson's voice comes onto the line.

"Hey, is Nora there?"

"Uhh, yeah." He hesitates. "Why?"

"I can't find Zoey and—" I hear a rustle indicating the phone has been dropped or...

"You can't find her? What do you mean?"

"Max called me after she had a big fight with her dad and now we don't know where she is."

"Shit." Nora echoes my earlier frustrations. "Maybe she went to a bar?"

"She didn't tell me she had a favourite bar, though. Does she?" I ask, but don't wait for an answer. "It could take too long to find her."

"Where would she go after a fallout with her dad?" Nora mumbles to herself, and as I listen to her, a switch flips in my head, I know exactly where she's gone.

"Nora, I'll let you know when I find her." I hang up and make my way back down to my car.

When I pull up at the shelter, the place is dark, the only light is the distant street lamps. If she isn't here, I have no idea where she would be. I tense to keep the hope inside me flickering as I open the car door and sprint towards the building.

And that's when I see her. A tiny figure slumped against the front porch, holding a bottle, glistening in the light from the moon.

I quickly pull out my phone and text Nora and Max to tell them I've got her.

As I get closer, her red rimmed eyes meet mine, and she dips her head back into her propped up knees. My heart drops to the floor with a splat. "Zoey, sweetheart," I say softly.

The need to comfort her overwhelms me as I sink down next to her and scoop her into my lap. Her sobs harrow through my soul as she leans into my chest, and I want nothing more than to absorb her pain. "Sssh, I've got you. You're okay," I whisper into her hair, holding her against me.

"He took it, Harrison. He's f-f-fucking it all up," she sobs. The defeat in her voice damn near shreds me apart because this isn't my Zoey; she's strong and resilient.

"Sweetheart, tell me what happened," I beg, needing to soothe her. She doesn't respond straight away, sobbing and babbling into my chest. The vice grip she has on the tequila bottle doesn't let me see how much she's had to drink, but I can't smell that much on her, so I'm wondering how drunk she actually is. If at all.

Minutes pass as I hold her. Letting her break in my arms.

When she quietens and stills, I briefly wonder if she's fallen asleep on me, but then her blonde head lifts. Her usually bright blue eyes have lost the sparkle that I love. Her cheeks are wet with her tears. I lean toward her without thinking and kiss the tracks on her face. The salty taste coats my lips, but I don't stop. I want to make her feel like she isn't alone. I feel her body sigh against mine as her heart rate evens slightly against my chest.

"I'm not going to ask if you're okay, but is there anything I can do to help?" I murmur, stroking her hair.

She takes a long, deep breath. "He sent a business proposal over my head, straight to the board of trustees, Harrison. He's trying to take it from me."

"Your dad?"

She nods.

"There's no way in hell I'll let him take this place from you, sweetheart."

"I emailed the board telling them that my father and I are no longer in contact, and the proposal wasn't approved by me."

"And how did they respond?" I ask, shoving down my anger for her father.

She sniffles and shudders against me, so I wrap my arms around her more to keep her warm. "Lance called me straight away to say he understood and if I wanted to change my mind, he has contacts, but I haven't heard anything from Maggie, although I'm guessing she's on Team Lance."

"That's good news," I say, but as I feel the deflate in her chest, my own heart breaks wide open for her.

The sounds of the quiet night drift around us; the buzz from the motorway, the rustling of the trees, the beating of our hearts.

"How have I made such a mess?" she says quietly. I'm not sure if she wants an answer to that question, but I refuse to let her feel like this is all on her.

I soothe her by moving my hand to the tip of her shoulder and rub my fingertips in circles over her jumper. "This isn't your fault."

"This *is* my fault. He said I dragged you into my mess and he's right. I mean, look at me. I'm the definition of a mess."

"Zoey, don't—"

"No, Harrison. Please don't be nice to me. I don't deserve it. You wouldn't have chosen me if it weren't for circumstances. Our arrangement was a lie and now everything is so fucked, I..." She buries her head in her hands on another howl that pierces the silent night.

Emotions pool in my gut and I can't pinpoint one that sticks before it shifts to another. She does deserve to be treated right and everything she's feeling now is because of her parents' poor treatment of her. The one emotion that sticks in my throat is rage for her parents. "Fuck the arrangement and fuck your father too. If he can't see how amazing you are, then it's his loss," I rush out, unable to tame the sneer in my tone when I mention her dad.

She pauses, raising her head slightly. "I-I'll never be enough for him," she whispers into the sleeve of her jumper, covering her mouth.

The fury that was stuck in my throat dies a death when I see the pure destruction on her face from her admission. Everything in me screams to comfort her, so I do.

"You're enough for me."

I hold her tighter, needing the material of her jumper in my palms because if I can be the one thing she needs in this moment, then I'll do it. I'd give her the world if she asked me. This strong woman deserves so much more than being treated second best. She deserves everything and I want to help her get that. I don't need to be her purpose, but I want to help her find it again because seeing her so defeated like this is destroying me as much as it is her.

My lips meet her forehead as I take a deep breath against her soft skin.

"Zoey, I'm so sorry that someone has made you feel like you aren't worth all the love you deserve. But sweetheart, let me tell you," I say, lifting her chin so our eyes meet. "Not all of us want to hurt you. Some of us just want to love you."

Chapter 44

Zoey

And in the middle of it all, he stood with me, unwavering.

Choosing me.

His love roared louder than my chaos.

Chapter 45

Zoey

It's been a week. One week of moping, one week of eating ice cream, like it's my main food group.

Harrison tried to take me to see the animals a couple of days ago to cheer me up, but I couldn't. Not yet. I will, but for now, I know they're safe and being looked after, so I need to take a minute. Or a week, it seems.

Unsurprisingly, I haven't heard a thing from my parents. Either of them.

I'm not sure what I expected, but the silence tells me I've done the right thing. They'll never be a part of my life again. Even admitting that to myself hurts. It feels like a million tiny knife wounds against my heart because aren't they the ones who should love me unconditionally? It shouldn't matter if I was the 'surprise baby', I should've never been treated differently to my brothers and I see that now. Letting go has been harder than I thought it would be but I'm processing slowly.

Hence the wallowing. I've binged every TV show and movie ever made, my favourite being *Red, White and Royal Blue,* and if I don't move soon, I'm going to become delusional and start thinking that I'm the Kings' son and I'm in love with the president's son. My Instagram is full of fan made reels of Alex and Prince Henry and it makes me cry every time I see the clips. Why couldn't I be a fictional gay man in another life? *Fuck, maybe I'm already losing it. I need to get out of this bed.*

My brothers have been blowing up my phone. Nora and Jess came over and force fed me a salad two days ago, but I've ruined their hard work with more ice cream. A lot more. In fact, I might never eat it again after today.

Aside from encouraging me to shower, eat and drink water, Harrison has mostly just sat with me and held me. He's even worked from home all week. He's been here for me and listened to me when I've been ready to talk, but also been silent with me and never once expected me to do anything other than just *be.*

Wallowing is good for the soul, especially when you shun your parents, lose your trust fund and realise that even with the renovations paid for, running that shelter isn't a long-term thing I can do without that money. To be honest, I've probably grieved that more than my parents. I need a plan to make sure I don't lose that place, which is why today is the day I'm done with wallowing. I'm making a plan, I'm talking fundraisers, organising family days.

Today, I'm *alive.*

I'm showered, which is a blessing, believe me. My week old hair was not the one. But now, it's sleek clean, and so am I. Determination fuels my steps as I walk out of the room I've been holed up in and step out into the fresher parts of the house.

"Harrison?" I call, scanning the hallway, waiting for him to respond.

"In the kitchen," he replies. I pad my bare feet to the place where he is and when I see him bare chested, sun glowing behind him as he chops strawberries, my chest fills with a warmth that only he gives me.

When he looks up, his expression falters. "Wow," he breathes, heat sparking in his big brown eyes.

I brush my fingers through the tips of my hair. "I know. I'm unrecognisable and clean. Come here and smell me. I no longer smell like despair and sorrow," I say, trying to hide the pain in my voice, but when he rounds the corner and pulls me into his strong arms, lifting me from the floor with such ease, my throat burns with that release that comes from crying your eyes out. *Damn it, I've done enough crying.*

"You always look beautiful, sweetheart. But you do smell incredible." He groans into my neck and squeezes me tighter. "A lot less like stale ice cream now, more like you," he says, inhaling deeply again. Something awakens in me that's been dead all week, a tingling, an awareness of him and how fucking much I want him.

My hands flex around his broad shoulders as I cling to him, and he gently sets me on my feet. When our eyes lock, we are mirrors of need, staring deeply at each other with unspoken words. *I want you. I need you. I love you.*

I can't be sure, but the night he found me outside the shelter, I think he mentioned something about love, but I didn't want to assume that he meant he loved me. But I felt it in the way he soothed me, in the way he pressed his lips against my tear-streaked face, and the way he looked at me like he would never leave me.

Longing pangs in my gut as I realise we need to have a conversation about everything. Now that neither of our original reasons for marrying are valid, things can change. He can leave if he wants, he doesn't have to be tied to me anymore.

But as I stare at this man in front of me. So strong, in body and soul, I struggle to think of *my* future without him.

His fingers stroke my hair as he stares softly into my eyes. "What's going on in that beautiful brain of yours?"

"I was thinking about us."

"Yeah?" I'm rewarded with my favourite beaming smile of his.

"And the shelter."

"You know, the work is almost done. Sam has been keeping me updated."

"I know," I say, mindlessly stroking his arm. "I need to make some plans to get donations and adjust the business model since I won't be getting my trust fund."

"I can help," he says without hesitation.

"Thank you," I reply, meaning it more deeply than a superficial 'thanks' because I really do owe him a lot.

His grateful smile is all I need as a response. "So, do we need to go to the shelter today? We can see Mouse and Jelly."

"Eventually, but first..." I pull him towards my lips with haste and kiss him.

His body melts into mine, and I feel his exhale against me as our mouths move slowly, tasting and softly re-exploring after almost a week of not kissing. And kissing Harrison Clarke is one of my favourite things to do.

When we stop, my hand strokes in his hair as I stare at him, and he stares back. Suspended in a moment where nothing exists but the two of us.

"I made you pancakes," he says softly.

"With strawberries?" I question, letting him go.

He winks, sending a jolt of need through my body again. "And Magic Stars."

My head flings back with a pleasure filled groan. "God, I love you."

Time stops as we both stand stock still.

Zoey, what just slipped out of your mouth? My mind asks itself.

No, that didn't slip out. It was a thought, right? Yeah, right, tell the awkward silence that.

Ohhhh balls. Right, time for some damage control.

"I-I-uh, I meant, I love Magic Stars and pancakes. They're great. And those juicy, juicy strawberries. Yum, they're really tasty too."

Oh good, I've made it worse.

Harrison turns to face me, amusement tilting the sides of his mouth as he watches me spiral into an oblivion of useless words that don't make sense anymore but want to escape my mouth in another incoherent babble.

He crosses his arms over his chest, popping those slutty veins for me, and uses one hand to stroke the scruff of his beard, which he's trimmed, and I like it shorter.

"So, is it the pancakes, the chocolate, the strawberries... or me that you love?"

My hands ache at the need to flap around and make more of an idiot of myself, but I manage to restrain them by clasping them together in front of me. I look down to my entwined fingers and then back up to Harrison. "All of the above?"

He nods thoughtfully and takes measured, slow steps towards me again.

When he reaches me, I'm panting. A rawness fills my veins that screams, 'Please love me too'. He uses his fingers to hold my chin and make sure I'm looking at him, but I'm not sure how I could look at anything else when he's in the room.

"For the record, I loved you first."

He swoops in, claiming my mouth and my heart, all with one pressing kiss that ends too soon.

"You love me, even if none of this has been conventional?" I ask, my voice full of trepidation.

"Being conventional is overrated." He kisses my nose. "I know we need to talk this out, but there's no way I'm letting you go. You and your post-it notes, your madness for eating Magic Stars in a certain way, your love for that shelter and your big heart. Let me keep you, sweetheart because I want to stay your husband for real and forever."

Joy springs around inside me like a little lamb.

"You're sure?"

He doesn't answer. Instead, he claims my mouth again. It's the kind of kiss that makes me want to stand on my tiptoes and flick a leg up, like in the movies.

And when he breaks away and wraps me in his arms, my head resting on his chest as the steady thumping of his heart immediately syncs with mine, I have this overwhelming feeling like I'm home. As he runs his hand up and down my back, I feel like he's mine and I'm exactly where I'm supposed to be.

Chapter 46

Harrison – Three months later

"Ophelia, bubs, what's wrong?" My niece buries her little head into my arm as she grips onto my hand. I crouch down to scoop her up into my arms.

"I wanted to walk down the aisle with you, Uncle Harrison," she sniffles, and my willpower trembles like my heart in my chest.

My sister pats her back and shakes her head. "Oh, Ophelia. The men don't walk down the aisle, it's just the women."

Her head snaps up, the tears and whimpers immediately stopping. "So, I can walk down with Auntie Zoey?"

"You can walk in front of her. How does that sound?" She smiles, her tears forgotten. "Why don't you go check on her for me?" I suggest setting her on her feet. As soon as her toes touch the ground, she bolts in the direction of my wife's suite across the hallway.

"Cass, will you go with her? Make sure she gets to the right room?" Katie adds.

Sweat trickles down my spine from the heat and humidity that is typical in Thailand. My linen suit should keep me cool, but I can't seem to keep it together. I blow out a breath, feeling the buzz of nerves dance in my body.

"You good?" Katie asks.

"I'm nervous."

She smirks. "The good news? You're already married, so technically, this is the easy part." She nudges me with her elbow, and I grunt a laugh.

"You're right. It just…"

"I get it. This feels real."

"Yeah, it does."

She shakes her head, smiling. "I'm still mad at you for lying to me about the first wedding."

"You can never stay mad at me, little sis." Katie wasn't the only one who was mad for a little while. Max had a lot to say about how we lied to him, but we gave him a couple of weeks to calm down and things are better now. He can see that even though it started out in the most nontraditional way, I love his sister with everything I have and not even a grumpy Max could scare me away. Owen, however? The dude is so relaxed he's horizontal half the time that he shrugged and told us to be happy.

"No, I suppose I can't." She seems to consider her next words with a frown. "You certainly make it harder to hold on to a grudge when you fly everyone out here for Christmas break based on a group chat your nieces made."

I scoff at the fact she thinks I had any other choice with those girls. "You say that like I had a choice. They begged me for months about a 'wedding do-over'." I laugh and she joins me.

"True. Still, Thailand on Christmas Eve-eve? Extravagant."

I shrug. It might be extravagant but when Zoey told my family, all those months ago, that her perfect wedding would be on a beach, and no one would be wearing shoes, that stuck in my brain, and as soon as the group chat was made that night, I knew then I'd do anything to make her happy.

So, here we are, getting married—or technically, it's a blessing since we're already married. My family, her brothers and friends. All barefoot.

"There's my boy." My dad's voice filters into the space. He's wearing a navy linen shirt and beige linen trousers.

"Hi, Dad," I reply as he wraps his arms around me.

Zoey met my dad officially the week after I told her I loved her, and the pair of them have been in cahoots ever since. I knew they'd love each other. They're both full of mischief and are always planning things. I think my dad and my sister even call Zoey more than me now, which I guess is fine if I'm still my niece's favourite. Although it wouldn't surprise me if Zoey snagged that top spot, too. She's so damn loveable.

"I've just seen your girl. She looks magnificent, Harrison." He pats my cheek. "You both look so happy, and that's all I ever want for my kids." I watch his eyes fill as he fights back tears. "If only your mum could see you today. She'd be so proud."

"Oh, Dad, don't cry," I say, pulling him back for another hug.

"These are happy tears. I'm allowed to cry happy tears. I just miss her."

"I know. We all do," Katie adds, joining our hug.

"Knock knock." Grayson's voice comes in through the doorway as he greets Katie and my dad. We all had dinner together last night, so formalities aren't needed today.

"Hi, Mr Clarke. Everyone okay in here?" he asks.

"Everyone is great," Dad replies, smiling at me. "We'll see you out there, son."

Once Grayson and I are alone, I get the biggest whoosh of déjà vu. "Wait, woah. We've been here before, right?" he says, smirking.

"Except this time, there's no tie."

"Hmm, how are you going to have a crisis if you aren't fidgeting with your tie? I can't fulfil my duties as best man if you won't let me fix something this morning."

"I'm hoping nothing needs fixing and this runs smoothly."

Grayson groans. "Why did you just tempt fate like that?"

"Nothing is going to happen. It's going to be fine," I tell him confidently. "We've got ten minutes until the ceremony and nothing, I mean nothing, is going to ruin today."

He pins me with a look that says, 'You better hope you're right'. "You know, I was thinking," he says, crossing his arms over his chest.

"Sounds dangerous."

"Ha-fucking-ha. But still, I was thinking. Letting me be your best man, twice, and over Max, might I add, almost makes up for not inviting me to Vegas."

I chortle. "Oh, please, Vegas wasn't my idea anyway. If you're still pissed, take it up with the twins."

He scoffs, but I don't tell him that the reason Max isn't my best man right now is because he's walking Zoey down this aisle with Owen. Her parents still haven't reached out and I think there's even rumblings between the whole Bancroft clan since the fallout, but Zoey and I have kept out of it so far.

"Speaking of being a best man, when am I going to be yours?"

He pales and his Adam's apple moves like he's swallowing bricks. "Dude, don't make me sweat. I'm doing enough of that in this heat without your input on my love life."

I leave it because I know he adores Nora, and everyone moves at their own pace, except Zoey and I, who dove in head first and did it all backwards.

"Today is about you." He checks his watch and smiles. "It's go time, man. Let's get you at the top of that aisle again." Grayson says, headed for the door.

I take a minute to breathe because when I go outside and my feet hit the sand, I'm going to be seeing my wife and I get to marry her all over again.

Zoey

Someone has jinxed me. Or tempted fate somehow.

How do I know? Because here I am, in the perfect resort in Thailand, and I'm about to walk onto the beach with my husband waiting for me... the flowers are perfect. The flower girls are perfectly dressed in their white dresses and waiting with their mum in the other room. No one has shoes on. I'm wearing the pink flowing dress Ellie picked out all those months ago on the group chat. My brothers are here and it's fucking raining. Not just a little drizzle, it's a full on torrential rainstorm. In Thailand, in December. It's supposed to be their dry season, and on my wedding day—second wedding day—it's raining. I watch the downpour through my window, staring at the beach as shallow rivers form in front of the steps I'm supposed to walk down.

"The rain should pass in the next half an hour," the wedding planner tells me.

I don't want to think about how ruined everything is going to be because nothing, and I mean nothing, will stop me from walking down that aisle.

"I don't want to wait."

Max and Owen both turn their heads, mouths open. "What?" they both shout.

"Oh, okay. Well, we won't stop you, but I need to check if the celebrant will go out in the rain." She walks off and I sigh. If the celebrant won't do it, then I guess I'll wait, but I won't be happy about it. My foot taps against the floor impatiently as I wait for the news.

"You know, you and Harrison are already married, right? So, waiting shouldn't be too much of an—" Owen stops when I whip my head to him, giving him one of my death glares. He holds his hands up. "Keeping my mouth shut."

Max chuckles next to me.

My foot taps again.

"I'm not nervous," I say indignantly.

"We know," they both say in unison.

"We're already married."

"We know," they repeat.

"And it's not like a little rain will scare him off." I pause, chewing my lip. "Christ, I'm more of a handful than a rainstorm and he's lasted six months with me so far."

No, everything is going to be fine. The rain isn't a bad omen. No one has jinxed me.

A light knock on the door has all our heads spinning to see. Max walks over to answer it but doesn't let the person in. I hear whispers but nothing concrete, even though I'm straining to hear anything.

When Max closes the door, he turns to me and smiles. "You ready for that walk now, sis?"

"We can get married in the rain?!" I practically shout.

Both boys chuckle as they walk over to me. "It's stopped raining."

It's stopped raining.

"And the sun is shining again."

Air whooshes from my lungs and something inside me settles. Everything is going to go exactly as we planned.

Getting all the girls holding hands in front of me is like herding elephants, drunk elephants. Kids are slippery little creatures.

The music begins playing from the hotel's resident ukelele player and my heart plummets to my stomach, I don't think I was this nervous before. Why does it feel different now?

"How do we get the girls to move?" Owen whispers, frowning at the precession of white in front of me.

"Try giddy up," Max snorts on my other side, stifling my own snigger as I jam my elbow into his ribs.

"You're both going to hell." I smile with them. "Cassie, go on honey, go find your Uncle Harrison for me at the end of the aisle."

Cassie turns to me, smiles and takes her first step with her brown hair shining and her flower crown sitting proudly in her hair. They all walk forwards, and as soon as my toes touch the sand too, I relax.

"You ready?" Max asks.

With my arms thread through my big brothers' and my hands holding the most beautiful bouquet of daisies I say, "I'm ready."

The cool sand crumbles beneath us as we move down the aisle. My husband waits for me and I want to run to him. Everything fades away as I move, watching the way his face takes all of me in. I'm floating towards him when I finally let my brothers go, he immediately pulls me to him for a kiss.

The ceremony begins and it's my turn to renew my vows.

Facing my husband, I take a deep breath and his smile warms me from my head to my toes.

"Harrison, falling for you wasn't what I expected at all. I always thought that falling in love would be like riding on a rollercoaster. But with you, it was like walking into a place and instantly feeling like I was home. Before you, I felt like I was swimming, barely keeping my head above water, with no one to grasp onto for help or support. And then you appeared in my life; calm, steady. Mine. I don't know what I did to deserve you, but I'm sure as hell not giving you up. I can't wait to spend the rest of forever with you, baby."

Harrison looks at me with complete and utter awe, his big brown eyes glistening with emotion as he keeps his focus solely on me.

"Harrison, would you like to say your vows?" He nods, never breaking our connection, and clears his throat.

"Zoey, I know everything we've done has been upside down, but truth be told, I'm okay with that because *you* turned me upside down. You collided into me on that plane, and deep down, I knew I didn't ever want to let you walk away. And I never will because I choose you, Zoey Clarke. I'd choose you every day without pause, without a doubt, over and over because you are my person. I love you, sweetheart."

And I believe every word that he says.

"You may now kiss the bride... again."

Chapter 47

Zoey

We stumble backwards into our honeymoon suite, our bodies slick with rainwater and our clothes entirely part of our skin now. Turns out the weather can be unpredictable in Thailand. It rained just before our ceremony, and we got caught in a downpour just as we were walking to get back here.

Despite the chill from the rain, my body pulses with piping hot want for my husband. The need to explore every inch of his body is the only thing I can think of as we paw at each other. Luckily, he has the same idea. His hands move over my wet clothed body as our lips collide, both battling for dominance over the other. When I begin to relent and give him a little control, I know he senses it. His hands grip me against his hard body as he walks us to our bedroom.

His deep brown eyes are almost black with desire as he looks down at me. I pause at his gaze, pleading silently to him. I want him to take control. I want to succumb to every carnal desire pulsing through my body right now. I need him. And just like always, it's like he knows exactly what I'm thinking.

"Do you need me to take control right now, Zoey? Do you need me to find out just how badly your pussy needs my dick?" His voice is laced with a roughness that I find completely consuming.

I nod feverishly, a blush creeping over my body, drawing out the most delicious heat, partly from the surprise that he is so dirty and how he changes from being a sweet, wholesome guy to someone who says pussy and dick in the same sentence with ease. *Props to the man.*

Honestly, no man has ever taken control of me like he does. I've spent my whole life making my own decisions, and that includes sexually too. I stay in control because that's what I'm comfortable with, but this freedom that whispers in the air, the power of saying yes and giving over my control to my husband is making me delirious. It's more than trusting him, it's having the knowledge that he knows exactly what I need because he needs it too.

Harrison spins me so my back is to his front as we walk forward. His hands trail roughly down my ribcage over my wedding dress, making my back arch into his touch.

"I've got you," he purrs into my ear, calming my erratic heartbeat, thrashing against my ribs. And I know with every fibre of my being that he's got me, he's always got me.

When we reach the bed, he turns me to face him again. His warm gaze captures me as I watch his tongue dart out, wetting his bottom lip. I mirror his movement, licking my own lips and before I can think, his hot, wet tongue is in my mouth, claiming my own.

He trails feverish kisses along my jaw, then he licks a trail between my collarbone to behind my ear. The cool air from the air conditioning touches my damp skin, sending a shiver directly to my core. I whimper as Harrison undoes the zip of my dress and more cold air puckers my nipples. His fingers move skilfully to remove my wet clothing and his follow shortly after with a slap to the wooden floor below.

"Damn, my wife is so fucking beautiful," he purrs, bending to take a nipple in his heated mouth.

My head throws back as I tangle my fingers in his hair, holding him to my body. "Ohhh my God," I whisper with a moan.

He pops his mouth off me, and I whimper at the loss of contact. "On the bed, arse in the air. Show me that beautiful pussy that I'm going to spend all night fucking."

I groan as I back towards the bed. When the backs of my legs hit the mattress, I turn and crawl, swaying my hips seductively, hearing him curse behind me. The bed dips, and the heat of him being near is almost as intoxicating as him actually touching me. The ache in my body intensifies with how close, yet far, he is from me.

Without warning, he slides one thick finger inside of me, followed quickly by another. "Oh God, yesss," I hiss as he stretches me. The burn turns rapidly into a white-hot jolt of pleasure that I crave. I drop onto my forearms, silently begging him for more as my nails dig into the duvet.

"I love how wet you are," he purrs behind me. Lowering his body closer to mine, enough that I feel his erection graze over my bare flesh. His weight causes my body to dip lower, and my nipples graze the duvet, but there's not enough friction. Sparks of need fire down my spine. I feel like I might combust if he doesn't give me more.

My head falls forward as a moan erupts from my throat, enjoying the feeling of being full of him as he strokes and curls his fingers inside me, taking me closer to the edge.

"Hmm, that's my girl," he coos in my ear, his hot breath fanning across my skin like wildfire. "Your pussy is biting for more from my fingers. I can't wait to sink my cock inside you, feel you tighten around me and coat me with your cum so I can fill you with mine."

My mouth is dry, my pussy is full, and my mind is losing the battle to give in to the pressure building inside me. I need to come.

"I... I need your cock, Harrison," I beg breathlessly. My walls flutter around him, teetering right on the cusp of my orgasm. But the moment he removes his fingers, my head snaps over my shoulder, and I watch him shift his boxers down his legs, freeing his cock, the silky tip rubbing against my skin. I torture my bottom lip between my teeth in anticipation. He lines himself up to my entrance, my body pulsing around him, already trying to suck him inside.

Desperation claws at my throat, feeling him right where I need him, but not inside me yet. I'm about to protest when he grabs the headboard above me and slams himself so deep inside of me that I have to open my legs further to accommodate him. "More," I cry, the plea tumbling so easily from my lips because I'll always want more from him, need more, crave more.

He hums with satisfaction. "You like taking all of my dick, sweetheart?"

I nod as he increases his pace. Every thrust echoes a bang of the headboard against the wall.

"You like it when I fuck you hard?"

"I like everything," I force out, lust filling my tone. The smell of sex and us lingers in the air like a drug I can't get enough of.

"Fuck, I'll never get enough of this of you," he growls, gripping my hips tight enough to leave marks. I clench at his words, mirroring my thoughts because I'll never get enough of him either. The way he claims me with soft touches but takes control like this, marking me as his. It's everything.

Suddenly, Harrison slows, his arms drop from the headboard to trail down my spine as he lavishly drags himself in and out of me. One hand tangles in my hair as the other ushers me upright so I'm sat on his lap. He snakes the hand in my hair around to grasp his thick fingers around my neck and lightly squeezes. My pulse thrums under his fingers as my hips move to feel him inside me still. The sensation of being full and consumed with him holding me in place is too much and not enough all at the same time.

"Fuck, sweetheart, you're so perfect," he whispers against my ear. "Rub your clit. I need to feel you come."

I brush my fingers over my heated skin until I reach my wet centre. My head is light with Harrison's hand firmly still around my neck as I rub myself in circles. I reach a fever pitch within seconds.

My orgasm crescendos like an unprepared symphony. It's relentless, loud, and obnoxious. Harrison takes no prisoners as he releases me, mid orgasm pushing me forwards as he resumes fucking me with wild abandon. He drives so deep I'm drunk on him, and when he his hand connects with my skin, I cry out, spiralling into another orgasm.

My legs shake from the sheer force of pleasure driving through my body. Every nerve ending is occupied by Harrison as he praises me. "That's it, sweetheart. Come back to me now because I want you to feel me fall apart for you too." His thrusts increase as his body pounds into me, his grip on my hips relentless as he growls and shouts my name. "Fuck, Zoey," he roars, his cock swelling inside me as his movement becomes erratic and spills inside me, pumping in and out a few more times before collapsing onto my back.

Breathing hard, we both come down from our orgasms. He slips out of me and rolls over until we're facing each other.

"Happy wedding day, Mrs Clarke," he smiles and my heart leaps.

"Happy wedding day, Mr Clarke."

"I have a surprise for you," he pants, moving strands of my slightly damp hair off my face.

"I love surprises," I hum, still trying to catch my breath.

"I know. Do you want it now?"

I nod, eyes closed, blissed out. The bed dips, telling me he's moving and then I hear his feet padding on the wooden floor.

I'm stuck in a dreamy, post orgasmic state when I feel his lips dust against my forehead. "No sleeping yet, gift first." He coos against my skin. I open one eye to watch him round the bed, butt naked, barely paying attention to the envelope he's holding because when he sways those thick hips towards me, that V shape carved into his hips is like an arrow pointing to his beautiful, still semi-hard dick, so I can't focus on anything else.

"Don't look at me like that. Here, open your present." He hands me the envelope that feels heavier than I expected.

"Can *you* be my present?" I ask, fluttering my lashes.

"Open it," he replies, his voice low and demanding.

"But I wanna lick you," I whine, trying to pull him closer to me but grabbing air instead.

He smirks, stepping forward, holding my chin and running his thumb over my bottom lip. "You can thank me by getting on your knees and licking me after we've showered and you've opened your gift."

I shudder, my skin erupting in goosebumps. I love it when he gets all growly with me. "Yes, sir," I pant, licking the tip of his thumb. In my peripheral, I see his dick twitch from the contact and my core pulses with need for him again.

Opening the envelope, I run my finger along the seam, feeling the paper rip as I move. There's a brochure inside that looks like it belongs in an estate agent window. I look over the glossy paper at the pictures of a beautiful farm with five acres of land and old stables adjoined to the farmhouse.

"What's this?" I ask.

"It's for us."

My head jerks up to meet his grinning face. "What?" I say on a forced exhale.

"It's our house."

Our house. The use of those two words together sends sparks of warmth into my belly because we are a we.

"But—"

"No buts, no fighting me on this. It's ours, just like you are mine and I am yours." He takes the brochure from me, places it on my bedside table and pulls me up to standing, wrapping his hands around my face. Our naked bodies brush against each other, skin caressing skin in the most primal way. "Do you want me to tell you about the plans I have for that place?"

"Plans?"

He nods. "It has land that we can use for animals. I thought the stables could be converted into pens like you have at the shelter, or it could become an extension of Paw Prints. I've already filed paperwork to officially adopt Jelly and Mouse because I know they'd both love that place."

I have to bite my cheek to stop the whoosh of tears threatening to burst free, but it's completely futile because the way this man is makes me feel so whole… I don't know how I ever existed before him. "Baby," I say. "It's too much."

"Nothing is too much for us. We've got our whole lives to plan adventures, and this is our first one, together."

Another tear falls free as I smile, looking up at my forever guy. "Let's go have some fun then, husband."

Epilogue

Zoey - Four years later

Kids' parties. They're a new form of hell that I didn't know existed. Probably because Harrison and I don't usually attend them. Every year up until now, with his nieces, we've managed to avoid the kids' party. This year though, there was no avoiding it. Poppy, Jess and Liam's little girl did one pouty look at Harrison, and he was putty in her hands. Honestly, *my* pout doesn't work on him, but any other female in his life? He bends over backwards as soon as they stick out a lip.

"Zo, would you grab the lemonade?" Jess calls as she sets up a table filled with snacks to make the kids even loopier than they are.

Poppy spins around in circles, her princess dress puffing out as she falls to the floor in heaps of giggles.

I turn to Harrison and lower my voice. "Is giving the kids *more* sugar a good idea?"

He huffs a laugh. "In my experience, sugar and kids equals chaos, but who are we to say?"

He's right, it will be chaos, but it's chaos we can walk away from, so there's that.

Walking over to the little kitchenette, I bend down to get the lemonade in the fridge when a loud thud startles me, and I almost drop the bottle. I still, wondering if it'll happen again. "What the..." I mutter to myself after the second noise, my gaze sharply flicking around the room in case the ceiling falls on my head because that's what it sounded like.

Moving my feet slowly, I set the bottle on the worktop and sidestep to stand in front of the pantry. Leaning forward, I press my ear to the door, a rhythmic sound echoes distantly as I step back, willing my pulse to slow.

What if there's a bird stuck in there and it flies out at me? Oh god, what if it's a rat? That would be worse. Or maybe it's a magical portal that leads into a land full of shifters that are wolves and dragons and... yeah, okay, maybe I'm being dramatic. My imagination runs away with me when I'm terrified.

I squeeze my eyes closed, moving my hand to grip the handle and yank the door open along with my eyes.

Oh fuck.

I should've kept the door closed.

"Oh, my God!" Nora shrieks. "Zoey, close the door!!"

I'm stuck in place, staring at Grayson's bare arse. That's still moving in rhythm. Oh God, I'm just watching my best friends fuck in a pantry cupboard. What the fuck am I doing?

"Oh." I fumble, whipping my head from left to right, unsure where I left the door. Grayson grunts and I panic more. *Ahhh, make it stop!*

"The fucking door, Zoey," Nora yells, still being rammed by her boyfriend.

"Right." I yelp, springing into action. There it is, the door attached to the doorframe. Fucking moron. I close it and my eyes, but a steady rhythmic thumping still plagues me, as does the image of Nora and Grayson having sex.

"Oh Jesus," I whisper, forgetting all about the lemonade and running out. As I turn the corner, I smack into a hard chest. The familiar smell of freshly washed clothes and my favourite spicy scent floats around me.

"Woah, where's the fire, sweetheart?"

"I-I-I." Stuttering isn't something that usually happens to me, but then again, neither is seeing my friends fucking at a kid's party.

Harrison's frown pinches his brows together. "Are you okay?"

I blink rapidly and then blurt, "I just saw Grayson fucking Nora in the cupboard. I'm traumatised."

"Wait, what?" he replies before erupting in a bout of laughter. "They're in there fucking?"

I nod, closing my eyes and seeing it again. *Nope, don't close your eyes.*

"I'm never coming to a kid's party again."

My husband hugs me, and I feel my racing pulse even out. "I don't think you'd usually find that at a kid's party, so future ones should be safe."

"I need to bleach my brain and my eyeballs."

He chuckles into my hair. "Or *we* could find another cupboard."

"No way." I shudder. "Not at a kid's party. My lady boner is gone."

His big hands drift down to cup my arse as he pulls me flush to him. "Mmm, I need to stop right now because I'm about to kick them out of the cupboard and take you in there," he growls with a fire in his eyes. I don't doubt that he would, but I'm far too traumatised.

I open my mouth to respond when Nora appears, looking dishevelled and covered in red marks on her neck. She may as well be a sinner in church with the way her cheeks are colouring before us.

"I'm sorry about that. Grayson has some…" She clears her throat. "Urges at the moment."

I tilt my head and hope to God the memory of his white arse fades soon. "Urges?" I ask, partly wishing I hadn't asked.

"We're…" She hesitates, blushing more. "Trying for a baby."

I gasp and tap my friend on the head. There's no way I'm touching her more than that right now. "Ohhhh, congratulations."

Grayson appears behind her moments later, looking equally as dishevelled. "Wait, did it work already?" he says, looking bemused.

Nora slaps his chest. "Are you kidding me with that? We talked about this already."

Harrison and I are a mess of shuddering shoulders as we try not to laugh.

"What are you all doing in here?" Liam says, breaking our little pow-wow up.

Nora flushes the darkest shade of crimson I've ever seen on her, and Grayson scratches the back of his neck.

"You two were fucking," Liam declares, crossing his arms over his chest, glaring at Nora and Grayson and when his gaze lands on me and Harrison with a frown. "Were you all having a foursome?"

"Oh God, no!" Nora shrieks.

"Dude, it's best you ask fewer questions at this point," Harrison laughs, slapping Laim's shoulder and directing him out of the kitchenette.

When we get into the large hall, everything, and I mean everything, is pink. The balloons, the streamers, the cake, the tablecloths. Even the bouncy castle is pink.

"Jeeeez, it looks like Barbie threw up in here," Grayson mumbles as we walk through.

Luckily, there aren't many kids here yet. We got here early to help with the set up, but Jess assures me it's only the children she's met through mum groups. I mean, how many can that be?

"Zozo!" My favourite little pink princess comes barrelling towards me with open arms, and I scoop her up, inhaling her warm, soft toddler smell.

"Hi beautiful girl, how's the birthday going?" I say, pulling back to look at her face.

"Pink!" she yells far too loudly for someone so close to me.

"No! Where's the pink?" I say, spinning her around.

She chuckles in my arms. "Pink!" she shouts again, pointing everywhere. Harrison ambles up next to us and Poppy all but leaps into his arms.

"Hi, Popster. How does it feel to be two?" he asks, kissing her cheek.

Poppy grins and wraps her little arms around his neck as she screams, "Aa-pane, Aa-pane!" She wants him to swoosh her around like a little aeroplane. It's something he's always done since she was tiny and... watching him with her, I suddenly feel that same feeling in the pit of my tummy. It happens every time he's with his nieces, too.

And I think it might be guilt.

We've hardly talked about having a family and now I feel this weight settling uncomfortably in my belly for not talking about it sooner. It's not that I don't want kids, it's just that I've always considered myself the fun aunt, not the Mama. But watching how effortless Harrison is with kids, I'm wondering if he feels the same or if he wants a whole brood of Clarke kids.

Truthfully, if he told me he wanted children. I'd have one in a heartbeat, but I just never imagined having one. But then I never imagined having a fake husband who turns out to be my real husband, either.

Poppy squeals as he sets her down and we watch her run towards the pink bouncy castle and catapult her tiny self onto it.

He takes my hand and kisses the back of it, breaking my trance I've managed to put myself into watching little Poppy. When I look at him, his eyes are slightly squinted in question. "What's that look?"

I shake my head lightly. "What look? I don't have a look."

Harrison eclipses my view of the room by stepping in front of me. "I know you, sweetheart. What's going on?" His voice is so soft and gentle and *God,* he'll make the perfect dad. But I just, I just...

"Do you want kids one day?" I blurt in the most uncouth way imaginable.

Harrison chuckles, and I can't figure out if he's smiling because I brought the subject up or if he's going to tell me he wants to get me pregnant right now. Either way, I'm sweating.

"Do *you* want kids?" he counters.

"I asked you first," I say pointedly, incredibly aware of the fact that I'm acting like a child myself.

"Sweetheart." He holds my chin between his thumb and forefinger, something he knows makes me so weak for him. "I want what you want. Mostly, I want you. But I'm not scared about any version of our future." He guides my face to his and softly kisses my forehead.

I feel my heart tumbling down to my feet and then swooshing right back into my chest. "How are you real?" I mumble, pulling him into a kiss that probably isn't that appropriate for a kid's party. I pull back and peck him once more, looking into his big brown eyes, I get lost so easily. "Would you be mad if I said I'm happy as we are?"

His smile doesn't falter, as he keeps me in his arms. "I'm happy too. We have some amazing family around us and cute tiny humans that we get to spoil. I'm really fucking happy."

The weight somewhat dissipates from my belly, and I let out a sigh. "Me too." I settle my chin on his chest, looking up at him. "Promise me something?" I ask, and he nods in response. "If you ever feel differently, you'll talk to me."

A big hand comes up to stroke a strand of hair from my face, dipping to kiss my forehead. "Likewise."

And for the millionth time since being married to my husband, I wonder how I got so damn lucky that the person who owns all of my heart is him.

Acknowledgements

Thank you for reading the final instalment of The Ladies of London series – there is a little more bonus content coming soon, so keep an eye on my socials for the link towards the end of 2023.

My readers – Thank you for sticking around for book three. It means the world to me. To all my incredible ARC readers, thank you for all the love for my books, when you care about my work it makes me feel like all of the stress is worth it.

My alpha/beta readers – You have all helped me in so many different ways. Mhairi, Natalie, Stacey, Tash – thank you for taking the time to read, listen, and help me out with early drafts of this book. It's better because of you all!

My editor, Sarah. Thank you for loving this book when I thought it was utter shit. Thank you for pushing me to be better at my craft. I hope you realise you're stuck with me forever.

My proof reader, Lisa. Your eagle eyes have been incredible with this book! Thank you!

To my family and friends for listening to me complain about these characters, just know that every single freak out has led me here to this point where I have published three books! So thank you for listening and supporting me.

Here's to more books in 2024!

About Author

Meghan lives in rural England with her family – husband, two children and a yappy dog!

She works in Education by day but writes smutty romances by night.

There are lots of plans for Meghan to write more books so if you enjoyed this one there are more on the way!

Follow Meghan Hollie on Facebook, Instagram, TikTok and Goodreads.

If you enjoyed this book, please consider leaving a review on amazon and you'll be thanked in virtual hugs forever!

Printed in Great Britain
by Amazon